POLICE PROCEDURALS RESPECTED
BY LAW ENFORCEMENT.™

"Carolyn Arnold writes realistic and entertaining police procedurals with characters so real, I lose myself in her books."
—*Deputy Rebecca Hendrix, LeFlore County Sheriff's Department Poteau, Oklahoma*

"For Police procedurals that are painstakingly researched and accurately portrayed look no further than Carolyn Arnold's works. The only way it gets more real than this is to leave the genre completely."
—*Zach Fortier, Police Officer (Ret.) Colorado, United States*

"I tend to shy away from Police Procedural novels because I get angry and frustrated at the lack understanding by many authors...I was extremely impressed by the amount of research she must have done."
—*Stacy Eaton, Police Investigator and Certified Crime Scene Investigator Pennsylvania, United States*

ALSO BY CAROLYN ARNOLD

Ties That Bind
Justified
Sacrifice
Found Innocent
Just Cause
Life Sentence
Eleven
The Defenseless
The Day Job is Murder
Vacation is Murder
Money is Murder
Politics is Murder
Family is Murder
Shopping is Murder
Christmas is Murder
Valentine's Day is Murder
Coffee is Murder
Assassination of a Dignitary
Hart's Choice

SILENT GRAVES

CAROLYN ARNOLD

HIBBERT
&
STILES
PUBLISHING INC.

Silent Graves (Book 2 in the Brandon Fisher FBI series)
Copyright © 2014 by Carolyn Arnold

Excerpt from *The Defenseless* (Book 3 in the Brandon Fisher FBI series)
copyright © 2014 by Carolyn Arnold

www.carolynarnold.net

2015 Hibbert & Stiles Publishing Inc. Edition

This is a work of fiction. Names, characters, places, and incidents are the
products of the author's imagination or are used fictitiously. Any resemblance
to actual events, locales, or persons, living or dead, is entirely coincidental.

ISBN (e-book): 978-0-9878400-4-2
ISBN (print): 978-1-988064-07-9

Cover design: WGA Designs

PROLOGUE

"THE GRAVES LAY SILENT. The graves lay untouched. The graves lay silent. The graves lay untouched."

He tapped his hand against his thigh as he repeated the chant. He had done everything right. He had made sure not to leave anything behind and had chosen only those who deserved to suffer and die.

The way they'd tilt their heads back in laughter, flaunting what wasn't theirs to own, draining their cocktails as if there was no tomorrow. No risk. Nothing to lose.

Chapter 1

He had promised her a time she'd never forget. It was why she sacrificed comfort and drove in her stuffy BMW into the countryside. The weather had such nerve to reach record heat waves in September. It scorched as if it were the middle of summer.

She glimpsed in the rearview mirror, angling it to better see her reflection.

"A woman has been reported missing…"

Those few words from the radio made it through to her ears. That was top news? Surely, there was a murder, or a stock market drop to report.

"…it's suspected that she may be the victim of foul play. Police are urging women of the Washington, DC area to be careful."

She laughed. *Be careful.*

A song came on, one she didn't care for, and she commanded the radio off.

She had never been where he had directed her to go, but she was excited to see this Wooded Retreat. Usually, they'd meet up at her house or the Marriott, but he had wanted today to be special—personal.

She had long given up on feeling guilty about her marriage. Her husband was too busy with his prestigious law firm in central Washington. Really, it was his work that killed their marriage—his love for revenue his priority.

Her focus returned to the road and where she was headed. She wasn't used to the country with all its color. She was accustomed to the shades of gray that were intrinsic to life in the city. Maybe there was something to be said for the simple things. She lowered the window and breathed deeply, ready to give the rustic experience a chance.

The air was fresh, despite the humidity, carrying with it the smell of greenery—but there was something else. She inhaled deeper, coughed, and raised the window back up. Damn blasted cows that polluted nature with their stench.

Why would he think she'd be in the mood once she got there?

The thought barely formed, and she had the answer. He was a fabulous lover. Thinking of his hands caressing her skin sent shivers through her and made her lower abdomen quiver.

She turned left when she noticed the rundown diner he had mentioned to her.

The gravel crunched beneath her tires as she went from the highway's asphalt to an unpaved surface. The strip was narrow, barely wide enough to accommodate two cars if one came in the opposite direction. She studied the edge, anticipating the need to do just that. The soft shoulder appeared unforgiving as if it would suck in her car given a chance.

Fifteen miles.

She found it hard to believe this stretch would continue that long. Her eyes went to the woods, being cautious, watching for any deer or other animal that may decide to become a hood ornament. She checked her side mirror. All the dust being kicked up would wreak havoc on the wax job.

So much for showing up looking perfect.

She glanced in the mirror again and touched her fingertips to her forehead. She couldn't let him see her like this.

Driving with one hand, she reached into her designer handbag on the passenger seat and pulled out her compact. She lifted the loaded brush and the air conditioning vent cascaded powder through the air. She blew to keep it from landing on her cream-colored pantsuit and began application. The scent of the powder made her sneeze.

As she reached for control of the wheel, the case dumped on the floor, going straight through her legs, barely missing her pants.

She slammed on the brakes. The mailbox he had told her to watch for, once a bright red, had worn from time. She almost missed the turn.

She couldn't see the house from the road, but her heart beat rapidly now, anticipating what awaited her.

She fished into her bag again, this time for her gloss. She smeared some on with a finger, smacked her lips, looked in the mirror, and declared herself perfect. She was ready to go to bed with her lover.

Chapter 2

A couple months had passed, but I was still getting used to sleeping alone. Most mornings I would roll on my left side, open my eyes, and expect Deb to be lying there. Every time I did this, it met with the same result. I was alone.

The mornings were hard to take. At night, my mind was usually preoccupied with the day's events, a current case, or the complicated relationship that existed between Paige and me. We had just closed a case a few days ago, and it was easier to let go of that than the continuing innuendos that remained, as fissures, beneath the surface of our relationship. I loved her, in a way, but not on the level she required. She acted as if everything was fine, but I knew—I sensed—it wasn't.

I rolled over and faced the clock. Five a.m.

I returned to my back and stared at the ceiling. It was hard adapting to the early mornings, but these days I usually beat the alarm. Even on days off, my body would wake me.

AC/DC's *Thunderstruck* came on, and, at the same time, my cell vibrated on the nightstand. I rolled over again and sat up. It wasn't like I would be getting more sleep anyhow.

"Rise and shine, Kid."

I rubbed a hand across my brow. Even though I had earned being called by name from Supervisory Special Agent Jack Harper, periodically old habits would resurface and, with it, the nicknames. "What's up?"

"What's up? Am I some friend now? I'm your boss."

"I'll save professional for office hours," I said the sardonic statement with a grin I'm sure he didn't miss. In this career, there was no such thing as set hours.

"Come in straight to the meeting room today. We've got a new case."

"Sure."

"What's that noise in the background? Have you been partying all night?"

I hit the button and turned it off. "It's AC/DC, classic rock."

"Well, it's not music. Music is—"

"I know—The Rat Pack, Natalie Cole, Michael Bublé."

"Don't knock it, Kid, and there's nothing wrong with Michael."

Yeah, I suppose if you're good with the crooner music in the first place.

"See you soon," I said.

"Don't be late."

I rolled my eyes, wishing the expression weren't lost on the walls of my bedroom, yet thankful he couldn't witness it, or I might be searching for a new job.

I rose from the bed and flicked on the stereo, turning up Nickelback's *Burn it to the Ground* until the glass in this old house rattled. I loved this song, and loud was the way I preferred it.

I had an hour to make it to the office. I wrapped my hands and wrists with tape, and then started beating on the heavy bag I had installed in the bedroom. Deb never would have let it happen, but I didn't have her to worry about anymore.

With each impact, I let it go—the stress, the anger, the frustration, the lack of control. The physical movement drained the negative and infused me with the positive.

Adrenaline pumped through me, and I embraced it, as I roundhouse kicked the bag. It swung on its chains. I reset the bag and had at it again.

The song changed to the next on the playlist—Poison's *Nothing But a Good Time.*

Damn. Now this was music.

I uppercut and jabbed at the bag mercilessly, going at it as if sucking its life force.

Thirty minutes later, sweating profusely, I headed for the shower. There was no better way to start the day. In a matter of minutes, I'd be facing the next monster to cross paths with the FBI.

I SMILED AS I ENTERED the meeting room just on time. How could one get any more punctual than that?

"You're late, Fisher." Jack was sitting at the table with the rest of the team.

"It's Pending, boss. He probably forgot to set the alarm." Zachery lifted a steaming take-out cup to his mouth, cutting his smirk short. Whenever he could poke at my probationary period with the nickname, he would.

"He even got a wake-up call," Jack mumbled.

"Brandon," Paige said. Her red hair hung in loose curls, serving as a soft frame for her face, but her eyes were cool.

I took all of them in, not sure how they did it. They were there, not just on time, but early. They were all alert, despite the caffeine they clung to as if their lives depended on it.

"Sit. We don't have all day." Jack patted his shirt pocket where he kept his cigarettes. He had probably already smoked a few since waking up.

"Hey." Nadia came up behind me and tapped me on the back as she walked by.

"Hey." I took a seat.

The screen was filled with faces of various women. On the left side, was their smiling before photos. On the right, was the aftermath—their remains, part flesh, part bones.

Nadia clicked the remote she held, and the screen filled with a picture of one woman. She was beautiful, with long dark hair and brown eyes. Nothing, in particular, stood out about her.

"Her name is Amy Rogers. Her husband is Kirk Rogers."

"Hmm."

I knew what Jack was thinking—money bought results. We were in the Behavioral Analysis Unit to stop serial crime, not for a single abduction. Why weren't the police handling this case?

"He owns the communications company Trinity," I said.

Nadia acknowledged me with a bob of her head. "That would be correct Brandon, but the man has lawyers, and he paid people to do some snooping around. They found out that a bunch of women have gone missing in the area over the past decade. He also has a tight friendship with the chief of police down in Washington. He had him call us in."

"So, we're looking for Amy Rogers? No real concern for the other missing women?" I knew I was being cynical, but the power of a buck, the control and sway it held, sickened me at the best of times.

"We're investigating this case because this is the one we've been assigned." Jack intensified the reprimand with a hardened facial expression.

"I'm not saying anything contrary to that. It's just--"

"I know what you're saying, Brandon. We have a chance to find Amy Rogers before it is too late. To accomplish that, a good place to start is investigating the older cases," Paige said.

I let what she said go. I didn't need another parental surrogate on the team. I already had a father figure in Jack. I addressed Nadia. "Who were these women you had on the screen when I came in?"

"Their naked bodies were found in ditches along I-95 between Lorton and a little west of Dumfries."

"No jewelry or anything?" Zachery asked.

"No."

"I-95 is a major highway, but it's not a huge stretch. What— twenty minutes," Paige offered. "It's likely someone from the area."

"How many women and how long ago do these bodies date back to?" Zachery asked Nadia.

"The oldest dates back to nineteen seventy. Her name was Melanie Chase. She was discovered along I-95 near Woodbridge by the Levine family who was on a road trip. The youngest, age three, had to go to the washroom. There were no rest stops for a distance so the father pulled over for the kid to go, and they got more than a number one."

Woodbridge? That is where I live. "How was she killed?"

"The ME ruled the cause of death as being pulmonary edema."

"Fluid in the lungs." Everyone gave me the once-over as if to say, *yes, that would be pulmonary edema.* "What about the other victims?"

"Another died of a severe stroke while yet another of a brain hemorrhage. These three old cases, the thirty missing women from Prince William County—"

"Thirty?"

Nadia nodded. "Yeah, that has our interest too, and that's thirty missing women in the last six years. Seems Amy Rogers wasn't the only target."

Zachery quickly compiled the math. "On average, that's one woman every two months."

"Holy crap." The words left my lips without thought, and everyone's attention was on me again. "What more do we know?"

"These three women were married, as is Amy Rogers. None of these women had children either. All were reported by their husbands. All of them were taken from Washington or PW County. It's too coincidental to ignore."

"I agree," Paige said.

Nadia turned to the screen, magnifying on their wrists and ankles. "The three women that were found all had these same markings. It appears the killer had bound them all with linked chain."

"I see there are different nationalities among the victimology." Zachery bobbed his head toward the screen.

"Yes, the only similarities are what I mentioned—married, no kids. Among the law enforcement community, by the time the third victim was found, he had earned the moniker The Silent Killer."

"And here, I thought that was cancer," I said implicating Jack's smokes.

Nadia continued as if I hadn't said anything. "Based on forensic evidence, these women were aware they were going to die but couldn't do anything about it." Nadia's face paled and she swallowed heavily.

"Ketamine?" Zachery lifted his cup but didn't press it to his lips.

"Actually, there wasn't any trace of that in their systems."

"Possibly something herbal then that would inhibit their ability to move and then leave the system quickly."

"If they figured one person was responsible for the death of these three women, why not call in the FBI?" I asked.

"They did, but the case was never taken on. The killer went silent, no pun intended, and there didn't seem to be any threat."

"We're thinking this guy's back and could have Amy Rogers?"

"That's exactly what we're thinking."

Chapter 3

The night before...
Dumfries, Virginia
Monday evening, 7:30 p.m.

The news was public now. Another woman's life summed up in the media—missing. Trent Stenson wished he could discredit it as something menial. He was surprised it was worthy of the news, and the reason was likely because she was the wife of some rich businessman—Kirk Rogers of Trinity Communications—and he was worth millions. According to the newspapers, Rogers even got the FBI involved.

His superiors made Trent feel that his contributions held little value. He had the official training and three years on the job, but he didn't rank and was kept under the label of officer. There wasn't much room for advancement within Dumfries PD, but he could always move up to captain. That was the only downfall about a smaller department. People typically retired before they were replaced. It had him considering a move over to Prince William County PD where they had about six hundred officers to Dumfries eleven. PWPD also got involved with the complex crimes—where he saw himself.

He already had a friend there too. Lenny Hanes, a detective from the Violent Crimes Bureau. They even had beers on occasion. Trent hoped that Hanes would put in a good word and help him transfer and advance, but things hadn't worked out that way yet. For the most part, shit floats to the top. At least, that's how some disgruntled cops saw things.

But none of this stopped Trent from doing the job. In fact, he was determined to excel. He subscribed to the advice "anything worth doing is worth doing well."

Amy Rogers wasn't the only missing wife who graced the missing persons database from the area. There had been many others before her. He suspected more would follow.

He looked beyond the front desk, and out the glass doors to the parking lot. It was a quiet night. The PWPD communications center had dispatched only a couple domestics calls and one drunk and disorderly at a local bar. Officer Becky Tulson had that covered.

Yes, it was the perfect time. Management had left for the evening—it was up for debate who benefited the most from their absence. He loved being left alone to do his digging, and these missing women had his attention.

He logged onto the missing persons database and searched the area for women ages twenty-two to thirty. It didn't seem race mattered so he let that parameter go. He searched Prince William County and surrounding areas as far as Washington on the south side.

Thirty faces came on screen. He searched for new ones. He had the others memorized and categorized in his mind—and in his filing cabinet at home. If his sarge found out about the latter, he could lose his badge, but it was worth the risk if it meant bringing even one woman home.

Most of their faces were familiar to him. He scoured this information every day, sometimes more than once day. It had become not a fascination, but an obsession.

Who would take these women? How did the husbands lose track of their wives?

Not that Trent had any experience being married. He was only twenty-four and preferred to hold onto his single lifestyle as long as he could. He didn't need a woman telling him how to live his life.

He dropped forward and cupped his forehead in the palm of a hand for a few seconds. His bangs brushed the back of his hand. Silly how, at a time like this, he thought of his mother and how she preferred his hair cut above his collar. He let it grow out, only trimming its length periodically. The women he took to bed liked to run their fingers through his hair.

The door opened, and a woman in her late sixties walked in. Her blue eyes stood out in stark contrast to her pale face and gray hair. Tears had dampened her cheeks.

"I should have called it in. I shouldn't have driven all the way here." She shook her head, and tremors ran through her body as if she fought off a chill.

Trent rounded the desk. "Ma'am. Slow down. You're safe now."

The radio crackled to life, and Officer Tulson confirmed she was returning to the station.

"Sorry about the interruption. Ma'am?"

In the time he listened to the transmission, the woman had collapsed to the floor. She sat there with her knees tucked into her chest.

"Ma'am. I'll call you an ambulance. You'll be fine."

She reached for his hand and tugged on it. "There's no time." Her eyes seeped fresh tears. "It's there...I found it. I should have called."

Trent agreed with her assessment that she should have stayed put at home and called it in, but he didn't verbalize this. "It's okay. You said, 'it's there' ma'am? It what?"

She nodded, slowly. Her eyes reached into Trent's. Her body heaved with another bout of crying. Her hand covered her mouth, her eyes pinched shut, and her head burrowed to her knees.

Oh, he thought, please don't be another crazy.

"Ma'am, I can help you, but only if you talk to me. Let me help you off the floor." He held out a hand to her, and she took hold. He helped raise her up, but when she reached about halfway, her legs faltered.

"You have a face like my grandson."

He pulled up on her, attempting to straighten her out—this time assuming most of the responsibility against gravity. He feared that, if he let go, she'd crumple back to the floor.

"I could go home and pretend I never saw a thing. I'll shut my eyes, and the body will be gone."

The body?

Morbid excitement pulsed in his veins.

A homicide case—in his lap? Maybe this was the break he was waiting for?

He reined in his emotions which were balanced quickly by the realization that this *body* was once a human being, or at least he hoped so, although, even that thought sounded wrong to him. He didn't need a crazy making a fool of him. If he took her seriously and an investigation revealed nothing more than a decomposing cow on a riverbank, or even worse, thin air, he'd never make detective.

He considered the empty station. If anyone came in, no one would be at the front desk. "Excuse me. One minute." He spoke into his radio. "Officer Tulson, what is your ETA?"

"Tulson here. Pulling in now."

"Roger that." He turned back to the woman. "We'll just wait for Officer Tulson and we'll make out a report."

The woman nodded. She understood. Good. She had some wits about her.

He studied her in those few seconds. Her eyes, although moist, were cognitive. There was awareness behind them. Her pupils followed his as he took in her face. They were not dilated or pinpricks. She wasn't on medication.

"Honey, I'm home." Becky walked in the front door, her steps coming to a standstill when she saw the woman.

He went over to Becky.

In the limited space of the station, her sexual pheromones sparked making it impossible for any man in her vicinity to ignore them. She had a uniquely shaped face, and, when paired with her confidence, it made her beautiful.

"I need you to watch the front for a bit."

"Sure."

The way Becky's gaze pierced his eyes, he wondered if she read his thoughts. Then she smiled, but only a partial display. The light in her eyes completed the expression.

Trent led the older woman to a conference room, thankful his sergeant wasn't there to take over. If he got in over his head, though, he had someone he could call—Hanes—but he'd reserve that as a final option. Technically, he should have driven her to PWPD, but why squander this opportunity?

"Would you like some water?" he asked.

She was already seated at the table. "Yes, please."

He poured a glass and sat beside her. "My name is Trent Stenson." He dropped the officer part, not because he lacked pride in his position, but what did it matter in here? If he wanted her to relax and feel like an equal, he needed to level the playing field. "And you are?"

"Audrey Phillips."

Holding a pen in his hand, he fidgeted with the pad in front of him. He would rather listen to her recollection of the situation and then make notes, but he had to follow things by the book if he would ever rank. He wrote her name on the form.

"Now, you said you found a body?"

Her face paled further, eyes blank and distant. She nodded.

"This was a human body, I assume."

Seconds had passed before she answered. "Yes."

This would take a long time if all he received were simple answers, direct, concise, and to the point. "Continue." His pen was poised, eager to spread some ink on the page.

"Most of her…" Shivers jerked her shoulders upward and her head twitched. "Most of her was a skeleton, but her face, her hair, it was there. And she was…gray. Is that normal?"

Excitement laced through his insides. Could this be one of the missing women?

"Where did you find her?"

"Out back. On my property." She gave him the full address and waited while he took down the details. "She was in the field. Just… just lying there." She covered her mouth with a hand, lowering it a second later. "We had flooding, but it's receded now. Do you think she came up in the river?"

It was too early to offer an opinion, and they needed men out on the scene. The longer the body remained exposed to the elements, the more contaminated it would become.

"How old do you think she was?"

She lifted her shoulder and nudged it against an ear. "Thirties. I took this. " She pulled out a plastic sandwich bag and extended it to him. Inside was a gold band.

He wanted to scream, *you touched the body*, but, instead, countered with, "She was a married woman?"

Audrey nodded.

He took the bag and pinched the ring between his fingers. Saying those words out loud caused images from the missing persons database to play through his mind as if on fast forward.

Could it be her?

He studied the ring and got the burning sensation in his gut, the one that contracted it into an acidic raisin. "Can you excuse me for a minute?"

"Yes, of course." Her brows sagged, and the corner of her mouth twitched as if she were confused by his rush to leave the room.

"I will be back. We need to get some officers over to your place."

His heart beat fast, the pressure in his gut not easing up, instead, intensifying. He pulled out his cell and dialed. "Len… you're at home…this is important. You know all those cases we've been talking about? How I think they're all connected somehow? Well, now we have a body."

DETECTIVE LENNY HANES STOOD IN the doorway of his kitchen. He watched his wife cleaning up the dinner dishes and loading what would fit into the dishwasher. Nicole and Brett, both under eight years of age, had been put to bed not long before. Lenny hoped the ringing phone hadn't wakened them.

"You're sure this is her?" he asked into the receiver.

His wife looked at him and he mouthed the words, *it's a case.*

"When isn't it?" She closed the dishwasher door and started the cycle, leaving him in the kitchen but kissing his cheek on the way by. "See you in the morning?"

Lenny made a sad face. He held her hand until it filtered out of his, keeping his eye on her until she disappeared up the staircase.

"The ring. It matches, I swear to you." Trent sounded out of breath.

"And she took the ring off the woman's finger?"

"Off Nina's finger? Yes."

"Before you get all caught up on—"

"I swear to you, it is. The engraving on the band matches the one noted in the missing persons database and there's—"

"There's what?"

"Audrey Phillips, who found the body and took the ring, she took some of the flesh with it."

Bile hurled up Lenny's esophagus. He swallowed—roughly. "What is wrong with some people?" His stomach tightened, compressing his dinner into a reduced space.

"Don't know. She seems like a sweet woman, but I don't get it."

"People do strange things when faced with extreme circumstances."

Lenny remembered one case where a woman leaned over her husband's body and open-mouth kissed him. She only admitted that he was dead when he didn't reciprocate. The hole in his head and the blood pool around him wasn't enough. He shook the memory from his mind.

"And you haven't told anyone else about this yet?" A couple of seconds passed. "Trent? You hear me?"

"Sorry, I was shaking my head." He let out a small laugh. "Guess you couldn't see that."

"No." Lenny sensed a mixture of emotion coming through the line. Trent was excited that his fixation on the missing women hadn't been in vain, but, at the same time, he came across as regretful that his assumptions might be correct.

"We're dealing with a serial killer, Len. It's obvious. Amy Rogers went missing just last week. They called in the FBI for her. They need to know about this."

"We can't rush to conclusions. I'm going to notify the chief to let him know about the find and contact crime scene and the ME. I'm heading out to her place now. Stay with the woman there, keep her calm, and let her know we'll take care of it."

"It?"

"The DB, Trent. The victim. You have to learn to think of them that way. Otherwise the job will eat you up."

"I'm not babysitting this woman. I'm going to the crime scene."

"Oh, no, you're not."

"Len—"

"There isn't room for debate here. You have to stay there. That's your job. This is mine."

"So you keep reminding me. Just remember, I connected everything before the detectives of PWPD even had a clue."

"Now you're resorting to digs? Come on, Trent, you know I've got your back. I always have."

"I still don't see detective on my badge, and, yep, I'm definitely in uniform."

Lenny laughed. "Stop sulking. I'll keep you posted." He hung up the phone, went upstairs, and told his wife there was another case. His hours around home would be hit—and more likely miss—for the next while.

"Just take care of you." She brushed a hand on the side of his face, and he kissed her forehead.

"That's why I love you."

"Love you." Her nose went back into her paperback. She would be carried off into a fictional world before he hit the front door.

CHAPTER 4

"I'm picking up on the smell and, according to the property owner, the body should be right over—" Detective Hanes cast the flashlight across the field as he walked and stopped just shy of making contact with the corpse. If it had been another second, he would have tripped over the thing. It's good that he didn't have any aversions to dead bodies because this one would top the list of gruesome finds.

Jimmy Chow, the lead crime scene technician, came up behind him. As his name suggested, the man was Chinese. He called things how they were, had a wacky sense of humor, and repeatedly proved more loyal than a canine. Chow gestured for a couple of his people to move out over the area. Portable lights were set up and turned on.

Chow pinched his nose and spoke. "Surprised we didn't pick up on this odor from farther back."

The smell of death occupied not only the sinuses but seeped into the skin and clung to clothing. This case would have them reeking of it from every pore and breathing it from their lungs. "You're acting like a newb. Isn't it worse breathing through your mouth? Come on, you've been around—"

"No, not quite this bad." He dropped his hand, swallowed deeply, and analyzed the body. "She appears to be mid-thirties. You said Stenson thought this was Nina Harris? I quickly looked at her file before coming. She's the right appearance. At least I can imagine it."

Unlike Chow, Hanes didn't need to study her file. Trent and he had shared many beers talking about the missing women from the area.

Hanes infused life into what had simply become a shell, a carcass. He imagined Harris smiling like she had in her wedding photo. He envisioned her eyes rolling back and the sultry expression piercing her lips into a subtle pout. He pictured her on the arm of her husband, being his pride and sense of accomplishment.

"It gives you a point of reference to ID the body," Chow said.

"But it can also limit perspective. One step at a time." Hanes circled the body, trying to take in every angle. Despite wafts of decomp tearing up his eyes, he pushed through. "There's the finger Audrey Phillips took the ring from. God, it is missing flesh."

"She took the finger with the ring."

Chow's rhetorical summation caused Hanes's belly to perform a flop like it had when he first heard about what Phillips had done.

What was left of the victim's skin was bloated and appeared to float over the bone mass beneath it, as if one could poke the flesh with a pin and have it hiss out air. Many of her fingernails were gone, and her eyes were missing. The decayed milky slime likely washed away in the river, or had been picked on by fish for food.

The flesh that remained was gray, and in some areas, the skin appeared waxy and held a brownish tinge. The body that would have once been considered beautiful and have garnered the attention of men, now, resembled something that could star in a swamp horror movie.

Animals hadn't disturbed the remains which Hanes found unbelievable due to the odor she gave off. Maybe even wild creatures had a tolerance threshold.

Around her wrists and ankles there were darkened markings. Hanes bent down next to her left ankle. The stench, being this much closer, stole his breath for a second.

"It looks like she was bound."

"I was just noticing that myself." Chow pointed with the tip of a pen to her wrists. "She was definitely held for a period of time to create these impressions."

"Agree. Also, there are contradictory signs as to the age of the remains. She has flesh in some areas, but even they don't tell an accurate timeline."

"Very astute, Detective Hanes." Hans Rideout, the Medical Examiner, came over to them.

He worked out of the Department of Forensic Science in Richmond. He was in his late forties with a full head of gray hair and a wash of white sideburns. He had a contagious smile, and the lines around his mouth testified that he shared the expression often. His work with the dead never brought him down. Hanes wondered sometimes if the man was clairvoyant due to the clarity with which he saw the victims.

"I'd also say she didn't die here. This is a secondary crime scene," Hanes said.

Rideout laughed, jacked his thumb toward Hanes. He spoke to Chow. "That's why they pay him the big bucks."

Chow smiled. "I keep trying to tell him."

The joviality in ME's eyes narrowed with intensity as he focused on the body. "She has been dead for some time. There is some evidence of adipocere." He must have sensed their energy and added the explanation. "That's the result of the chemical process saponification. The body's fat petrifies into a wax-like substance, kind of like soap."

Hanes cast a glance at Chow. He was surprised the man held onto his stomach contents given his earlier reaction.

"I wouldn't suggest exfoliating with her." Rideout's sometimes inappropriate sense of humor garnered a smile from Chow. Hanes suspected it helped him fight the urge to vomit.

Rideout continued. "This process results in what you see here." He pointed to the areas that appeared waxy and brownish gray in color. "The victim appears as if she were in good physical condition. It might be why there isn't more of it, or it could simply be the length of time to discovery wasn't significant enough to complete the process over her entire body. This tells me two things immediately. She's been dead for months, and the body's spent time in a warm, damp area, deprived of any oxygen."

"So, she died in the river, or on the side of the river?" Hanes asked.

"Not necessarily. Even moist soil. She could have been buried. It's possible the high waters eroded her burial site, swept her into the river, and voila! She's before us now."

Voila! Like it was a magic trick, Hanes thought.

"How much time would you say she spent in the river?" Hanes asked, considering timeline and estimating distance traveled. If they could figure that out, maybe they could pinpoint an entry location.

"It's hard to say for certain. If she was buried, her decomposition would have started in the soil, and, as I've stated, the soil would have been moist and contained bacteria that would result in adipocere. She's missing most of her fingernails. Based on submersion in water alone, that takes approximately eight to ten days. The water around here, on a blanket hypothesis, would be temperate, but, like I said, time of death would date back months."

"Could we narrow down where she went into the water?"

Rideout let out a small laugh. "You have a body that has been through the gamut. She's been buried, and she's been on a trip down the river. Now, you'd like me to give you a point of entry? Think of it this way. She could have been in her grave for X number of days and then went into the river, or she could have been in the soil for a longer period and then got swept into the river. She could have hurried down the river like she was on a white water rapids excursion, or she could have gotten snagged along the bottom. Predicting an entry point based on the circumstances in front of me, would be a crapshoot."

"A crapshoot," Hanes repeated.

"Yes, but don't quote me on that because that's not too scientific." He smiled and hunched down next to the body.

CHAPTER 5

THE NEXT DAY...
WASHINGTON, D.C.
TUESDAY, 10:00 A.M.

JACK HAD SENT PAIGE AND Zachery to speak with Albert Patton, the chief of police in Woodbridge, about Melanie Chase, who was found in nineteen seventy. We were going to talk to Kirk Rogers about his missing wife, Amy, and Stanley Fox, the chief of police for Washington, was to meet us there as well.

Trinity Communications boasted a thirty-story, glass building in downtown Washington. They were a leading Internet provider, but their product range also included cell phones and television satellite service.

Inside, the lobby ceiling was three stories high. A wide staircase, with escalators to the sides, led up the back wall to the second level. The space had a modern and fresh feel to it with brushed metallic accents and marble flooring. Oversized steel structures, some might consider art, were dispersed in the space, likely to instill a sense of awe in visitors. Large screen televisions dangled from above, giving the appearance of being suspended by nothing. They broadcasted commercials for Trinity.

A huge reception desk was located in the middle of the modern design. Two guards were stationed to each side, and one woman sat there. A kiosk near the desk had a sign above it that read *Learn where it all began.*

"Welcome to Trinity Communications." The receptionist offered a sincere smile. "What can I assist you with today?"

Jack held up his creds.

Her smile faded. "What can I do for you?"

"We're here to see Kirk Rogers."

"Well, I don't know if…" She adjusted her seated position. "Do you have an appointment?" She tilted her head to the side, her salon haircut which had the front tips of her hair longer than the back, reached her shoulder. "I couldn't possibly disturb him. If you don't have an appointment, I can make you one."

"We have one for ten."

"Oh." Relief washed over her expression, and she straightened her head. "Your names?" Her eyes went from me to Jack.

"Special Agent Harper and this is Agent Fisher."

I noticed how he dropped the special part when it came to me. I don't think it was lost on the receptionist.

She made a snapping noise with her mouth as she typed into the computer. A few seconds later she looked up at us.

"You take the South elevator to the thirtieth floor." She gestured to the bank of elevators on her right. "When you get up there, you will have to check in with Helena. I will notify her that you are on your way. Good day gentlemen, and remember, choose Trinity and get far."

I saw Jack roll his eyes before he left the counter in the direction of the elevator.

"Get far. It's kind of an ingenious slogan really," I said.

"Hmm."

"Well, it implies a lot without spelling it all out."

Jack tapped his shirt pocket.

I was determined to help him with his addiction. There was no way that chain smoking was good for his health in any fashion. Maybe, if I could get him addicted to exercise as a form of stress relief, he wouldn't feel so inclined to put those sticks in his mouth at every turn.

"When did you start smoking?"

The elevator chimed its arrival. He loaded onto the car. I followed.

"Were you young? My guess is you must have been."

Jack turned to face me, not with his entire body, or even his upper torso, just his head.

"You smoke all the time. You had one on the way over here. You're wanting one now. It's coming off of you."

"Hmm."

"What's that for?" I still didn't always understand his expression, which, in my defense, wasn't a word but a guttural sound.

"You should be focused this much on the case."

It was maddening trying to communicate with this man at times. But I should have known better than to even try to obtain personal information from him. He had it wrapped up tightly to his chest. Paige once told me Jack wasn't afraid of anything. I think he feared letting anyone get close.

"Mr. Rogers." The random thought verbalized, and I laughed. I thought of the children's television show and the man in the gray tweed suit.

Jack raised his brows. "Am I missing something Kid?"

"Oh, don't start with that again." I wasn't sure whether to say what I was thinking or not. "And what was up back there? You introduced yourself as Special Agent and me as just an Agent."

"It's for reasons like that the nickname slips out."

"Come on, Jack. Haven't I proven myself enough?" The cases we worked in the last three months flashed through my mind.

"What's left on your probation? Twenty-one months, give or take?"

"You're going to need all that time to make up your mind about me?"

"I'm saying that until you have proven yourself," he held up a hand to silence me, "until you have done so repeatedly, and until your attitude improves some, I can't help the nickname, and I am old enough to--"

"Yeah, yeah." He always had a way of reminding me of the age difference. I was only twenty-nine. He'd have me believe he was on the earth when the dinosaurs roamed.

It took less than a minute but felt much longer, and we made it to the thirtieth floor.

The reception area was a scaled-down version of the main

lobby. It was also inlaid with marble and accented with brushed metal. The reception desk was a half circle, and the lettering *Trinity Communications* was mounted on the wall behind it.

Helena, I assumed, sat behind the desk, a headpiece situated over one ear.

She smiled as we walked toward her. "Good morning. Welcome to the thirtieth. Is there something I can assist you with?"

It was obvious by her expression, by the way she took us in, that she knew who we were, but she wanted us to announce ourselves.

"Agents Harper and Fisher with the FBI." Jack passed me a glance, and I picked up on his wording. Apparently neither of us was special now.

"Of course. Mr. Rogers is expecting you. I will take you to the conference room." She flipped a sign on the front desk that read *I will be back to service you in a moment.* The company's slogan was beneath that.

She led us down a hallway where she opened the fifth door on the right and gestured for us to go inside.

"Please, have a seat. Make yourselves comfortable. He'll be with you in just one—" She pressed a button on her headpiece. "Trinity Communications, thirtieth floor. How may I direct your call? Certainly. One moment, please." She pushed the button again and then addressed us. "I apologize for the interruption. He'll be with you shortly." She smiled and excused herself.

"Gentlemen." No sooner had the receptionist cleared the doorway when Kirk Rogers walked into the room. Two men shadowed him. One was a lawyer, as evidenced by his expensive suit and haircut. The other would be Chief Stanley Fox.

Rogers had a wide smile that appeared more caricature than real. His eyes pinched into dark lines with the expression narrowing his eyes to slits. His brown hair was trimmed short, and he had a high brow line, his hair coming to a subtle V mid-forehead.

I found it strange the man was smiling, given the circumstances. He must have been bred to put on the expression regardless of a situation—an indication of pride and arrogance. The report showed him to be thirty-three, only a few years older than I am, yet there was the equivalent of many more years' experience in his eyes. Maybe it came with owning one of the largest communication companies and from working in a building he owned.

"This is Hugh Pryce, my lawyer, and this is Chief Fox with Washington PD." Rogers gestured toward Fox.

We all shook hands as the formal introductions were made. The lawyer and the chief had a firm shake, as expected, but Rogers's was even more so. As he shook my hand, I sensed a silent communication that said, *just find my wife*. There was pain that resided in his eyes, although he buried it behind the winning smile and confident demeanor.

Rogers undid his suit jacket, laid a flattened hand over his abdomen, and took a seat across from us with his lawyer and the chief of police. He leaned forward, clasping his hands on the table in front of him.

"Have you gotten any further with your investigation?"

Pryce took a legal pad out of his briefcase and then poured Rogers a glass of water for which he never received acknowledgement by means of a thank you or a nod.

Rogers was a mogul. He was used to being spoiled, used to getting his way, and, when things went off track, well, maybe that's why we were called. He wasn't worried as much about his missing wife as he was his reputation. Those other murdered women who his investigator found out about served simply as the metaphorical icing he needed to involve the FBI.

Fox steadied his focus on me, and it made me uncomfortable, as if he were assessing me negatively. He was in his late fifties and had very little hair on the top of his head. He was dressed in a checkered suit with a cheap tie.

Jack leaned back in the leather chair, crossed his leg, and clasped his hands over his knee. "Tell us about your wife, Mr. Rogers."

"My wife is everything to me, Agents. She is really what gives my life any calm at the end of the day."

I knew what the media said about this man. On one hand, he

was a philanthropist who followed in the shadows of his father, but I gauged the monetary donations and charities were made solely to benefit one person—himself. Opposite of the positive projection, the rumors were he slept with many women, and, according to some sources, the man possessed no morals.

"How long were you married?" Jack asked, even though we knew the answer.

"Two years."

"Guess it doesn't take long, does it? When you know you have the one, you know."

"Are you mocking my feelings in some way? Implying that, because we haven't been married long, she can't mean that much to me?"

"I'm simply making a statement. Continue."

Rogers pulled out on his collar. With the motion, I knew what Jack was doing. He was testing the man's anger threshold.

"She would never cheat on me if that's what you're implying. I know what the papers say. Did you know that five publications are being sued by me, as we speak, for defamatory statements?"

Maybe it came from working with Jack for the months I already had, the cases that required the team connect their psyches to find a killer, but I sensed what Jack was thinking right now. At least, I was thinking it. There's usually a shred of truth that these magazines build on.

"Were you faithful to your wife?"

Rogers glanced over at his lawyer.

"Relevance? It's like he's on trial here. Mr. Rogers simply wants the disappearance of his wife and her safe return to be given top priority," Pryce articulated and twisted a large gold ring on his finger.

"And, of course, justice found for those other missing and murdered women," Jack added.

"Goes without saying."

"Hmm."

"What is that?" Rogers's eyes went between Jack and Pryce. "You don't believe us when we tell you that this case is larger than my wife. You think this is a media stunt to draw more attention to Trinity?"

"I never said that."

"But your demeanor does."

We weren't going to get anywhere with him as long as he and Jack played largest cock in the room.

"Mr. Rogers, we believe you." It warranted a corrective glance from Jack. I pretended not to notice. "When did you last see your wife?"

"I assume you'd have all that in a file." His face went expressionless. When neither Jack nor I spoke after a few seconds, Rogers did. "It was the end of last week—Thursday morning before work. I was headed into the office as normal. I kissed her good-bye. She barely acknowledged it. It was five in the morning. I left and never heard any more from her."

"Do you know what her plans were for that day? Does she have an agenda book?"

"She does." Rogers gestured to Pryce who pretty much tossed the leather book across the table.

I put a hand on it but didn't move to open it.

"She had a weekly appointment at the salon on Thursday mornings. My investigator confirmed she arrived at nine-thirty. Her hairdresser was questioned by him."

"And did she—"

"He. His name's Paulo. Suppose that doesn't matter."

"Did Paulo mention anything about her state of mind? Did she seem to be in a hurry or stressed?"

Rogers seemed to give it some thought. "He did say she was more fussy than normal. The color didn't turn out quite the way she wanted, and she made him re-do it and then complained about the time it was taking."

"Do you know why your wife would have been in a hurry?"

Rogers laughed and turned to his lawyer, who smiled. "Agents, my wife has the life of a dog. By that, I mean I love my wife, and, because of that, she is pampered and spoiled. She doesn't have to lift a manicured finger for work. She has my money to spend. Oh, and I loved spending it on her."

"Loved?"

"I just—" His voice faltered disclosing emotion for the first time since he entered the room. "Sometimes, I'm not sure we'll get her back, especially considering what happened to those other women and then the others who went missing over the past six years. They were never found."

"You let us worry about that," Jack said. "Do you have—"

"Anyone who hates me?" Rogers smiled. "You don't get to the top and not have the haters."

"We're going to need a list of names."

Rogers gestured to Pryce. He slid a sheet of paper across the table.

"Daniel Wade is the highest on my list, but I don't think he's capable of something like this."

"And he hates you because?" Jack asked the leading question.

"We've already spoken with Mr. Wade," Chief Fox interjected. "He was cleared in this case. He had an alibi that checked out."

"All right." Jack's words came out slowly and evenly, "and you haven't received any request for a ransom?"

"None."

"We set up surveillance in his home after he came to us, but it was of no use," Fox said.

"How did your investigator find out about these other women, and what makes you think they are connected to your missing wife?" Jack asked Rogers.

"Just a feeling after my contact started researching the history in the surrounding area."

"Going back to your wife at the salon, you have no idea why she would have been in a hurry?"

"You have her agenda book. You'll see nothing was written in it for the day she went missing."

"Is it possible she ran off with another man?"

"As I said earlier, why would she?"

"HE'S ONE ARROGANT BASTARD. I'll give him that." Jack pulled out a cigarette.

"You don't think he's involved with her disappearance?" I studied his profile. He didn't seem inclined to face me.

I pushed the button to close the elevator doors, and the car started its descent to ground level.

"It's too early to assume much of anything. We can't run this investigation wearing blinders. Mrs. Rogers might be connected to the cold cases, and then she might have nothing to do with them." Jack's words of caution from a past case ran through my mind, *everyone's a suspect until you rule them out.*

CHAPTER 6

"GOOD MORNING, BEAUTIFUL."

He unlatched the bedroom door, cracking it open cautiously, as if she could fight back. She wouldn't of course. She'd welcome him to her. If she didn't, then he would take care of things to ensure she did.

Her naked body was sprawled on the bed, spread eagle. Her wrists and ankles bound to the posts. Her blond hair cascaded over the pillow as an angelic covering, yet she was poisonous.

She deserves to die. What are you waiting for?

He ignored the voice that kept him teetering on the brink of insanity—so would say the mental institutions, those who would prefer to poke him and run tests on him as some lab rat. They would force pills down his throat and tell him to remain calm as they did so.

You are a man? Do it!

He gripped his head, covering both ears momentarily. He had to do this. It was time for him to handle things like a man. He approached her, watching her sleep. Soft snores reverberated up her throat.

He tapped his hands against his thighs.

Tappity, tap. Tappity, tap.

He opened the tattered curtains that hung from the rusty metal rod. For a few seconds, he appreciated the view of the back woods. He heard the birds singing and caught a glimpse of a squirrel running across the yard. He didn't fear anyone seeing anything, not out here in the middle of nowhere.

His thoughts went to the hill, down the makeshift path that had become that way over time. Each time he had to take care of business in the woods, he had tried to take a slightly different route so as not to make an obvious impression. No sense taking unnecessary risks. Still, despite his efforts, there was evidence of a regular passing.

He heard a deeper moan escape her throat and turned from the window to the woman.

"Sydney. Sydney." He said her name twice, calling out as one would to a child in deep slumber.

Her head lolled side to side and her eyes shot open.

There was recognition there, followed by fear.

Her eyes were bloodshot, her pupils dilated. She said something from behind the silver duct tape, but it wasn't audible.

"Now, if you're a good girl and cooperate, everything will be okay." He sat on the edge of the bed. He ran a hand down her inner thigh. She quivered beneath his touch. He wanted to experience pleasure in response, but his feelings were void.

She mumbled again, and this time he was tempted to remove the tape.

He pulled out a vial and a needle.

She screamed—more like muttered—from behind the tape. Her head rocked back and forth, and her body thrashed as much as her constraints would allow.

He saw it in her eyes as he had witnessed in all their eyes. Their pleading with him to have mercy be shown—but who was he to deny them the pleasure of the flesh.

He plunged the loaded needle into her neck, and, within seconds, the movements stopped.

Her eyes rolled back, and her body fell limp.

"There you go, baby. Good as new." He rose from the bed and unzipped his pants, taking his time with the buckle of his belt, and then lifted his t-shirt over his head. He would take control again.

Tears seeped from her eyes as he got on top of her.

Chapter 7

Chief of Police Albert Patton sat behind his desk, tapping a pen against the edge of it. "Glad there's finally some attention being paid to this case. The FBI didn't want it years ago."

Paige and Zach were seated across from him.

She put assorted crime scene photos on the desk. "We're aware of that, but we're interested now, and it's not just the case of Melanie Chase but other similar cases in the area."

He lifted one and held onto it. He shook his head. "What a waste. Unbelievable how sick of a world we live in. Every day, when I don't think it could get any worse, it does." He put the photo down. "Her face is vaguely familiar. What was her name again?"

"Lena Swanson. She was found along I-95 around Lorton back in seventy-three."

Patton shook his head in silent meditation. "You know, I remember Melanie Chase's case very clearly. Some of them stick with you more than others."

"What made this one stick?"

"You mean besides the fact she was a beautiful woman? Just that there was nothing for us to go on. Everything led to a dead end. Everyone in her world was removed from suspicion so we thought maybe it was a truck driver, you know because she was found in a ditch along I-95. Yes, as I gather from your expressions, that's like finding a needle in a haystack. There weren't the man hours required for it, and then the doubt comes into play. What if it wasn't a truck driver we were looking for? There was one guy, though, a Frank Wilson, but the evidence wasn't there. He worked with Chase and happened to be a short-distance driver for a meat packer."

"We'll need the name."

"Of course. Straightline."

"How long did you investigate the case?"

"Years, but when everything kept circling, we had to move on." The chief's face reddened. "Sometimes there's just nothing you can do." His eyes hazed over.

"Anything you remember that stood out from witness interviews, or who was the last to see her alive?"

"Her husband. He said he dropped her off at work in the morning. Everything was normal, but, if you've read the file at all, you already know things didn't play out like that. Her workplace said that she had quit her job. Being dropped off there was all an act."

"She could have been having an affair."

"Absolutely, but that, like so many other things, was one of them circles. It couldn't be proven. The husband adamantly dismissed the idea as being inconceivable."

"Yet, she withheld the fact she quit her job from him. It wouldn't take much more lying ability than that to cheat."

"Well, like I keep saying, nothing was proven." He paused a few seconds. "Since I heard about that woman Rogers on the news, I've had a few sleepless nights wondering if I had missed something and could have stopped it. I take it you're thinking these old cases are connected?"

"Is there anything else you think we should know about Melanie Chase?"

The chief rubbed his chin. "She was a married woman with no children. You likely know that from the file. What you might not know is she was described by her friends as worldly and outgoing. She wasn't shy."

Paige wondered if her 'worldly ways' were what ended up with her on a metal slab and then six feet under.

"The killer was profiled as a male. There wasn't evidence of sexual assault, but she had been bound. The forensics team figured for about a day."

"It was enough to leave the bruising?"

"She was a fighter. We even lifted epithelial from beneath her fingernails, not that we could do anything with it, but we were hopeful for the future. DNA wasn't considered reliable evidence until over a decade after Chase. There were abrasions on her hands. Maybe you'll be able to do something with it now and find a match for the DNA."

CHAPTER 8

ALL OF US WERE IN the briefing room at headquarters. Jack had an unlit cigarette in his mouth. I wondered what the man would look like without one. Zachery hugged another cup of coffee, and Paige scribbled notes into a file.

"Are you going to share with us?" Jack asked her.

"Sure. I just wanted to get my thoughts together." She pried her eyes from her notepad. "Zach and I spoke to the chief in Woodbridge. The first victim, Chase, wasn't raped, but she fought back. There was foreign skin trace found beneath her nails. They collected DNA, but it was fairly useless in that day and age. On the way back, I called in a favor to the lab. They pulled it, and entered the parameters into the database. No known match at this point."

"And Frank Wilson was their number one suspect?"

At first, I questioned where Jack had gotten the name from but remembered Nadia mentioned it in our briefing.

"Yes. He's since passed away with cancer." She consulted her notes. "Two years after Chase."

"Well, that rules him out for the second victim found in seventy-three." The cigarette bobbed as Jack spoke.

She nodded. "Partially why he was eliminated as a suspect for Chase."

"The other reason?"

"His wife swore under oath that she was with him at the time of the disappearance. These two factors were enough to cast suspicion from Wilson. With Chase and the second woman, Swanson, neither was sexually assaulted but were both bound. They were only missing a short time."

"If he were a truck driver, he'd have scheduled stops to make. He couldn't risk getting caught," I said.

"With a truck driver, we'd be looking at a short-run route." Zachery lifted his cup for a sip.

"You said the first two were not raped? What about the other one?" I asked Paige.

She lifted her folder. "She was. Trace of semen was found. No match in the system."

"It didn't tie back to DNA from the first two? You mentioned Chase had epithelial under her fingernails."

She shook her head. "Well, obviously not. I just mentioned that we had that run through on the way back here."

I disregarded the bitterness in her tone. "Are we considering it being a team?" The revelation, even though it had been mentioned during our briefing, had my stomach shrinking into a knot thinking about what those poor women had been through—and so close to my home.

"All these women were ages twenty-two to thirty and married with no children, as we had discussed. Melanie Chase had quit her job not long before her disappearance and death. Amy Rogers didn't have to work a day in her life."

Jack removed the cigarette from his mouth, tapped the end gently on the table, and stuck it back into his shirt pocket.

Apparently, I was jumping ahead.

"Continue. What else do we know about the victimology?" Jack asked.

"They were different nationalities—Caucasian, Asian, and Hispanic. The unsub isn't limited by race, but he doesn't seem to be picking his victims at random either." Zachery gestured to the screen where the before and after pictures were displayed. "They were all beautiful women with a vibrant age range, but all of them were healthy and took care of themselves. They didn't subscribe to raising a family with their husbands but wanted to keep the power of their sexuality with no childbirth."

"You're saying mothers aren't sexy?" Paige lifted her eyebrows.

"Not what I'm saying, but it lends itself to the criteria to which the unsub is attracted. These women were aware of their beauty. You can see it in their eyes. They were confident."

"But not powerful in the sense of the corporate world."

"Yet, powerful in their own domain. They claimed ownership over themselves and didn't transfer this power to their husband."

"You think he targets adulterous wives?"

"It could fit the profile."

"There are still a lot of questions to answer. Like what made him change his MO?" Zachery asked. "Was this second person there from the start?"

"Good question. Why go from not sexually assaulting the victims to rape? And the DNA not matching..." Her words trailed off for a few seconds. "We mentioned a team. Could be that the first unsub was perfecting his method of torture and murder. Maybe he wasn't capable of rape? What if it wasn't a mutual decision for the second person? What if he forced them to rape on his behalf?"

"You're talking a surrogate? Our unsub used someone else to live out his fantasies? Killing them was no longer enough. It wasn't enough defilement."

I traced a circle on the table with my index finger—my mind in thought. "It was likely someone close to him, a long-term friend, or a child?"

Paige shook her head. "Nothing turned up among Chase's long-term friends. Wilson's wife was interviewed at length about her husband and her possible involvement."

"Her involvement?" I asked.

"Yeah, with no sexual assault with Chase, it lent itself to the possibility that a female could have been the unsub."

"Just because of that?"

"Because of that and the fact women don't typically sexually assault other females. Of course, for every statistic, there's a contradictory case."

"A good one would be the Canadian case of Carla Homolka.

She took part in the sexual torture and murder of her own sister."

Paige cocked her head at Zachery as if to say, *did you really need to bring her up?*

Jack pulled the cigarette from his pocket and stuck it in his mouth. "Let's focus on the unsub. What does all of this tell us about him?" His eyes went to me for an answer.

"He likes to be in control, making him a narcissistic-type personality. He binds them, drugs them to have power over them. Maybe he's lacking it in his everyday life."

"Agree with Brandon. I also think that he knows the type of woman he wants. Amy Rogers fits that profile," Paige said.

"We must remember the average age for a serial killer is early thirties. Assigning that age to the unsub from the seventies—"

I quickly did the calculation. "That would make him in his seventies today."

"He could be as young as mid-sixties. We could dig into short-run truck drivers who would have taken I-95 during the years of nineteen seventy to two thousand."

"You're kidding right?" The words gave birth before I had time to think about them or reel them back. Now I was left to defend my statement. "That would seem like an impossible feat. The list of potential suspects would be too large for us to investigate all of them. Wouldn't it?"

"Pending does have a point, boss."

I could tell it killed Zachery to agree.

"We need more than this to narrow down a truck driver Jack," Paige added.

"Well, what about this other guy he may have started working with back in—" With all the years being mentioned, I was quickly losing track.

"Two thousand," she said. "She was the one that was raped."

"Assuming that the original killer worked with someone younger, maybe that person took over for him, or maybe they are working together?"

"If the two of them are still working together, the older man could be luring them. The victims would think him a harmless old man and come closer. He drugs them, and the rest is history."

"We're spinning here. We need more to go on." Jack's voice carried the exasperation we were all experiencing. The room lay thick with tension and deep thought. "Let's go at this a different way. If this unsub's come out of hiding, why and why now? Even just taking the last case from two thousand where the sexual assault took place, there is a huge cooling off period from the second victim in nineteen seventy-three."

"The original could have had health limitations? Maybe he died, or maybe he changed his MO or means of disposal? Maybe there were more victims, but we don't know about them. Then you consider the number of reported cases of missing women in the area over just the last six years. Something's triggered him, or his surrogate, to get going again." Jack rubbed his forehead. "This case is already giving me a headache. Zach and Paige, I want you two to go talk to Wilson's wife from the time. Brandon and I will go to see Chase's husband." Jack pulled out his lighter and left the room.

Chapter 9

Trent Stenson trailed behind Hanes through the corridors of The Department of Forensic Science. "I deserve to be in that room."

"The autopsy really isn't that much fun." Hanes kept moving toward the morgue. "Shouldn't you be taking care of business for Dumfries PD?"

Trent stopped walking.

Hanes turned around. "What? Don't be like that. You know how this works."

"If it weren't for me, we wouldn't even have an ID on her. I'm the one that's been watching these cases over the years and putting everything together."

"We don't even know if it's her yet. I'll keep you posted."

The doors swung shut behind Hanes as if engulfing him into its keep.

"I'll keep you posted." Trent mumbled the words, wishing he could have gained access to the case he was certain would advance his rank, but, more importantly, he wanted this bastard stopped and caught.

Hans Rideout stood over the body wearing a teal green smock. His instruments were lined out beside him on a silver tray, organized in an amazing fashion. The metal of his tools refracted the bright lighting of the overhead bulbs. His glasses were resting on the top of his head when he came in, but he pulled them down as Hanes approached the slab. "I assume we're ready to get started here."

Hanes's focus diverted from the corpse that, given its twist on decomposition, had his coffee threatening reappearance. He made eye contact with Rideout. "You seem ready to go."

"This case intrigues me. This is my first cadaver that has signs of adipocere. These are a rare find."

Hanes dared to take a glimpse at the body. His stomach unmistakably tossed. He hated this newfound reaction. While Rideout termed it "a rare find," as if it were something to be treasured, Hanes would have been happy to never come across it.

"You will be pleased to know that we were able to obtain her fingerprint. It has yet to produce us with an identity, but it is running through the system. All right, let's get started."

Rideout made external observations of the body and spoke them for the benefit of his recorder. He would compile them into his written report afterwards.

"The body is that of a Caucasian female and appears to be well-nourished. Height is sixty-six inches, and the body weight is one hundred ten pounds. I would estimate her age between twenty-six to thirty-three."

He moved the body to its left side and then its right, peering beneath it.

"No signs of lividity, but, based on the age of the body, that's expected."

"So, we don't know what position she died in?" Hanes asked.

"That would be correct. Livor mortis is long gone." Rideout continued on with the external examination, noting all the physical attributes of the deceased. Her hair was brown, shoulder length, both ears were pierced—no earrings. He listed the details of the decomposition and the stages as he worked over the body.

Hanes made notes of what Rideout was saying, even though he'd get the full autopsy report to view later. He normally didn't have a problem standing in for autopsies. He saw it as part of the job, but he could never shake the feeling that everyone became catalogued, as if inventory, by the process. He wondered how the ME would describe him when he was the one lying on the gurney—mostly bald with brown stubble on his head, measuring in at seventy-four inches, weighing two hundred and thirty pounds. Hanes shook the thought that he often revisited.

"Now, here is an interesting find, and one I know we noted at the crime scene." Rideout lifted her left wrist. "Contusions on both of her wrists and ankles."

"Bruising?"

Rideout smiled, which seemed sickly out of place with his gloved hands covered in the deceased's fluids.

"I'm wondering if we're looking at a serial killer. He binds his victims and dumps them in the river?" It sounded ridiculous to Hanes when he said it out loud. They only had one body. Technically, they needed three to classify it as a serial. Maybe he was listening to Trent too much.

"You're forgetting one thing. This body was buried, based on decomposition. We also pulled dirt trace evidence from it."

Hanes let out the breath he was holding. "We'll need the soil tested for future comparison. It will be useful when we narrow in on a location. Love how things work backward sometimes."

"That's life, and of course, the test will be done."

"Anything more you can tell me about her?" Hanes couldn't help but think Trent was right about all this. Maybe the missing women were connected, culminating in this recent discovery. There was a serial killer out there.

"Toxicology will be run on her to find out the time of her last meal. If possible, what it was and if she was on drugs or alcohol. Although, I hold little hope of finding anything in the latter regard. I also pulled an insect from her that I will have processed."

Over the next twenty-five minutes, Rideout finished up the autopsy, pulling apart the deceased as if she were a bucket of parts and not a once-living person. It was the job and a necessary one. He weighed the organs, including the brain, noted the appearance of the head, the neck, the body cavities such as the ribs and sternum, the lungs, heart, liver, spleen, pancreas and adrenal glands, the genitourinary system, and gastrointestinal tract.

He took pause at the brain and the lungs.

"There is evidence of hemorrhage in the brain. The lungs show signs of pulmonary edema."

When he was mostly finished, he stepped back from the table and lifted his face shield. "I have a theory on how she may have died."

"What are you thinking?"

"A brain hemorrhage, pulmonary edema. I'm thinking she died from being hung upside down."

"Upside down?" Hanes repeated the doctor's hypothesis, not really believing it. As a kid, he was always cautioned by his parents that being upside down would cause the blood to rush to his head. He didn't realize he could die from this.

"Yes, and it's quite likely. So our vic was bound, hung upside down to die—"

"Like a butcher." Rideout interrupted Hanes. "To drain the meat of blood, they hang it."

"You think our killer's a butcher?"

Rideout shrugged his shoulders.

"If he is, he doesn't use his knives for killing or torture."

"It is an interesting thought process, however, don't you think?" Again, a smile started to light his face, seeming out of place among the canvas in front him stained in red when the phone rang. He pulled his helmet off, peeled his hands from gloves, paused his recorder, and headed to the phone.

"We have one sick bastard to catch," Hanes mumbled. He thought about the location of where they found her. Was she placed in the river or buried on a riverbank? The waters had been high.

Rideout replaced the receiver in the cradle.

"Was there evidence of sexual intercourse?" Hanes asked.

"DNA would be impossible to obtain at this point, unfortunately. I did, however, note contusions around her inner thigh and vaginal opening so I would conclude forcible entry not long before death."

"She was raped." Hanes let out a deep breath.

"I'd guess repeatedly." Rideout gestured to the phone. "Now we have an ID as confirmed by both her prints and DNA. Seems she had this information placed on record from when she was a kid."

TRENT STENSON WENT BACK TO his duties at the front desk. He had spent most of the week as a desk jockey. While he got to meet some interesting people who walked in, he would have preferred being out making a difference.

All his interest in the missing women didn't seem to amount to anything. Even his friend dismissed his input by shutting him out of the autopsy and making him feel useless. He spent most of his time watching out the front doors to passersby on the sidewalk, and it wasn't even like there was much to see in this small town. This was ridiculous. He should be at the morgue. This was his case. He knew it. He felt it.

The victim's age was right. The timeframe was right. The wedding band was right.

He pulled up the missing persons database again. Why did he do this to himself? It wasn't getting him anywhere, but he didn't give up easily. He was made to persevere when the odds were against him.

Chapter 10

THE ROOM AROUND HER KEPT getting darker—or was it her vision? Her headache's intensity had ratcheted to the point of unbearable pain. Her thoughts didn't line up, no matter how hard she tried to concentrate. The chill had become a familiar backdrop, tinged tepid. Its warmth encased her body, enshrouding it in calmness—it was her body preparing for death.

Tears fell down her face, past her forehead, to the concrete below. Before, she could hear the soft tap as they made impact. Now she knew their destination without the auditory confirmation.

She couldn't remember how long she had been down here but figured it had been days. Days of endless rape by a man she thought she knew.

A stab of pain burrowed into the back of her head, and, with it, her vision went black. Within seconds, everything turned dark.

OUTSIDE OF WOODBRIDGE, VA

JACK AND I HEADED TO talk to Melanie Chase's husband from nineteen seventy. He was seventy-one now and, according to records, he had re-married and resided in a small community just outside of Woodbridge.

"We're here from the FBI, Special Agents Harper and Fisher." Jack showed his creds, but it wasn't really needed.

The woman at the door had a petite frame and trusting eyes. She smiled warmly. "You're the one who called and said you were coming. Come in."

She led us to the living area.

"Jed, the FBI's here."

Jed Chase sat, reclined in a sofa chair. An oxygen tank was beside him, its mask on the side table with an ashtray and a package of cigarettes next to it.

I struggled not to glance over at Jack. Did the habit have man wanting to reach from their grave for a few puffs?

Jed's face was wrinkled, and his white hair held a yellowish tinge. His hand gripped the arm of the chair. His fingernails were stained from nicotine. His blondish eyebrows appeared nearly transparent against his pale skin.

"Yeah, I see 'em, Anna."

She waved a dismissive hand at him and smiled at us again. "Go ahead, take a seat where you like. Would you be interested in some tea?"

"Anna, they won't be here long. They've wasted a trip."

"Nonsense. We have them as guests in our home, they get tea." She addressed us. "I'll be right back."

Jed rolled his eyes and let out a haggard breath. "Health ain't what it used to be." He referred to the apparatus situated beside him. "Emphysema."

"We want to ask you a few questions about Melanie," Jack started. "We've read the reports, and your interview with Detective Patton."

"Then I don't know what else to say. Like I said to Anna," he paused for breath, "your trip's been wasted."

"Can you tell us what Melanie was like the last time you saw her?" I asked.

Jed's head turned to me. "She was stressed out. Said she had all these reports due at work."

"But she quit the week before."

"I'm only telling you how it was."

Jack leaned back into the sofa, hooked a finger on his shirt pocket and dropped his hand. "We know that she quit. It's been testified to by her boss."

"I don't believe a word of it. Maybe they killed her. Maybe they're trying to cover it up."

Melanie Chase worked for an accounting firm as an intern at the time she went missing. Everyone had been cleared.

"They were interviewed at length," I said.

"But you're not there reconfirming their statements. You're here and that makes me—" He wheezed, and it had him reaching for the oxygen. After a few seconds, he took it down. "Makes me mad. You come into my home after all these years questioning me? I loved her. There's no woman I've loved more."

Anna came into the room holding a tray with a teapot, four cups, sugar, and milk. Her steps slowed, and I sensed she had heard her husband's words. She was rather quick to resume her pace, though, so maybe this wasn't news to her. She was used to being second place—even if it were to a dead wife and a haunting memory.

She put the tray on the coffee table, prepared her cup, told us all to make our own as we liked it, and sat in another reclining chair. Maybe her husband's comment had thrown her off a little because the energy in the room tingled between the couple, and it wasn't until she sat that she shot back up to make a cup for him.

"Anna, she is the spark in my eye now—the reason I don't just curl up and die." He pointed to the oxygen tank. "But Melanie...I want to see justice for her. Something horrible happened to her. Her life was stolen—and our future."

I thought back to the file. "You never had kids."

"Never got to that point. The killing bastard took that from us." He lifted the oxygen mask again for a few hits.

About twenty minutes later, Jack and I excused ourselves from the Chase home. We sat in the SUV in their drive talking the situation over.

"They didn't have kids either." I made the quick summary. "It definitely seems to be a solid connection with the victimology."

"We knew that from the file before we went in, but what did we learn?"

"That the man's a bitter coot who takes his new wife for granted."

"Kid, get serious. Something useful."

I'm not sure why, but being called Kid in that moment made

the realization hit.

"He said that she was stressed that morning."

"Keep going."

Sometimes I wondered if he already knew the answer but was testing to see if I knew how it fit together.

"Amy Rogers's hair stylist had commented on the same thing."

"Continue."

"Both women were stressed and in a hurry for something. For what? For the same reason? For a different reason?"

Jack didn't speak so I carried on. "Both husbands claimed their wives had never cheated on them. I'm starting to believe that's a bunch of BS."

Jack lit a cigarette and expelled a puff of white smoke. "It could be to save face. Maybe they did know, but they're not sharing it with us."

"Even in light of an open investigation? We don't know if Rogers is dead yet." I stopped talking. I didn't know all the answers. I was trying to piece things together the best I could.

The onboard system in the SUV rang.

Jack connected the call. "Harper and Fisher here."

"Jack, it's Nadia. There's been another abduction. Her name is Sydney Poole, but that's not all. One of the missing women, from three months ago, her body was found."

CHAPTER 11

"HOW DO I LOOK? Do I look okay?" Trent straightened his tie.

Hanes shook his head. "It's not prom. It's the FBI. Cool it."

"How can I when I put all this together? I'm the reason—"

"Audrey Phillips discovering the remains of Nina Harris, that's the reason."

"Let's not forget the missing Rogers lady. Also, let's remember I'm the one that connected it before they did. I've been studying these missing women cases for months, years even, tying them together and recognizing how they were connected."

"Is there some reason you are talking so loudly? I could hear you down the hall Officer Stenson. Is your sergeant not missing you back at Dumfries PD?"

Chief Nathan Steele came toward them, his stride centered and determined. The loose skin below his brows hooded his eyes and gave him an untrustworthy appearance. His hair was light on the top of his head with fine baby hair on the crown surrounded by a wreath of brown.

"I wanted to thank you again for referring the case to the FBI," Trent said. He had been able to secure the day off. He told his sergeant what he was doing and the man just shook his head.

"Referring?" Steele laughed. "All we did is report this case. They were already working it, really, with the Rogers woman missing."

"They were already working it?"

Steele's eyes went from Hanes back to Trent. "Are you hard of hearing?"

Trent took a deep, steady breath, attempting to calm himself, to cleanse his system. He didn't need to mouth off to the top guy and blow any chance of a transfer and of making rank.

"Your lack of knowledge may be why you're an officer. We do the real work."

Hanes turned to Trent and his eyes read of an apology.

Trent wasn't sure why his friend was sorry for Steele's demeaning attitude. He also didn't understand why Steele was determined to sweep in and claim credit for the connection. It's not like he was the one that pieced things together or made the request to call in the FBI. If they had waited on him to "do the real work," how many women would die? How many more would go missing?

The anger boiled in his system, but he had to abate it. The only calming thought was shit floats.

THE FBI AGENT, who went by the name of Supervisory Special Agent Jack Harper, wore his confidence well. He had seen a lot. Trent saw it in his eyes. They always disclosed the truth. People could tell you whatever they wanted to spew off, but the truth was hidden within the pupils.

They were all in a conference room at The Department of Forensic Science in Richmond.

Steele settled back into his chair. "Serial crimes are not our job. It's that of the FBI."

"Hmm."

Trent wanted to smile but was hesitant of basking in this. Steele had, in effect, admitted negligence. He liked this guy Harper.

He assessed the rest of the team who had come with him. There were two men. One was a guy who didn't appear much older than Trent. He had light red hair and eyes that jabbed about the room, taking in everything. The other man was intelligent, possibly even a genius. Again, it was in the eyes. They assessed and analyzed.

Then there was the woman. She was trim with red hair that reached past her shoulders. Her hair was more fiery-colored than the guy's and fell in soft curls that framed her face.

She caught him looking at her and smiled. Trent returned it.

"Why do you say it like that? Hmm?" the chief asked.

Trent caught the smirk on the male redhead.

"We have two missing women to save who need our focus."

Trent loved how the Supervisory Agent didn't ask for things—he demanded them—but the finesse with which he carried it out, at word value only, initially came across as a proposal. The mental fortitude behind the statements cemented them as directives.

Trent knew who he wanted to be when he grew up. The thought made him smile in his mind. "Two missing women? Someone besides Rogers?"

Harper turned in his direction.

Trent smiled awkwardly.

"I understand you're the one who connected the recent body to the missing women cases?"

Trent nodded. "I knew that something was up—just the sheer number of missing women in the area. I've been looking into them for years."

Harper scowled.

"But what am I supposed to do about it? I'm just an officer."

Harper's face contorted, as if he caught the smell of rotting flesh.

Trent should have stopped at "for years."

"Well, I'm not just an officer. I am a member of Dumfries PD. They let me sit in today because I have some knowledge of the missing women cases. That's why I knew Nina Harris. Someone had to care about these women." He wasn't sure why he was compelled to impress the man or had the impulse to ramble.

"You're excited because you were able to connect a missing woman to a body, or are you're excited because another has gone missing?" Harper's eyes went through him. "For certain, one woman has lost her life. It's up to us whether another two do as well. This is not even mentioning all those other women who may have been saved if we had acted sooner."

Trent's tongue went thick. "You said two women?"

"Yes. The husband owns a prestigious law firm in Washington. His wife was last seen the day after Rogers was reported missing. Her name is Sydney Poole."

Trent leaned across the table. "When did you find out about…" His words stalled under the SA's glower.

"You leave that worry to us." Harper turned to Hanes. "We'd like to start with seeing the body of Nina Harris and then the crime scene."

"What kind of person do you think is capable of something like this?" Trent asked. Why couldn't he keep his mouth shut?

"Based on the statistics we've already gathered, the unsub is a male, likely in his early to mid-thirties—"

"That's the ripe age for a serial killer."

The agent's staggered exhale disclosed that he wasn't impressed with being interrupted. "He likely fits into society and holds a job."

"You know all that already?" the chief asked.

"He's attracting beautiful women with successful husbands. The fact that he fits in is an easy conclusion. There's no doubt he's also a ladies' man—probably more popular with them than his male counterparts. He may feel incompetent in the presence of his peers. With women, he has the power and control."

"He binds them," Trent added. He knew this much from Nina's body.

"Yes, to reinforce that they are to be submissive to him. He takes their fight away because he has a God complex."

The genius agent at the end of the table contributed. "You see, he's been at this long enough, he believes he's getting away with it, and will continue doing it."

Trent knew he had to get their names down. He remembered the guy's in charge and the woman's—Paige Dawson. She smiled at him again and he returned it.

Harper didn't miss the interaction as evidenced by the slightly narrowed eyes. "He won't stop until someone stops him, and that's what we intend to do."

"Should we be arranging for a press release on this? Warn the women in the area? I think something was on the radio after the Rogers woman went missing," the chief said.

"There's no need for an official release at this point. We cannot tell women what to be on the lookout for until we have more evidence and facts to support a profile. We also don't want to cause undue panic. It seems these women are targeted and specifically chosen."

"Right. They have wealthy, successful husbands."

"Only in the two recent cases. This dates back decades."

"Decades?" Stenson knew his eyes widened. He only knew about the women from the last six years.

"Any other questions, or can we see the body now?"

CHAPTER 12

ZACHERY READ THE AUTOPSY REPORT in its entirety on the way to the morgue. I knew because I walked beside him while Jack and Paige were in front with the Steele, Hanes, and the Dumfries officer.

"You have this thing solved yet?" I smiled at Zachery.

"Pending, wouldn't you love me to do your job for you."

"I do my job quite well, thank you. I'm making small talk."

"Why?"

Why. Good question. Maybe it stemmed back to the conference room and the way the officer kept making eyes at Paige. It shouldn't bother me. She didn't belong to me, but watching his attention on her, imagining what he was thinking…

Jack stood to the side of the morgue door, letting the rest of us go in ahead of him.

"So, you be the FBI." A graying man of about six-foot-five held out a large hand, first toward Zachery. "I'm Hans Rideout, Medical Examiner."

As he made his way around to all of us and the introductions were made, it didn't appear the ME had the same stigma toward us as did the police chief. I got the impression that, to him, we were outsiders, here to take the credit for a case they should have been left to solve.

Only a few seconds passed in silence as Rideout pulled the appropriately marked slab from the wall and its frozen cocoon. "The family's been called. I hate cases like this, when they demand to see the body."

As the ME lifted the sheet, I understood why he said that. My coffee swirled into sour bile and threatened to burn a hole through my stomach lining.

"It's adipocere." Rideout must have noticed my facial expression or picked up on my energy. He leaned over the cadaver to level his face with mine. "It happens under unique circumstances—moist soil, for example, and it takes months to form."

"The report says she was found in a field." Zachery held onto the folder, his one index finger pressed between its manila covers. The group turned to him, and the ME's mouth twitched like he was going to say something but refrained. Zachery continued. "She was buried, swept into the river when the water was high, exposing her grave. Her burial would have started the process before the river claimed her."

"Yes, very good. We found trace of soil on her. It's being tested, along with an insect we found on the body."

Zachery held his expression during the doctor's condescending praise, and I was impressed by his ability to keep it cool. His intelligence could rival that of the ME's.

Zachery held up the folder. "Now the report shows no evidence of lividity, and that makes sense based on the age of the remains. It also notes that you believe she died from being hung upside down."

"Correct. Look at her wrists and ankles." Rideout pointed to bruising in those areas.

"I'd say she was bound with chain, as you can make out that impression, but have you taken photographs under ultraviolet lights? It would enhance the visual. Maybe we could confirm exactly what the unsub used and track it down to a supplier," Zachery said. "It might take more time than we have right now though."

I took in those in the room. The officer's face disclosed more fascination over the body than disgust. The chief stood back from the group of us, his hands tucked under his arm pits. The detective's body language wasn't communicating much.

"Anything else you pick up on?" Rideout asked Zachery.

Zachery leaned in closer to the body.

My sinuses were singed enough from the smell of death standing a couple feet back. The acid in my stomach rolled again.

"With her wrists being bound the way they were--" Zachery moved around the gurney and the rest of us stepped out of his way, "she was laid out, connected to a sort of pulley system."

"Excuse me?"

Zachery laid his one palm, flat out, pointed to the heel of his hand. "She was bound at her wrists." He pressed a fingertip to the pad of his index finger. "Bound at her ankles." His eyes were on his hand and the vision he was conjuring in his mind. "He kept her hostage for a while, and she was unable to fight her constraints at all times."

"Unable to fight her—"

"Yes, we believe that the unsub uses some sort of drug to subdue his victims, but these markings show that he didn't keep her under. He gave her hope she'd escape."

"One sick bastard," the chief said from the side of the room.

Zachery continued. "That's why there are some deeper impressions—the struggle. Going back to the victim being laid out." His attention went back to his palm. "The pulley system would connect the chains in a systematic manner. As the unsub cranked the ratchet, the body would move along the table until it ran out of surface." He demonstrated the thought with his hand by lifting his palm upward.

"She died upside down," I mumbled.

The members of PWPD watched Zachery. The officer's eyes kept going to the body.

Rideout took a step closer to the slab. "I concluded that she died upside down, but what you propose, well, the entire method seems quite plausible."

Jack tapped his shirt pocket, no doubt a cigarette calling out, tempting him to light up. It had been about an hour. I was surprised he wasn't shaking.

"Brilliant." Rideout's eyes went to the body, an odd smile on his face.

"We have to think about chains, hanging bodies…" I introduced the audible brainstorming session. "Could be our unsub is in the meat packing industry."

Detective Hanes, who had been quiet up until this point, stepped forward. "Initially we were thinking the same thing, but there's no indication that they were hung by hooks."

"Unless the chain was just fastened to them? It's seems coincidental. Who else uses chain and hangs bodies upside down?"

Paige let out a deep breath. "It could explain the old cases too. We mentioned the possibility of a short-run truck driver who frequented I-95."

Chief Steele stepped forward. "Old cases? What are we talking about, exactly, here?"

"Yeah, you had mentioned it dates back *decades*," the officer said.

Jack provided a quick overview of the old cases.

The officer's eyes scanned over each of us. "You think a meat hauler from the nineteen seventies is still abducting and killing women?"

"It's possible."

I noticed Jack didn't share that the third victim was raped. Like he always said, *only share what you have to, so they think you're giving as much as you take.*

"One more question, was there evidence of rape?" I asked.

Rideout looked up from the body. "My guess is repeated assaults."

THE FOUR OF US LOADED into the SUV and followed Hanes and the Dumfries officer in their department-issued sedan. Jack had the hands-free system connect us to Nadia.

"I need you to look into meat packers and distributors who would have had trucks running along I-95 between Greenwood, Maryland and a little west of Dumfries, Virginia. Narrow it down to the years nineteen seventy to two thousand. That would at least cover the first three victims."

"That's narrow?"

Jack disregarded her. "The driver likely would have been in his mid-thirties at the time, but only use that parameter if there are too many hits."

"Anything else?"

"For now, that should be it. It's likely the guy had a bad attendance record or other marks against him."

"This driver would be—what?—in his seventies now?"

"Yes, but it should get us closer."

"You believe a seventy-year-old man is luring these women?"

I wished I could read the expression on Paige and Zachery's faces. Not many questioned Jack's decisions.

"Maybe he entices them with candy." Nadia laughed and so did everyone else, except Jack.

Jack continued. "It also goes back to the highway murders. The last one was raped. We could also be after a younger counterpart who helped him years ago."

"You're not leaning toward a child?" Nadia asked.

"Not necessarily. It could be someone younger than he is but considered a peer."

"Maybe the old guy brings in the women. We know how you attract the ladies, boss." Nadia's smile infused her voice.

Color touched Jack's cheeks.

"What can I say? When you got it, you got it. Now get to work."

Jack disconnected the call.

I turned to him. "Going back to our first thoughts on this, if we go to the victim from two thousand and factor in a younger counterpart, possibly a child, working with the original unsub, he would have had to at least be in his teens at the time. Maybe the old guy died or retired, and something triggered the younger man to start up again. Although, it's possible he never stopped, remained active, but no bodies were found. Either way, guessing him to be about fifteen then, that would put him in his mid-twenties today."

SHE PULLED AGAINST THE CHAINS secured around her wrists and ankles. The metal links slapped against the bed frame.

Where the hell am I?

She should be able to remember, but her mind was so foggy.

Thoughts were impossible to form in any logical progression.

She remembered champagne, but nothing else was coming to her.

Frustrated, she thrashed against the restraints, but there was no give. She stopped moving when she heard the front door.

Oh, God, he was back.

Her heart paused beating, and she held her breath.

Please go away. Leave me alone!

She heard his steps coming closer.

"Hello, beautiful I'm home." He spoke from the other side of the door.

His voice, the one that used to tempt her to stay in bed all afternoon, now riddled her body with chilled tremors that fired through her being. With them, came the clarity that she was still naked.

"Hope you didn't miss—"

His speech was clipped. Had it always been that way?

Images flashed in her mind, rapid-fire, like the shutter on a paparazzi's camera. He had been her lover. She had risked her marriage on this man, and now she faced the possibility of losing so much more than that to him. He had always had such a delicate touch, the way his hands would trace over her body, admiring every inch.

The vision crashed with the recollection of the intensity that boiled beneath his skin, making his body feel as if it quivered with nervous energy. The signs had been there all along. There was a buried hunger that singed through his fingertips and seemed to propel him to ravage her, as a starving man would a plate of food. This used to make her crave him.

"I'm here. No more waiting." He pushed the door open with a foot. He was lifting his shirt over his head as he came into the room.

No! No!

The words wouldn't give birth audibly but instead ricocheted in her head, a relentless nightmare. He was going to defile her again, further exceed her physical tolerance. The stickiness between her legs was more than sexual fluids. Blood smeared her thighs.

"Don't." She struggled so hard to even get that one word to form. Tears stung her eyes. A headache pounded in the back of her skull.

He kept advancing toward her, his eyes not on her face but on her naked body. He tapped his thighs and then worked at unbuckling his belt. "I have a surprise for you, but first—"

She screamed in silence.

CHAPTER 13

THE CRUISER PULLED DOWN A gravel road and kicked dust up in its wake. Jack followed closely, and the dirt cloud coated the black hood a charcoal gray while stones pelted the underside of the SUV.

"It's always in the middle of nowhere," I said, thinking back to the horrifying case in Salt Lick, Kentucky, of eleven graves and ten bodies. With that, came the remembrance of the tight underground passageways, although, those were never far from mind.

No one commented on my observation, instead, we traveled in silence. I believe each of us was contemplating what awaited us. With the thought, I was thankful Jack couldn't read minds. He chose, then, to glance over at me, making me question my assumption. Maybe he could.

The cruiser pulled into the driveway of an old farmhouse. It had a dilapidated front porch which didn't appear sound enough for a toddler to walk across, let alone support the weight of an adult. The roof bowed in the middle, sagging, as if burdened by the passage of time. The barn was painted a bright red, a gold star mounted where its front peak formed a triangle. It was in better shape than the house.

The cruiser pulled to a stop. Detective Hanes and the officer met up with us halfway between the two vehicles.

"We've got to go the rest of the way on foot." Hanes gestured with a pointed finger to a place beyond the barn.

There was a wooded patch to the far left, but most of it was open field.

"It's not too far, closer to the river. I'm going to let the homeowner know we're here."

We waited for Hanes who returned in a couple of minutes. The officer spent the time studying us. His eyes squinted in the sunlight, causing his forehead to wrinkle.

"Are there any other houses nearby?" Jack asked Hanes.

It was an interesting question. I couldn't remember passing one for miles.

"Well, there are a lot of houses along the river, and it runs for miles. It wouldn't be practical to knock on all the houses along the river if you had that in mind. Rideout's not even certain on TOD at this point, and we can't pinpoint where the body entered the river." Hanes took a few steps in the direction he had pointed to earlier.

We followed along behind him. The walk took about fifteen minutes from the house.

"What was the homeowner doing out here?" I asked, figuring it was a viable question.

The officer turned around and walked backward as he spoke. "She said that she walks her property regularly. Something about clearing her mind."

"She happened upon it?" I heard the skepticism in my own voice. The officer didn't miss it.

"Mrs. Phillips is a sixty-one-year-old woman. Do you figure she's involved with this?"

I noticed the sideward glance from the rest of the team.

Zachery's eyes read, *oh, you've gone and done it now.*

"I never said she was, but it needs to be explained."

The officer stopped walking. "It needs to be explained why an individual would go for a walk on their own property?" He shot a look at Jack.

"Again, I never said that."

If this guy wanted to get into a dick-measuring contest, I was game. I went through the academy, through the training. I had the badge of a special agent of the FBI. I gave his uniform a once-over.

"You think because you're the FBI you can question anything and everything?"

"I thought you wanted us here." I raised my eyebrows. "I thought it was you who pushed for us to come and help find these women."

"A little too late for this one."

The hairs rose on the back of my neck. "Surely you can't hold the FBI responsible when officers didn't do their job and report the case of the missing women years ago." I wasn't even referring to the victims found along I-95.

His cheeks flamed a bright red, and he ground his teeth.

"Next time you feel the need to question everything we do, think about it." I brushed past him to Hanes. "We almost there?"

"Right here actually." Hanes drew an imaginary circle with his finger to take in a portion of the field. "She was lying on her back here." He pulled a photograph from a folder he carried and extended it to me. "We have everything at PD. We can go over it later."

In the photograph, the remains of Nina Harris appeared like a page from horror fiction. Despite the gravity that death carried, her bloated features and coloring had her resembling something alien, not human. It was tragic how in death our dignity was stripped and laid bare. We became nothing more than a travel case for a soul.

Before photos had shown Nina Harris as a beautiful woman, fit, with a seductive glint in her eye that fed the camera. In this picture, as she had been in the morgue, Nina's appeal had been stolen.

Knowing that we stood where she had come to rest, the area had a tangible quality to it. I was a relatively new FBI agent, but, being around the burial sites in Salt Lick and at crime scenes elsewhere, I was beginning to realize there was a common feel to the places where people had lost their lives. While it was true Nina Harris didn't have her life taken here, there was that feel in the air.

Zachery walked around the area where the body had been found. His eyes took in everything, including, I figured, each blade of grass.

"Her wedding ring was on her finger before the landowner took it off, along with part of the finger," Hanes said.

My stomach tightened but didn't toss. Blame that on Salt Lick as well. It had toughened me up from the start.

"The killer likes isolation." Zachery spoke, his eyes not focused on any of us. "He's ashamed by what he does and that's why he buried her. She wasn't supposed to be found, but he might be happy to be stopped."

"You can tell all that from staring at the ground?" Detective Hanes shifted his weight to the left.

Zachery still didn't make eye contact. "He buried her with her ring. The three victims from the highway weren't wearing their wedding bands." He glanced up at us.

"With the three, original homicides, the unsub stripped them of their commitment in life," Paige added.

"He didn't feel they lived up to it or deserved it. Maybe they were cheating wives?" I stepped closer to Zachery. "All the victims were beautiful women with busy husbands, even the highway victims."

Revelation lit in Zachery's eyes. "The first three victims were found naked, without their rings, and there wasn't evidence that they had been buried. They were just found along the highway. We're only after one unsub at this point. The original is no longer in charge, possibly not even alive. I bet that he is motivated to continue because of him though."

"Smart." Jack nodded and added, "He picks them out and gets close to them. He takes his time with them as evidenced by what they undergo."

"Rape and murder doesn't come naturally to him. He feels a compulsion." Paige bobbed her head. "Probably because of what you just mentioned Zachery, but the question of why remains."

I nodded in agreement. "Maybe the original guy is alive and has more influence than we originally thought, leans toward it being his child."

"The original killer is now the spectator. We estimated him to be in his seventies. Maybe he's involved and picks the women, like we mentioned before, but our unsub carries it out?"

"Whatever the case, he's getting more daring. He's going after wives of successful businessmen."

Detective Hanes's attention went between us as we discussed the mental state of the man we hunted.

"He has a low regard for women, no doubt learned at an early age. Despite feeling regret, as evidenced by the ring and burying of the body, he leaves them naked, a state of disgrace," Zachery said.

"He's more ashamed for them than for his actions." I verbalized the thought as it occurred to me.

Zachery's eyes went from me to Jack. "It's possible."

"So, why here, why now, and why Nina Harris?"

Jack finally gave in and lit up a cigarette. A stream of white smoke ascended on his exhale. "It could be as simple as because he could, or it could be more complicated. He could like here because of the isolation. He's able to keep the women, do as he wishes, and then dispose of the bodies. Something's definitely triggered this guy back into action. After the killings seemed to have stopped in two thousand," Jack addressed the officer, "who was the next woman reported as missing that fits the profile?"

"Leslie Keyes, two thousand and five."

Everyone stared at him. Jack took another puff, his eyes never leaving the officer. "Six years ago. Was the report filed in Dumfries?"

The officer shook his head. "Prince William County PD."

"When the husband was interviewed, what did he say?"

Hanes flushed. "We didn't interview anyone. It was a missing persons report. You know how they are. They get filed, and they're not actively investigated unless there's evidence of foul play."

"Did the husband have a life insurance policy on his wife, or would he benefit in any other way from her disappearance and pronouncement of death?" Jack's eyes fixed on the detective, his suction tight around the cigarette.

"She hasn't been pronounced and wouldn't there be better ways to go about it? A faster route if monetary benefit were the goal?"

Jack looked out over the field. His jaw muscles went as taut as violin strings. He took a dramatic inhale from the cigarette. "My question was, would he benefit?"

"I…we…don't know."

"It might be a good thing for us to find out then." Jack turned to the team. "We also need to speak with Nina's husband."

The officer shook his head again. Hanes was avoiding eye contact with all of us.

Jack continued. "Our unsub started up again with Leslie Keyes six years ago. Brandon and I will start with Keyes. While we're doing that Paige, I want you and Zach to visit Harris's husband."

"At one point, you wanted us to visit the wife of the first suspect in the Chase investigation," Paige said.

"We'll leave her 'til a little later." Jack directed his next words to the detective. "When Mr. Harris was told about his wife, how did he take it?"

"Like one would imagine. He was distraught but relieved to have some closure. It has been months since Nina went missing."

Jack studied the detective's face and nodded. "What is his line of work?"

"He…" Hanes turned to the officer.

The officer picked up. "He's not successful like the husbands of the two recent victims. He's not the owner of some law firm or a telecommunications giant."

Jack flicked ash from his cigarette into the grass. "To the point kid."

I swallowed the smile that would have enveloped my face given a chance. I liked hearing someone else get the nickname.

"He's a satellite dish installer. He doesn't work for Trinity if you're thinking they're connected that way."

"There goes the thought that all the husbands are busy and important," I said.

"Hmm." Jack turned to me. I thought that was one in my favor, and then his words confirmed it. "Fisher's right. We'll meet back at PWPD to discuss what we found out once we're finished with the husbands." He addressed the detective and the officer. "Make sure to have a crime board set up laying out the missing women, starting with Leslie Keyes from two thousand five. Start with noting their husband's line of work and their alibis for the day their wives went missing. Include anything and everything we know."

Detective Hanes passed a glance to the officer and then took a step forward. "That's thirty-two women including Rogers and this latest one."

"I said it back at the station, but her name is Sydney Poole. I'll get you some help. Her name is Nadia Webber." Jack extended a business card and told him the extension to reach her desk. "Give me fifteen minutes to let her know you're going to be calling."

"That won't be necessary."

We all turned to the officer.

He tucked a strand of hair behind an ear. "I have everything you'll need to know on the thirty missing women from the last six years."

"All thirty?" Jack's brows rose.

"Yes."

The team shared looks. Jack responded to him. "All right then."

"I know from your faces what you're thinking."

"You can tell our thoughts from our faces? Wow, you're better than us." Jack stamped the butt of his cigarette on the ground.

"Well, what I believe you're thinking. I knew something was going on with these missing women years ago. I've told you that." He turned to the detective again, as if for backup. "I have all the information you've asked Detective Hanes for, maybe more. I'll even get you everything on the latest two."

"Hmm."

The officer's cheeks flushed. He must have experienced what I did on the end of Jack's famous, *hmm*.

"I would like to be a detective someday, Agent, maybe even work at the FBI."

Jack studied his face. "You help Hanes get the board together." He gestured to the card. "If you find out your information isn't as complete as you think it is, call Nadia."

HE SHOVED THE HEEL OF his palms to his ears hoping to mute

the voice. Maybe it would stop calling out to him, telling him it disapproved, directing his next step, but it didn't matter. It summoned him even through ear plugs. He had tried. He attempted to drink himself unconscious—it got louder. He feared the results of mind-altering drugs such as cocaine, assuming the voice would take on an even more dominant presence. Doctors had tried to remedy him, but the voice was persistent—it prevailed and came out stronger.

She squirmed beneath him. He dropped his arms and rested his hands, one on each of her thighs.

"Please…off…why?"

He had let her ride the last dosage almost to its completion. The fact that her words were making it through told him her strength would also be coming back, and he couldn't have that. He brushed a hand down the side of her face. She turned away.

Make her look at you.

He cupped her chin and forced her to face him. When she did, the fighting spirit had left her eyes. It was replaced by tears.

She doesn't respect you. Make her.

His heart pounded.

Make her!

The image of another man pulling into her driveway and kissing her in the front window had been imprinted on his brain. His hands formed fists at his side.

"I thought you loved me."

She didn't move. She didn't even appear to blink.

Make her respect you!

"How? To do that?" His eyes searched the room for the source of the voice—the one he started to believe was lodged in his mind.

She tensed up beneath him.

He got off the bed and slapped his hands against his thighs.

Tappity, tap. Tappity, tap.

She ain't ever going to respect you.

The taunt was followed by laughter.

Even the voice ridiculed him and knew he didn't deserve a woman's love—if a whore were even capable of dispensing unconditional and loyal love. They gave what wasn't theirs to everyone, flaunting it.

She said his name. Her weak voice still made it through to his ears. Anger pulsed in his core. No one had called out to him by name—not after he had brought them here. Did she think she could appeal to his soft side? First one had to exist.

Make her respect you! Be a man!

He spun on his heels and headed to the cabinet in the corner. He loaded a syringe and came at her. "You are a fucking slut, and, for this, you will pay."

Her eyes enlarged as he pierced her skin and filled her veins with the serum.

CHAPTER 14

PAIGE POINTED OUT VICTOR HARRIS'S house, and Zach parked the SUV at the side of the road in front. Cars lined the driveway, two wide and three deep. A speedboat occupied one spot.

"It costs a lot of money to have a boat like this. It probably cost forty-five thousand, or more, to buy, and that's not even getting into the matter of fuel to use it." Zach touched it as they walked past.

"Maybe that's why it's in the drive and not at the marina."

"Could be." He moved around it. He pointed to silver lettering announcing the boat as Lady Speed. "Well, that's original."

Paige laughed, but it was stifled when the front door opened.

"Can I help you?" A black man of about thirty stood there. He matched the DMV photo they had of Nina's husband.

Victor had a high brow line, a wide, flat nose, and a day's worth of stubble on his face. Paige would consider him attractive if it wasn't for the pain that had etched into his features. It had taken the genetic predisposition of a handsome man and tinged it with madness. The loss of his wife under such violent circumstances had stamped darkness into his eyes and the energy he exuded.

Zach held up his credentials. "We're agents Miles and Dawson of the FBI."

"The FBI." His tone of voice made the inquiry a statement of fact. He walked down the front steps toward them. "Now you show up."

"Is there somewhere we can talk?"

"We are talking." Victor blinked, his eyes misting with tears.

"There's nothing left to say though, is there, Agent? My wife is dead. You didn't save her. The police never saved her."

"We're sorry for your—"

He turned to Paige. "Save your speech. There would be no need for apologies if everyone had done their jobs."

Paige stepped forward. "The only man responsible for your wife's death is the one who murdered her."

Victor let out a puff of air and his eyes read, *go ahead and shift the blame around.*

"We're here because we want to find this person and hold him responsible for what he's done, for the pain he has caused."

Rage veiled over his eyes, and he pressed a flattened palm over his heart. "It's not my pain I worry about. It was Nina's. What did she go through up until—" His hand snapped up from his heart and covered his mouth.

"We can find who did this to her, and you can help." Paige put a hand on Victor's shoulder. When she made contact, he seemed to shrink under her touch, almost as if melting beneath it. The man was undergoing extreme grief.

He pressed his fingertips to his eyelids, and then glimpsed heavenward. "I'm not sure how. Everyone loved her. She had a way about her, you know. She was confident and full of life. Women loved her. Men loved her. I wished they didn't so much, but I knew what I was getting into when I married her," his chest heaved, "but she loved me." His eyes connected with Paige's. "What more could a guy like me ask for? What more could any guy ask for?"

With the intensity in Victor's eyes, and the declaration of love for his wife, she believed him. The emotion even tapped a place deep inside of her she thought had died a long time ago—the need for a committed relationship. The excuse she chose as her primary arsenal, that she was too busy for a love affair, vanished when she tried to conjure it for validity. She hadn't found the right person. She thought of Brandon and amended her thought—the right *available* person who shared her feelings. Paige removed her hand from Victor's shoulder.

A shadow graced the front doorway, and a woman, appearing

to be in her fifties, stepped outside. She eyed Paige and Zach. "Victor, baby, are you okay?"

Paige saw the similarities. The woman was his mother.

Victor turned around. "I'm fine. Go back inside. I'll be right in."

She bounded down the stairs toward him and squeezed him.

"I mean it, Mom, I'm fine."

"Okay." She directed a fierce glare at Paige and Zach. "You find the bastard who did this to her."

Paige nodded. "We'll do our best."

With the woman back inside, Victor led them to the backyard and a patio set. Paige sensed eyes watching them, but, when she turned to the opened windows, no one was there.

"The day Nina went missing," Paige began.

Victor put his hands on the table. "Tuesday I had to get to work. I was running late. I'm always running behind, but the boss doesn't seem to mind."

"You said your good-byes in the morning, and then went to work? Do you know what Nina's schedule was for that day?"

"We didn't even say good-bye that morning." His eyes took in the yard. "We fought a lot, but I never would have hurt her. I never would have done anything like this. Neighbors had called the police on us a few times. Nina and I are, were, both animated people. When we saw things differently, well, the place wasn't any library, but I would never raise a hand to her. Ever." He paused, as if assessing whether they believed him. "The cops asked if it were possible that she was sleeping around on me and had simply taken off with her lover. I guess it's obvious that's not the case now."

"You said women and men loved Nina. Any man in particular?"

"You mean who gave me the creeps? No."

"We were noticing what a nice boat you have," Zach said. "It must have taken a year's wage to get it."

Victor rolled his eyes. "Surprised you don't know this, but Nina won a local lottery. She wanted the boat. I couldn't care less about it. That was one of our heated arguments. Between taxes and that damned boat, there went the money. That's why it's in the driveway now. No sense paying the docking fees at the marina. If you're interested, I'll give you a deal."

"Would Nina have any reason to be out near the area where she was found?"

"Nope. I've been racking my brain on that."

"Run us through her schedule for that day."

He ran a hand across his brow. "We had been fighting. If she told me, I wasn't listening."

"Did she have any regular appointments she kept—the spa, the hairdresser, a gym?"

"She worked out all the time. I tried to get her to concede with a home gym, but she said she liked getting out. She liked the attention she got." The implication of his words must have hit home. Tears pooled in his eyes. "Maybe she was cheating on me. I guess I wouldn't know."

"We're going to need the name of that gym."

"Last I knew she was going to Fitness Guru."

Back in the car, Paige and Zach discussed what they had learned from Victor.

"He's in denial about her cheating on him," Paige said.

WE TRIED REACHING BRAD KEYES at Fitness Guru, the gym he managed, but were directed to his house. He answered the door with a cell phone held to one ear. "You're going to have to figure it out. I'll be in as soon as I can. Listen, I've got to go." He disconnected his call. "What can I do for you?"

"We're here about your wife, Leslie Keyes." Jack fished out his creds, and Brad led us into his house.

"It's not a good time right now."

"It's not a good time? This is about your missing wife." Jack's face took on hard lines. I knew the expression all too well.

"She went missing six years ago. I've had to move--"

"Daddy! Daddy!" The words came from the sugar-coated lips of a boy of about six or seven.

"Come here. Let me wipe your face." Brad hunched down to rub a thumb across the boy's small mouth, wiping away what appeared to be white sugar powder from doughnuts. "This is

Tristan. Say hi to our guests."

"Hi." His voice was low, and he rocked his torso, his eyes cast downward.

Brad rested a hand on top of the kid's head. "He's shy around strangers, and, as you can see, I've got my hands full today. Work's falling apart without me, and hunting down a babysitter at the last minute like this is almost impossible. He'd be in school if it weren't for the fact he isn't feeling well. As you can see, that seems to have passed."

"We won't be long," I said.

Brad bent down to Tristan's level. "Why don't you go play in your room? I'll join you soon."

"'Kay." He waved a pudgy hand at us. "Bye."

"Bye Tristan." I smiled at the kid, and I sensed Jack picked up on my soft spot. Actually, if things had worked out differently with Deb, I could have had a kid about Tristan's age.

When the kid's steps reached the upstairs landing, Brad said, "I've just given up on her ever coming home. For years, I held out hope she'd walk back in that door. She never did. I told myself I'd get a phone call, and she'd confess she ran off with someone but missed Tristan."

"He was yours and Leslie's?" I asked.

Brad nodded. "He was a baby when she disappeared. Maybe she just couldn't handle being a mother. I've been through it so many times, to the point of exhaustion. The same questions, the similar scenarios rolling around, until I realized I can't live like that." He gestured to a sitting area off to the right of the entryway. "I had Tristan to care for. It wasn't just me. If it were, I probably would have let myself fall apart."

"When you filed the report, you were asked if she cheated on you. Your answer was, 'Les would never do that to me,'" Jack said, quoting the last part verbatim from the report.

"She wouldn't. At least, I never thought she—" Brad's cell phone rang. He held a finger up to us and then answered. "Hello... yes, I'll be there. It will be fine...good-bye." He shook his head and stood. "Listen, I don't know what I can do to help with this. I have to move on with my life. Tristan has to move on with his too."

Jack studied Brad's facial expression, and I knew he was also taking in the man's energy.

"Other women have gone missing," Jack said.

"Here?" He pointed a finger downward. "In this town?"

"Thirty-two now, including Leslie, and taking in the surrounding areas."

I noticed he didn't include the first three known victims.

"Thirty-two?" Brad took a seat again.

"We believe the abductions accelerated after your wife."

Seconds of silence passed.

"You believe they are all dead." Brad's eyes appeared moist. "Guess I always figured she was dead, but to really think about it…you think it started with my wife? Did you find her?"

I studied Jack's profile, curious what he would disclose to this man and what he would hold back. At this point, Brad Keyes wasn't a suspect, but no one rose above suspicion until cleared of it.

"We believe some old cases may factor in, along with some new ones."

"Does this have to do with that rich man's wife? I should have known. When my wife went missing I was told that missing persons reports were not actively investigated. I guess now that it happened to someone important, well, it gets the FBI's attention."

Neither Jack nor I said anything.

"You mentioned old cases. That means this son of a bitch has been out there for all this time? You could have stopped him years ago?"

"Your wife was the first missing persons case in the area since two thousand," I said.

"Do you think my wife triggered something to make him start up again?"

"We do."

"What? I mean what could have possibly made this sick asshole snap when he saw her? What made him take her? Did he kill her?"

"It's likely she is dead," Jack said.

"Based on statistics." I tried to lessen the blow, but Brad's eyes were glazed over. "Did you know of any man who was obsessed with her, maybe stalked her?"

He shook his head. "She didn't even leave the house much. She was a good mother." His voice faltered, and *mother* came out in fragments. "All this time I convinced myself I must have had it wrong, that she did leave me and take off with some other guy. I need to have more faith in people."

"Sadly, as humans, we're not made that way. We tend to judge first."

His eyes spoke a silent, *thank you*.

"Did your wife frequent a spa or hair salon?"

"No. I don't think so anyway. Like I said, she was home a lot. After Tristan was born, she came to the gym a few times, but otherwise she stayed around here."

"And the day she went missing?"

"Just like any other day. Nothing stands out to me."

Jack stood. His hand was already at his shirt pocket, fidgeting for his cigarettes. "We may have more questions for you so don't be going anywhere."

"Sure."

When we left the house, Brad Keyes was sitting on the sofa, a truly broken man.

Chapter 15

She was so cold. Her toes and fingers had lost feeling. The shivers had her pulling on her restraints and desperately wanting to curl her naked body into a tight ball for warmth.

Tears flowed down her cheeks. She knew the man who was doing this to her—at least she thought she had. Not that he ever talked very much, but she had been with him numerous times before. As her mind cleared in segments, she realized she was no longer on the bed. She was on a stern, flat, and unforgiving surface. A table?

She forced her eyes open and found herself facing a wood ceiling. Beams ran lengthwise, the same direction as she. Wires ran like snakes through holes cut into the wood.

She was underground.

The last thing she remembered was him talking to himself as he came toward her. After that, the rest went black.

Why was he doing this?

No matter how many times she thought that question, the answer remained a blank line. She had trusted this man. She had given herself to him, willingly, numerous times in the past. Why violate her in this manner?

It was as if he no longer saw her, but his eyes went through her.

Her eyes traced the chains that came down from the ceiling to her arms. They were coiled around her wrists. Following them back up, they went along to a ratchet where two more came down.

She lifted her head and confirmed her fear.

Shackles bound her ankles as well. It was as if the sight of her restraints had tightened them, suddenly making her feel as if they were biting into her flesh. She looked back at her wrists—it was reality. They were dripping blood.

She screamed at the top of her lungs which chilled her even further. No one would hear her cries.

CHAPTER 16

WE ALL GOT BACK TO the PWPD station about the same time. Detective Hanes and the officer had done a great job of setting up the board. Even though some of the women didn't have captions beside their names, things were coming together. They had information for all the missing women since, and including, Leslie Keyes.

"And you had most of this information already?" Jack asked the officer.

"Yeah."

"Hmm."

For some reason, the praise that vibrated through his exhaled expression had me feeling jealous of the officer. If I gave him merit, though, he did do an amazing job. Guess he'd earned a name from me, and I'd start thinking of him as Stenson.

"I also looked into whether Brad Keyes would benefit from the pronouncement of his wife, and there was only a standard policy on her that was taken out not long after they were married," Stenson said.

I acknowledged him as I walked past and closer to the board.

The far left showed the picture of Leslie Keyes, the one filed with the missing persons report. Beneath her picture it noted, *victim number 1*, along with her name and the last date she was seen in 2005. For all purposes, in this room, she was the first victim in recent years.

Occupation: house wife.
Husband's name: Brad Keyes.

Husband's occupation: Manager of Fitness Guru.

Last seen: at her house.

Last known scheduled appointment: unknown.

Beside her, more women were displayed in much the same manner. There were thirty-two women in all, and the boards took up the perimeter of the room. Where the whiteboard ran out, old-fashioned rolling chalkboards of the double-sided variety were utilized.

The last board showed pictures of Amy Rogers and Sydney Poole.

I pointed to their faces as I spoke. "Both victims were last seen at their hair salon—Rogers at Hair Fantasy and Poole at Sweet Cuts. Could it be he's picked these latest victims based on this criterion?"

"What? That they liked to have their hair cut Pending?" Zachery laughed.

Anger flickered inside of me, not so much due to Zachery's words but the smile on Stenson's face.

Why did it feel like a competition between us?

"I find it to be an interesting connection. None of the others were last seen at a salon." I knew there was something more. I needed a few seconds to think about it.

"And Keyes manages Fitness Guru where Nina Harris was a member, at least according to her husband. Has this been verified with the facility itself?" Paige tucked a curly strand of red hair behind an ear.

Detective Hanes pulled out a cell phone.

His motion sparked my memory. "When Jack and I were talking to Kirk Rogers, he said that his wife was last seen at Hair Fantasy, but that her hair dresser, Paulo, commented on the fact she was fussy and in a hurry."

Paige shifted her weight, jutted her hips to the left, and placed a hand there. "Maybe she was getting ready to see the unsub. I'm leaning toward him being the one these women are having the affair with. I don't think he's watching them from a distance. I think he's up close and personal before he kidnaps, rapes, and murders them."

"One sick son of a bitch." Stenson's words brought everyone's attention to him. "Well, these women may have been unfaithful to their husbands, but their lives shouldn't be measured by that. They don't deserve to die because of it."

"To our unsub, they do." I dismissed his comments with five words. I turned to Zachery. I knew he would have read all of the boards by this point.

Jack stood back and pulled a cigarette from its package.

"Keyes is only connected with two of these women—his wife and Nina Harris."

My words fell on a silent room.

Zachery paced the perimeter and stopped in front of Nina Harris. Her before picture was posted beside a photo of her remains. "I can't believe this didn't stand out to me earlier. The fact he buried her with the wedding ring doesn't necessarily mean regret for having killed the victim. It could be a statement of sorrow for the husbands left behind. This mixture tells me our unsub may not even be sure why he kidnaps, rapes, and kills."

"You can tell all that from looking at the pictures?" Stenson took up position beside Zachery.

"I can tell all of that from the collective. Consider his victim set—all beautiful women who were unfaithful to their husbands. None of these men can imagine his wife as adulterous. These women were good at what they did. Either their husbands are lying when they say there was no way they'd do this to them, or they were too busy to care or notice. The unsub was close to the victims. He became a part of their world, even if for a brief time, before he decided to carry out his directive."

"His directive?"

"Based on the timeframe of the cooling-off period, from the last highway killing in two thousand until the abduction of Leslie Keyes, it seems our unsub was dormant."

"Couldn't it be we just haven't found similar cases?"

"Always possible, but based on the expedited rate he is abducting women at this point, unlikely. Something changed when it came to Keyes. She was special to him. She likely hurt him, and it brought back his violent past."

"You believe he had a horrible childhood?" A glint in Stenson's eyes said, *it's always the parents' fault.*

"We believe he was involved with the rape and murder of at least one woman in his teen years. You decide." A cigarette bobbed in Jack's lips as he spoke.

"Our unsub is controlled by his past. Whatever happened with Keyes reactivated that part of his mind. It made him want to kill again, assuming he wasn't somewhere else doing this," Zachery said.

Detective Hanes came toward us, clipping his cell back to its case. "Nina Harris wasn't an active member of Fitness Guru. She hasn't been since six months ago."

"So she changed clubs about three months before her abduction." I studied the before photo of Harris. She had a healthy glow to her cheeks. "She would have joined somewhere else. I mean look at her. She was beautiful, healthy, and, obviously, placed a high importance on her physical fitness." My statements provoked a glare from Paige, not that it really mattered.

"We need to find out where she started going." Jack turned to the detective. "Are you able to take care of—"

"I'll call all the gyms in the area right now," Stenson interrupted Jack and was already to the doorway by the time Jack replied.

"While you're at it, inquire about Rogers and Poole."

Stenson tapped the doorframe. "You got it."

"He's a little overeager with this case, isn't he?" Jack used his cigarette to point toward the hallway.

"He's been working on these missing persons cases for years. Pretty much since he became a cop," Hanes said. "Don't think any more of it. I know Trent, and he's not your unsub."

"Hmm." After a few seconds, Jack pulled his eyes from the detective.

Chief Steele came into the room and latched both thumbs onto the belt loops of his pants. "Do we have a profile we can share with the public at this point?"

I knew what Jack was like when it came to public announcements. Depending on the case, it could be best to investigate behind the scenes without the added complications of the media's light, but there were times when either the public needed to be made aware, or it would help draw out the unsub.

"First, gather all your detectives and officers. We'll have a conference at eight to tell your men the type of man we're looking for. Then, we'll go public."

"There are some officers not on shift," the chief said.

"Call them in for this."

The chief nodded.

Chapter 17

She was standing in front of the window as a vision—one he had witnessed many times. Her brown hair was pulled back into a soft french braid, her back was to him. She wore a flowing white dress with embroidered daisies lining the straps. The sweetheart neckline accentuated full breasts that were always swelled and perky. She rested one hip against the glass and had one hand placed beneath her chin, as if she were in deep thought.

The sun shone on her, radiating her with a white glow as if she were an angel. She turned to face him. She never spoke, but she held out her hand.

Her brown eyes were captivating. Her eyelashes long and full. No makeup adorned her face. She was a natural beauty.

He went to her and took her hand. She smiled at him, as only she could—the innocence of a child, yet with eyes possessing the experience of a woman.

She proclaimed her love to him again. They had just made love, as she liked to call it, and she went to the window to watch the deer feeding in the field behind the house. She loved watching them. She'd laugh and call them gifts from God.

He maneuvered behind her and nuzzled into her neck, breathing in her scent and caressing her spirit with his energy. They would become one—again. As his lips brushed her skin, the tender part behind an ear, a baby cried.

Excitement raced through him, a mostly foreign euphoria. It was their child, their life, their future.

"I will get him." He attempted to smile but the expression

always felt forced.

She reached for his hand and pulled him back. Tears were in her eyes, and she shook her head.

"But he is ours. I will find a way to love him like my own."

She brushed a hand down his cheek, and, as she did, the softness in her eyes steeled over. Her chestnut eyes were now the color of pitch blackness and devoid of a soul.

"We will be together," he pleaded with her.

She left him, drifting away, her dress swaying with her movements—a soft fluidity contrasting against a cool aura. She never turned to wave good-bye, but she kept on walking until she disappeared.

"I believe I loved you!"

She didn't stop.

Anger raged, pulsating within his veins.

"Get back here!"

Then he heard her laughter, and the image faded.

He was in front of the television, and his fists formed on the arms of his chair. He could only see one thing—her face, her mockery, her belittling of him. She was a whore. She deserved nothing, but he had offered her his love and she spun it around, denying him. He would never forget her. Ever.

The reoccurring vision haunted him. Yet it was so real. She was responsible for who he had become. Their lives were on her head.

He picked up the TV remote and flipped through the channels until he reached a local news broadcast. The caption at the bottom of the screen made him stop surfing.

FBI called in for missing women cases.

He returned the remote to the side table and watched with interest as they showcased his work. A queasy fear entwined his insides. He spoke to the voice that had left him alone while he was with her.

"I will make you proud. I am no longer a boy."

Then her picture came on the screen.

"The remains of Nina Harris were recovered earlier this week…"

"No!"

How did they find her? How did they get her?

He knew the broadcaster continued, but he no longer heard her words. The chant he repeated as a prayer went through his head as he ran out the door toward the woods.

The graves lay silent. The graves lay untouched.

CHAPTER 18

"THE UNSUB WE'RE AFTER FITS into the community. He'd be attractive, in the age range of mid-to-late twenties," Paige said.

We stood in a room at PWPD, full of officers and detectives from both that department and Dumfries PD. They all watched us as if we were the most excitement the area had seen in a while.

"Women wouldn't be afraid to approach him. They may actually be drawn to him," Zachery said.

"It is possible he was having an affair with the missing women," I added.

"You believe he had a relationship with them? All of them?" A ruddy man of about fifty had his eyes on me. I sensed irony clashing inside him. How could the feds know all this and not have their man?

"We believe it is possible—yes. He's dangerous and unpredictable," Jack added.

"We don't believe he's motivated by a hatred of women, but we do believe he's had a hard childhood," Zachery added.

"You believe he was sexually abused?" Another officer asked the question.

"Not directly. However, we believe he had been encouraged, or forced, at an impressionable age, to rape a woman found in two thousand. We don't believe this is who he wanted to be but rather who he's become."

"You said he was encouraged by someone? Do you think it's a father and his son?" the officer asked.

"Possibly. Or a man and his nephew. There is a definite

connection there that made the duo feel untouchable and, at the same time, bonded them." Zachery put his mug on a nearby table. "The victim from two thousand was taken in the summer, during school break. The ones prior took place at different times. One in the spring and one in the fall. Also, the latter victim was sexually assaulted, whereas the first two were not. We also have another reason to believe that we are only searching for one active unsub at this time."

The fifty-something officer stood from where he had been leaning on the edge of a table. "And what is that?"

"The first three victims, starting with the one in nineteen seventy found on the side of the highway, were not buried. We have evidence that shows Harris was."

"What made him start up again?"

"We believe it is linked to Leslie Keyes. His relationship with her was close and special. It's likely she did something to hurt him, causing his past to resurface," Jack said.

"He realized he couldn't have her and made sure no one could," Paige added.

Every time we briefed a police department, it occurred to me how we categorized everything into a neatly presented package, whereas reality often dictated something entirely different.

Paige continued. "Now we believe he's abducted thirty women, including Keyes, plus two more in the past week—Rogers and Poole."

"Thirty-two women? That's—" The older officer's face scrunched up as he went to do the math.

Zachery interjected. "A woman approximately every two months. Now we have Rogers and Poole missing within a week. He's starting to fall apart. The man he has become is not what he wants. It's something he does, whether it's to please his father, uncle, or someone else entirely. He could even be holding himself accountable to a memory at this point."

"What makes you think he wants to please someone?"

"Well, based on Nina Harris and assuming it holds true for his other victims, she was buried with her wedding ring. It seems his targets have all been married women who may have been cheating on their husbands. He buried them naked to disgrace them but left on their wedding bands."

"That question begs why."

"That question tells us we're dealing with an unsub that is organized in his killing method, in getting the women where he wants them and how he disposes of the bodies, but he is not organized completely. He is capable of feeling regret, fear, and anger—unlike a psychopath who would feel and think nothing of rape and murder. The initial killer lends himself to that profile."

"We don't believe he gets pleasure out of what he's doing." Paige crossed her arms, and I noticed she swallowed deeply. As a woman, I could imagine this case would affect her more profoundly.

"Why does he do this then?" another officer asked.

My attention was on Stenson. He stood at the back of the room, his focus on Paige. He must have sensed me watching and averted his eyes to Jack when he answered.

"As my team has made clear, he feels a compulsion and has a desire to please someone. It is possible he hears commands to do what he does."

"He hears voices?"

Zachery answered. "Auditory hallucinations are more common than most think. Of those who do experience them, most say the voices help them become better people. Our unsub may be on medication to silence the voices, but, sadly in a lot of cases, this makes them louder and any good voices are muted while the darker ones take over. It would suit the suspected age of our unsub as well. Auditory hallucinations start up between the ages of sixteen to thirty and it can even be younger for men."

"A demon is telling him what to do?"

Zachery smiled. "It has nothing to do with the spiritual realm. These types of hallucinations are brought on by abuse, an accident, or the loss of a loved one. This is the case with seventy percent who confess to hearing voices."

"That would also fit with our unsub," I started. "Because of a childhood that started out with rape and murder at the approximate age of fifteen, this experience would qualify as a trigger for the hallucinations."

Paige nodded. "A lot of times these voices are those of the abuser. It's quite possible the man who guided him in the rape and murder is the voice he hears or that guides him now. Because of this, it can affect his sense of self-esteem and self-worth."

"These voices, based on the speed at which he's now abducting women, are getting louder and becoming more dominant. He may have once come across as having his life together, but things are, or quickly will be, falling apart for him. He may have recently lost a job or be close to losing one. He won't necessarily be as kempt as he once was."

I took in Stenson's longer hair. I wondered if he always wore it that length. This time, when he saw me watching him, he pressed on a fake smile.

"Sum it up for us then, agents." An older officer hiked up his pants.

Jack laid out the overview. "We're looking for an attractive man, age mid-to-late twenties, who may be holding down a steady job but may now be at risk of losing it. He may appear disheveled, but, for the most part, could be the guy next door."

"I should add this as well," Zachery said. "With the experience of auditory hallucinations, our unsub's line of thought will be disorganized. He may start sentences and leave the thought unfinished. He also is quite likely to appear agitated at times. He may repeat a certain movement over and over."

"Either way, we're out of time here. We've got to get moving on this case before there's another murder victim or another woman abducted."

"Do you think they're still alive to save?" Stenson asked the question from the back of the room.

Paige answered him. "We have to believe that."

CHAPTER 19

THE WAY I SAW IT, I had two options. One was to go home and get some sleep or at least go through the motions. The other was to stick around and analyze the crime boards until the victims' faces and stories melded together. I chose the latter. Maybe it would be seen as a desperate craving for Jack's approval, but that wasn't the reason. I knew the truth, and that was all that mattered.

Going home to the empty two-story house no longer held the comfort or served as the retreat, it once had. Deb had arranged to take several pieces of furniture with her. I didn't really care—furniture was only material possessions. It was more what the empty rooms represented. My marriage was over. There would be no amendment to that statement.

The rest of the team had left a few hours ago. I had told them I'd find my own way back. Now I sat in the room straddling one of the chairs backward. My attention was on the board with the two recent victims. I had taken down the photo of Leslie Keyes at the start of the timeline and posted her picture near Rogers and Poole. The women didn't share much in the way of similarities.

Leslie had the appearance of an innocent housewife. Her photo, cropped from one of her and her husband, showed her makeup tastefully applied with hues of mauve and beige dusting her eyelids. Her hair was brown and shoulder-length, worn straight. Her smile held sincerity. She was enjoying herself at the time the picture was taken. I believe the report said they were in the Dominican Republic for their two-year anniversary.

If I were to take the woman at face value, I would conclude she was someone who was really in love with her husband, a truthful person, not one who hid behind jewelry or other such things for false charm. She came off as the typical wife next door who was both beautiful and respected.

Thinking about Leslie on such an intimate scale, had my mind shifting periodically to Deb. I thought we had everything together. She seemed to be happy, but I suppose appearances can be deceitful.

Next, my eyes shifted to Amy Rogers. She had the spark of a tigress, her eyes carrying the come-hither look, but that could have been meant for the man taking the photograph—her husband? I made a note to check into this later.

Rogers had chestnut eyes and brown hair like Keyes, but that was as far as the resemblance went. I could imagine Rogers cheating on her husband, but I wondered if part of the reason was because I knew who her husband was—top in a communications business, a man who every simple-minded and easy woman would want to be with. There was no doubt in my mind the man was unfaithful. From there, it wasn't a far stretch to imagine his wife having her own fun.

Sydney Poole. She was a stark contrast to the other women. Her hair was a platinum blond, her eyes green. Like the other victims, her hair was long and reached past her shoulders. She had high cheekbones and knew how to apply her makeup. The coverage was light and noticeable—a fine line for women to balance, or at least it seemed so to a man. When some applied the dark shadow and smack-me-in-the-face lipstick shades, it didn't do anything for attracting my attention. Less is more, and, in this case, that motto applied. Poole never worked outside of the home, like Rogers.

With the three women, there was one thing that connected them all. Besides the fact they were all chosen by the unsub, they were all beautiful, married women. They had long hair. None of them had children except for Leslie Keyes. She was where things became personal for the unsub. He loved her.

Could it be as simple as the fact that she didn't reciprocate those feelings?

"You look deep in thought." A female officer came into the room. I had noticed her during the briefing, but she never made a comment, and we were never introduced.

"You have no idea."

She came toward me, her hips swaying enough for me to notice the curvature was more than a natural heave.

"Name's Becky Tulson. I'm actually with Dumfries PD, but I'm curious about how things are coming along." She extended her hand and smiled. Her hair reached the middle of her back, even pulled into a ponytail. A few loose strands hung over her shoulders.

"Brandon Fisher." When our hands connected, our eyes latched. She released her grasp hesitantly, her fingertips grazing mine.

"Where did the rest of your team go? You do something wrong and are being punished?" She paced the perimeter of the room, her arms loosely crossed. She stopped in front of the crime scene photos of Nina Harris.

I stood beside her. "It was either this and get something done or go home and stare at the ceiling."

"Ah, you're not a sleeper? Some sort of insomniac?" She smiled.

"Well, I'm not sure I'd go that far." Maybe if I were being honest.

"Tragedy, what happened to all these women." Her attention was no longer on me but on the spread of photos, specifically the one of Harris's remains. "I can't imagine what she went through up to this point."

I didn't really know this officer, but I detected a hint of underlying emotion. Her voice took on a gruff edge. This case was personal for some reason. "Did you know her?"

Becky turned to face me and shook her head. She swallowed deeply, her eyes probing mine. I sensed she was deciding whether I was trustworthy. She faced the photo again.

"When I was a teenager, there was this guy—"

She paused, and when she seemed content that I was listening, she continued. "He seemed great. He gave me gifts. My first gold necklace came from him."

I noticed, with her comment, she didn't wear one now.

"He spoke of getting married and having kids." She let out a small laugh. "Me with kids? Can't even imagine. Anyway, it all sounded wonderful at the age of sixteen. I loved him. I was the envy of my girlfriends."

I had a feeling where this headed and wondered why she was inclined to share such personal information with an essential stranger. The intimacy of this confession had me wishing I had left for home.

"He told me his parents were out of town and that I should come over." She smiled at me. "You know where I'm going with this?"

I nodded.

"Well, I'm telling you anyway. It wasn't movies and popcorn that were on his mind. He raped me." She went quiet for a few seconds. "I was in such shock, you know. Here was this guy who I loved, who was supposed to be my future, and he robbed me of everything. I had never been so humiliated in my life. Not before, not since. I walked home that night. It took me about an hour, and I cried the entire way. Not one person I went by even gave me a second look."

"Sorry—"

"Oh, no," she dismissed me with a wave of her hand. "There's no reason you need to be sorry. You're not the one who raped me. I'm over it now. I've dealt with it, but I will never forget it."

My eyes were on the picture of Harris, my mind on the information Becky had shared with me. "I don't understand what makes these men do this."

Becky laughed. "I thought you were a profiler. Isn't that sort of the job?"

I smiled. "Not really what I meant. I meant, I know why, from the standpoint of what makes these bastards tick, but not the why from a human standpoint. I don't understand how a man could hurt a woman."

The way the words came out made me sick with the vulnerability. Blame it on the hour. My stomach growled. "What time is it anyway?"

"From the sound of you, time to eat."

I was happy that she didn't latch onto my sentimentality, and I hated the fact it even surfaced. "Sounds about right. You know any good places to eat around here?"

"The Earth and Evergreen Restaurant." Her eyes pinched with a large smile. "They especially like their military types. It's a nice place—for around here anyway. Their prime rib is pretty good."

"Prime rib. Sounds delicious."

"Come on, I'll go with you. They also serve cold, imported beer."

Chapter 20

HE SWEPT HIS FLASHLIGHT ACROSS the dirt path that was littered with small twigs and leaves from the surrounding trees. The weather had been unpredictable lately with high winds setting in without warning. He heard the trees howling above him, but the voice made it through the rustling leaves, reprimanding him, and scolding him.

You are a failure.

You have to make amends for this.

Be a man and make it happen.

You let it come to this.

You were careless.

I knew you didn't have it in you. I knew all along.

His heart beat rapidly. Something snapped behind him.

He spun, casting the pinpointed light to the bushes. They shook. Something was in there. A few more steps, taken while walking backward, he kept his eyes on the shaking leaves. Was the source of the voice here to haunt him?

The doctors told him it lived in his head—the source of it simply a mental condition. But there were moments when it was so real that he swore he could reach out and touch the root of it, as if it were coming from a living being.

He hated coming out here at night. It gave him shivers down his spine and tickled the hairs on the back of his neck. He swore he could feel each of them rise in sequence.

"Go away."

The bushes stopped moving.

"I mean it. Go away!" He turned and hurried his pace. There was more noise behind him. There was a pounding in his ears.

The voice was closing in on him, advancing from behind and the sides.

"Go away!"

You are a loser!

He plugged his ears—one with his free hand and the other while holding the flashlight. Its beam now cast off-center from the trail.

You are never going to be a man!

The voice surrounded him now as if inside his mind. He needed the constant ridicule to stop and leave him in peace.

"The graves lay silent. The graves lay untouched." He repeated the chant aloud hoping it would keep the voice at bay, and it seemed to be working. Only a few more feet, and he would reach the burial sites. He heard the river before he saw it.

He fell to his knees. The flashlight dropped to his side. He pulled on his short hair and let out a scream. He wasn't this man, not the one he had become. How did it all get started? He couldn't remember now.

"You! You did this to me." He rose to his feet, the light casting out in a half circle from him. He spun, looking into the woods, into the bushes. "This is your fault!"

You made this happen.

Prove you're a man this time.

"No! No more women. It has to stop—"

You will never stop. This is who you are. This is when you're most happy.

Flashbacks paraded in his mind, all the women, all the rapes, and all the murders that took place, that he had orchestrated—or had he?

"You do this. Not me."

He crumpled to the ground, his head level with his knees, and he curled inward. His hands were fists, and his arms wound around him—still there was no comfort to be found.

The grave that had belonged to Nina Harris had, in fact, been disturbed. The ground, now dry, had served as a mudslide to the river and revealed his horror. He had lost one.

Shaking, he rose to his feet and visited each of the other sites. None of them had been disturbed.

I told you—too close to the river.

"Shut up!" He spun again, trying to find the source of the voice, even though he never would.

You can't do anything right. You never could. The voice laughed at him.

He held his hands over his ears. He couldn't seek asylum anywhere. The voice would find him. He dropped his hands. "I will prove to you I can."

You are a loser!

"I will!"

He chose to ignore the rustling in the bushes and the trees on his way back to the drive shed. His mind focused on one thing—proving himself a man.

Chapter 21

THE EARTH AND EVERGREEN RESTAURANT could have been a remodeled funeral home, but I never shared that opinion with Becky. With its cream stucco exterior, wood shingled roof, and a tower at the back side, it also had the appearance of an old, modest church.

Inside, it was like Becky had said. They liked their military. Patches from police departments from all over the world were mounted to the ceiling, and Marine Corps plaques were on the bulkheads. The flooring was a green carpet overlaid with a plaid runner. Everything dated back decades, from the dark wooden bar, to the tables that matched, along with spindle-backed chairs.

"Well, you were right about the prime rib." I stuffed in another forkful. "Very good."

Becky smiled and turned away.

I swallowed. "Guess it was rude of me to talk with my mouth full."

"No worries. You don't like to take your time with your food, though, do you?" She glanced at the plate that had been set in front of me only a few minutes ago. There were barely two forkfuls left.

"Maybe you should be a profiler." I smiled at her.

"Oh, please." She further dismissed the comment with a wave of her hand. "As if I'd want your job."

"You never know. The paycheck—"

"Yeah, probably stinks and isn't anywhere near what you deserve. Just like the position I'm in, but I deal with less sickos than you would." She lifted her coffee mug to her lips.

She hadn't ordered anything to eat, saying that her stomach couldn't handle food within two hours before bed. I found irony in how eating would disturb her sleep but coffee wouldn't. She said she drank it more for flavor than for any effects from the caffeine.

"Oh, I don't know, you get used to it." I put the last of the prime rib in my mouth. With the swallow, I knew I might regret my decision to eat so heavily this close to calling it a night.

"Really? I thought you were still under your probationary period."

"I am, but trust me."

"Yeah." She bunched up a napkin and released it on the table. "A lot of sickos in a short amount of time."

"Yep, pretty much."

Her eyes glazed over again, like they had at the station.

"You never get used what these people—if you want to call them that—do to other people. It would almost be easier to accept an evil spirit at work rather than that of a fellow human being."

"Coming from the man who analyzes the human psyche."

"No, it's true. While illness and preconditioning play a role..." I let my words drift into thin air. I thought about how this job had changed me. Before my first case, the one that had the team and me in Salt Lick, Kentucky, I didn't even want to think about spirit creatures. Now there was a dark side of me that contemplated how involved they were in our daily lives—how much control they held over our thoughts and our actions.

"You know why I told you that, back at the station?"

I put down my fork and knife and pushed the plate away. "Not really."

"You were probably wishing you were someplace else."

"Never."

"Yeah, right." She pointed a finger at me. "It's written all over your face. You're not a good liar, Brandon."

"Call it a weakness."

"Huh, I would have called it a strength."

There were a few seconds of awkward tension between us, the

kind that existed in a halt of banter between strangers, unsure of which direction to steer the conversation, whether to continue down the path it started on or take an entirely different course.

She broke the silence. "I told you in order to give you a bit of understanding into the mindset of these women. You are so focused on the unsub, and what he is or isn't, what his past was or wasn't. I think it would be easy to overlook the victims' mindsets."

"What are you thinking exactly?" This woman intrigued me. She was a combo of beauty and brains.

"A man cheats on his wife, big deal. Maybe it's even a sign of being a man, getting out there. The world idealizes them as being worldly and sophisticated. Even though, in a lot of respects, women have advanced in the twenty-first century. We can vote now." She took pause to toss out a sardonic smile. "However, women are still viewed as inferior. Wages for women continue to be less than their male counterparts. Women are expected to remain fit and active, while men can let themselves go around the middle."

"Hope you don't think less of me for eating all that just now." I laughed, and she tossed the bunched-up napkin onto my plate.

"No, be serious here."

"I'll try." I wasn't in the mood to be serious. I was fed, though hungry. What would it be like with another woman? I had only been with Deb and Paige. Modern society would view me as naïve and inexperienced. I liked to think I had values. With that thought, my failed marriage and images of Paige's naked body mingled together.

"These women were all married. Respectable, right? I mean a lot these days don't even go as far as making a commitment. Whether people adhere to their vows or not isn't what I'm focusing on, but there had to be some level of morals there for them to enter into a marriage."

"Amy Rogers married a rich, powerful man. Sydney Poole was the wife of a prestigious lawyer who owns a firm. It could have been something as simple as them seeing dollar signs. Women do like the finer things."

"I take it you have experience in that regard?"

I took her question as a challenge. "I know for a fact."

"What? You? Married?" Her grin faded when I didn't form one. "Oh."

"Never mind. It doesn't matter. Continue."

"Okay." She drew out the word. "Let's assume they married for love as well. Women do adore being doted on, no matter how independent we claim to be, and we still gush inside when we get a dozen roses."

"Good to know."

"I don't think you're that naïve, Agent." Her eyes drifted from mine to the table. I didn't think she possessed an ounce of shyness. I was wrong.

"What more are you thinking?"

"Just that these women had some sort of moral compass. If they cheated, perhaps they felt neglected. This other man, possibly your unsub, was there to fit the bill."

With her saying that, things aligned. "You think that the man we're looking for may have had connections to the men initially and not the women? You are a genius. He saw these women weren't getting the attention they needed at home so he saw it as his opening."

Becky leaned back into her chair, the wood creaking with the movement. "Could be. So, would I make a good agent?"

I flagged down our server and ordered a beer. "Hope you'll join me."

She consulted her watch. "It is getting late."

"Come on, one beer, and it's on me."

She nodded. "Sure, why not? Beer and coffee. Interesting combination."

She laughed, and the sound of it transformed into a soothing resonance. Becky Tulson was already beginning to feel like a close friend.

Chapter 22

The next morning I beat the alarm. It was becoming too much of a habit—under the sheets late but rising with the sun. The owner of The Earth and Evergreen Restaurant had accommodated us by staying a little after hours. Before returning to the station, Becky and I ended up having a couple beers and talking like we were childhood friends, separated by years of circumstance. It turns out she almost got married but decided the lifestyle wasn't for her. I told her I used to be married. Even saying the words aloud reinforced what I wished to forget—I had failed.

She must have seen it on my face, evidenced by the way she diverted the topic of conversation to sports, baseball specifically. I was thankful for her intuition, almost as much as I was for the insight she provided into the case. She gave it an alternate point of view.

A couple hours after waking up, I was back in the room down at PWPD. Jack, Paige, and Zachery were all there and appeared more rested than I felt, even if Paige nursed a cup of to-go coffee.

"How late were you here, Kid?" Jack came over and stood beside me as I studied Nina Harris's picture again. At this point, it felt like I was looking through it.

"Late." I caught a whiff of Jack's cigarette-saturated clothing. He didn't miss his stick on the way over here that was certain. If I inhaled deeply enough, would this air count as second-hand smoke?

"You're no good to the team if you run yourself into the ground."

"I thought that's how you liked your team, Jack."

The way his brow lowered and his eyes fired, I wished I could reel the words back.

"That's how I like my team?" Jack turned toward Paige and Zachery, who took the cue and left the room. With them gone, he didn't say anything. He just stared at me.

"You want the answers. You want the case solved," I said.

"Well, imagine that Agent Fisher. That is the job, but we also have to know when to call it a day. I'm going to ask you one more time. How late?"

"I was here for the case, and I found an interesting perspective." I wasn't about to share the fact it was brought to me by a police officer—at least not right now. A few more seconds of his glare, and I answered his question directly. "Somewhere around midnight."

"Then you went home?"

I had thought about propositioning Becky, but I couldn't bring myself to do it. "What does this have to—"

"Everything."

Here I thought my putting in the extra hours would impress the man and further prove that I deserved to be a permanent member of his team. In the process, I had accomplished the opposite.

"There are a couple things I don't care for." Jack's eyes went quickly from Nina Harris's picture, then back at me. "One—"

"I know. You hate tardiness."

His eyes narrowed and said as much as, *don't interrupt me when I'm talking.* "Tardiness. Two, I don't like a showoff."

"I—"

He held up a hand. "That's what last night was really about, wasn't it? You wanted to show the team how well you could do solo? If that's the case, you need to adjust the attitude. We are a team. We act as a team. We think as a team."

"If you hated the fact I was staying, why leave me here?"

Jack fished a cigarette out of the package. "I knew it would tell me a lot about you."

"And, what did it tell you?" I was angry now, and there was no way to bury the depth of it. The tone of my voice and energy would convey the truth.

"It told me you may act better solo."

I let out a deep breath. "Last night wasn't about any of what you're implying." There was no way I would tell him it started in a desperate need to avoid going home, and then morphed into a need to prove myself. Why did I always feel I needed to?

"I hope it wasn't." He slipped the unlit cigarette between his lips. It truly was the man's pacifier.

"It wasn't."

"All right then, let's get to work."

Paige and Zachery walked into the room the instant after Jack said that, and I wondered how much of the conversation they had heard. I sensed all of it.

Jack addressed me. "Let's have it."

I studied his eyes trying to ascertain whether this was a trap or a sincere inquiry.

"Pending was here for hours and came up with nothing."

Paige slapped Zachery on the arm.

"Actually, I'm wondering if we're going about some things the wrong way," I said. "We've analyzed our unsub but not our victims."

"Hmm."

I disregarded Jack's guttural response. I was determined not to let him throw me off course. I walked to the picture of Amy Rogers. "I wonder who took this photo."

"You were here for hours, and that's your question?"

"Zach," Paige said.

"It's the way she's looking at the camera. There is lust in her eyes. Was it her husband, or does this tell us something about her character?"

"Don't tell me you think these women somehow deserved what happened to them?" Paige's green eyes, which were normally soft, could have slit silk. She crossed her arms, hoisting up on her bosom as she did.

"Absolutely not."

Her arms relaxed.

"I do believe it may lead us somewhere, but that's not the big discovery." I paused, certain that Zachery would say something smart, but he didn't. "What if the unsub isn't connected with the women so much as with the husbands?"

All of them turned to each other. They were taking the suggestion seriously. My smile faded when Jack spoke.

"Where's the proof of that statement?"

"I still—we still—have to find that out."

"Hmm."

"It's just that we are so focused on the unsub's state of mind—"

"That's what we do Pending."

This time I shot a look at Zachery. "By extension, applying our analysis to the victims opens up another realm of possibilities. These were married women. They had some morals or they wouldn't have married in the first place."

Paige laughed. "Or they knew how deep the pockets went on some of these men. People marry for money every day. It doesn't always have to be about love."

I shook my head. "I think there was more of a reason and we know that Keyes and her husband planned on being together. They had a child. He wasn't, and isn't, wealthy."

"She felt it was her duty to have a kid. Maybe there was pressure from her parents, the in-laws."

Why was Paige bucking me like this? A minute ago she was defending me.

"I'm just speaking my assessments out loud." I wanted to add, *I don't need the judgment.*

Jack must have picked up on my thought. "This is why we operate best as a team. We talk things out and reason on them. It doesn't mean everyone needs to be in agreement."

My cheeks heated from anger. "All I'm saying is that these women didn't deserve this."

"No shit."

I hated this side of Paige, and, prior to now, I didn't remember having been on the receiving end. I refused to let her have the upper hand with this one. "What I'm saying is our unsub could have seen that these wives were neglected and swept in as the doting man they wished their husbands were."

Jack paced a few steps.

"I'll give it to you. That's an interesting perspective. He could be close to the family," Zachery said.

Paige let out a deep breath and rolled her eyes.

Detective Hanes walked into the room holding a clipboard. "I have the list of fitness clubs where our vics belonged."

Officer Stenson came in behind him and went to the boards that lined the room. He was basically on loan from Dumfries PD to help us with this investigation. He started writing down the names of the gyms. As he scribbled in the abbreviations for the fitness centers, I noticed a pattern. There were similarities.

Hanes continued. "Leslie Keyes was a member of her husband's gym, Fitness Guru. No other clubs in the area had a record of her ever being a member. She was an active member at the Guru up until her disappearance." He pointed the tip of a pen to Nina Harris's picture. "She was a former member, but, as we already know, she wasn't at the time of her disappearance. We did, however, track her down to Health Heaven, a smaller, retro club located at the other end of the city."

My attention went back to Stenson. He had made his way through about eight of the missing women including the ones of active interest—Keyes, Harris, Rogers, and Poole.

"None of the other women were members of Health Heaven?" I asked.

Hanes shook his head. "No."

"It's possible the unsub is an employee at a fitness club," Zachery said.

Paige tucked some of her red curls behind an ear. "I could imagine a high turnaround in employment in that field."

Jack had his cell phone to his ear. "Nadia, I need you to—"

I only heard part of what he was saying as my focus was on the boards and how they were filling in. It was plain to see that our victims were all health conscious.

Jack hung up. "Nadia will be pulling the employment records for all of these fitness centers." He gestured to the boards then looked to us. "She's still gathering employee information for shipping companies that took I-95 on a regular basis. She said it's a large pool."

I could only imagine. Jack seemed to think Nadia's capabilities were above human, but she did always come through for us.

"How many different gyms?" Paige walked up beside Stenson.

"Six." He stopped writing and faced Paige.

"Our victims were all active members at the time of their disappearance—"

"No, that's not the case." Stenson finished noting the gyms and pointed the tip of the black marker at Paige. "There are five who didn't hold active memberships at any clubs."

"Five?"

Stenson walked around pointing to the photos of those women. "They used to be members of clubs but not at the time—"

"Of their disappearance."

"Correct."

Paige spun to face us. "There goes the theory of them being connected to a fitness employee."

"Not necessarily," I said.

Her eyes shot to mine.

"Maybe the unsub wasn't working at the time or offered in-home services?"

"Hmm."

"With the number of different gyms noted, six, it proves our unsub is unstable. While employable, there are times he loses touch with reality. Maybe it's the voices he hears or something else, but, periodically, he unravels and holding a job is too much effort. Once Nadia has employment records, if we can track it down to a single name, we'll have to develop a timeline to coincide with the victims."

Jack pointed his unlit cigarette to Paige and Zachery. "You two are going to talk to the wife of the suspect from the highway killing in nineteen seventy. Mrs. Wilson. We still need to dig into why he was in the spotlight. We need to know if he had any close younger friends, nephews, or sons who could have taken his place for the murders in seventy-three and two thousand."

"Don't you think our time would better be spent speaking with the husbands of the women who didn't belong to clubs at the time of their disappearance?" Paige asked.

Jack's eyes snapped to Paige. They glazed over with a spark of anger. "Brandon and I will visit the husbands of those women."

The way Jack's jaw set, I knew he didn't appreciate Paige's attitude and, for a second, I felt responsible for it. I'm not even sure why. She seemed hurt, as evidenced in the way her eyes avoided contact with mine and the reddish hue to her cheeks.

Did she know about my going out with the female officer? Was she jealous?

If she were, she'd have to get over it. Paige and I would never be a couple, despite any feelings we might hold for each other. She reminded me of my past, not a future I had planned. On top of it, we worked on the same team. A relationship between us could jeopardize everything, and quite possibly lives, if given the ideal situation. I was also pretty sure one of us would have to leave the BAU.

Chapter 23

PAIGE LOADED INTO THE PASSENGER seat of the SUV. She didn't feel much like talking and was happy that Zach was normally good about not prying into her personal life. Today was definitely one of those days she preferred to remain quiet. It was about putting the hours in and calling it a day. While she was driven to find the truth, to bring justice to the victims, and hopefully save the recently missing women, she wasn't naïve about the likelihood they were already dead. Based on the short cool-down period, the unsub was likely stalking his next victim already.

He had carefully chosen his prior victims, picking women whose husbands were busy and away from home a lot, but, based on the speed at which he was abducting them now, he worked on impulse not logic. His world would be crumbling around him.

"I'm thinking once we get a name, if we do, that is connected to each of the clubs, we should inquire why he left. If we find out where he is currently working, if he is, we need to find out what his record is like. Is he on time? Is he a valued employee?"

Zach glanced over at her briefly before focusing on the road. It would only be about a twenty-minute drive to Woodbridge where Frank Wilson's widow lived.

"I agree. He's got to be falling apart. To take two women in the span of a week, a couple days really, when his record was approximately one every two months, he's got to be losing control. The auditory hallucinations must be getting louder and taking over."

"Maybe he's not even hearing voices but just feeling the

compulsion," Paige said.

"Why?"

"Like we thought before, a father figure to him, someone he wants to please. We have yet to find out if that person is alive or if he is trying to please a memory."

Zach pulled off the highway and followed the directions of the GPS to the house of Barbara Wilson.

Paige faced out the window when they stopped at a light.

"The thing I don't understand is that Frank Wilson died two years after the first victim, Chase. The change in MO didn't come until two thousand. What does Jack expect us to uncover with this woman?"

"Guess we'll find out, but he's the boss Paige so we do what he says."

She let out a deep breath and shook her head. She didn't need him to say the words, but she didn't feel like herself today. She needed to rein in her feelings for Brandon before they destroyed the career she loved and had worked so hard for. What no one else knew, nor was privy to, she had shown up at the police station the night before and was told Brandon had left with a female officer by the name of Becky Tulson. Paige didn't remember meeting her, but she already disliked her.

CHAPTER 24

WE WERE QUICKLY MAKING OUR way through the list of five husbands. We were on our way to speak to the last one now—Justin Parks. His wife, Lindsay, disappeared back at the start of two thousand eight. She was last seen in the morning when he left to go to work.

Parks was a successful businessman who owned a prospering franchise business for lawn care and handyman work that reached into several states. It was known that while he no longer got his hands dirty with the day-to-day work, he never missed a day at the office crunching numbers and scheming new marketing avenues.

Perfectionist Landscaping was a two-story building located in Woodbridge on a commercially-zoned property. Other corporations had nestled in the area, some larger than Perfectionist but with most of them around the same size.

The woman behind the counter was average-looking—the only distinguishable feature being a black mole on her right cheek. She offered a sincere smile. "Good day."

Her soft tone indicated a shy nature. My guess was she hadn't been at this post long and might not even be sure if she liked it.

"We're here to see Justin Parks." Jack flashed his creds.

"Oh, the FBI." She smiled and stood up. "I love that show."

I sensed Jack's energy emanating in tidal-wave-sized proportions.

"This isn't a show."

Her smile faded. "I just respect what you do. You're very

intelligent the way you go about solving mur—" Her hazel eyes went between us. "Why do you want to speak to Mr. Parks?"

"That is confidential." Jack gestured to the phone on her desk.

"Yeah, yeah, of course. I apologize. I'm getting carried away." She dropped back into her chair and picked up the receiver.

Jack's feelings about this woman were written all over his face. The receptionist was an FBI groupie, one of those people who idolized us but didn't really know what we did.

"He'll be out in a few minutes if you want to have a seat." She pointed to a sitting area.

Jack turned his back on the receptionist and faced the front windowpanes.

"Thanks." I offered a smile to compensate for Jack's aloof response.

Light shone into the lobby from three of the four sides. The fourth side being what led back into the offices.

"Hello gentlemen."

The man's voice had both of us turning to greet him. He wore a brilliant blue collared shirt paired with black slacks. Despite my initial assumptions that he'd be a stuffy businessman, perched behind a desk, squawking out orders, Parks had the type of friendly air about him that instantly put people at ease. Most women, I imagined, would find him attractive. His physique was kept tight and lean, likely from a regular gym regimen. His dark hair had sprinkles of gray on the sides, similar to Jack, giving him a distinguished look.

Parks held out his hand to us.

After the introductions, he said, "Did you find her?"

I passed a quick glance at the receptionist, and her head turned quickly back to her monitor, as if she thought her rapt attention on us would go unnoticed.

"We'd like to talk with you in private," Jack said.

"Of course. This way." Parks led us to a conference room where he sat at the head of the table. We sat on each side of him.

"Your wife, Lindsay," Jack began.

The smile that had been on Parks's face disappeared.

"She went missing back in two thousand and eight."

"Correct." Parks clasped his hands on the table and leaned forward. He repeated his first question. "Did you find her?" His cheeks went ashen.

"No, we haven't."

Parks leaned back, his focus unfixed. "I had to move on with my life, but not one day goes by that I don't think of her. Not one. Everything I do is for her." Seconds passed with him studying us. "What do you want from me? I'm the one who had the report filed. I answered everything then. When I last saw her—"

"We don't show that your wife worked out at a fitness club."

"No." He dragged the word out, skeptically. "Why would she? We had a gym in our home. I had it custom built for her. Lots of windows." He smiled, apparently caught in a memory. "She loved sunshine. She thought it was God's way of smiling at us and telling us that He loves us."

"Did anyone come into the home, an in-house trainer, for example?"

I noticed how Jack skipped right over the mention of God, not that it surprised me. The man always withdrew at the mention of a supreme being. The pass being, when a person had seen what Jack had, it was hard to keep on believing.

"If she had, I didn't know anything about it."

"You don't know if she had a trainer?"

Anger marked Parks's expression. "Am I a suspect in her disappearance now? I file the report, and I'm told these are not actively investigated. In other words, my wife's abduction doesn't mean anything. Can you believe they tried to imply she was cheating on me and ran off with her lover?" His voice rose with each word. "Tell me how that makes sense. They're not investigated, but I suppose it's just like the innocent who end up behind bars because the eager cop is more interested in his record than the truth."

"You mentioned abduction," I said. It earned me a glare from Parks.

"Of course, I did. There's no other way to explain it. Linds and I loved each other. Sure, maybe we had our small arguments, but what couple doesn't? You get over it, move on with your life. It doesn't mean you bed a third party."

"There were never any ransom calls?"

"None."

"Have you ever cheated on your wife?"

A small twitch tapped in Parks's cheek. He disregarded Jack's question and addressed me, "There are a lot of marriages with problems. Ours, mine, wasn't one of them. Please find her so that my side of the story is proven the truth." With the last two words, he looked at Jack. "Now, if that will be all."

"Actually, it's not."

Parks raised his eyes to the ceiling and let out a deep exhale.

"You said you didn't know if your wife had a trainer. How is that? You haven't answered that question."

Parks clasped his hands and leaned forward like he had when we first sat at the table. "She was given her own allowance, if you want to call it that."

"She had her own bank account?"

"Yes. Between that and my working twenty hours a day, we weren't together often."

"You were a happy couple though." Jack rose, and I followed his lead. He tossed a card across the table. "We will be in touch with a warrant for her financial records."

"I could just give you a copy of her statements."

Jack turned around. "Get them ready. We'll be securing a warrant."

I had a feeling he'd say that. As the FBI, we liked to do everything by the book. Everything ran through a local DA, any piece of evidence backed up by enough paperwork to keep hundreds employed.

When Parks flailed his hand in our direction, we took that as our dismissal to leave. I could tell he didn't understand the warrant when he willingly offered the information we sought. We reached the SUV when Jack's cell rang. "Harper. What is it, Nadia?" Seconds ticked off. Jack faced me and spoke into his phone. "Let me put you on speaker."

CHAPTER 25

BARBARA WILSON ANSWERED THE DOOR dressed in purple cotton pants and a floral t-shirt. Her white hair was worn short and permed. Deep creases traced her blue eyes, but the years hadn't dulled their gleam.

"Yes?" Her voice was frail, as if her vocal cords would snap if projected beyond a low volume. They attested to her seventy-plus years.

"Barbara Wilson, we're FBI Special Agents Dawson and Miles." Paige gestured to Zach.

Wilson's eyes scanned them, as if assessing whether they were who they said they were.

"Can we come in?"

The older lady looked behind them to the street with such intent that Paige turned around.

"I suppose."

"Thank you, Mrs. Wilson."

"You are welcome dear." She withdrew into the house and held the door open. She latched the deadbolt behind them. "The neighborhood isn't what it used to be." Her eyes connected with Paige's. "Not that I likely have to tell the FBI. What can I do for you?"

"We're here about your husband."

"Frank's been dead for years now." She moved toward a sitting area which suited her age group. She had likely bought the pieces when they were brand new. A gray coating of dust covered the end tables, a bookcase, and the television screen.

Zach remained standing, but Paige took a seat and crossed her legs.

"We want to know more about him."

"Why? Why now?" She tapped a hand on the arm of the chair she sat in and then moved the lever on the side to recline. "All the police wanted to do back then, when that girl got murdered, was interrogate him. They accused him outright. Probably why he's in the grave already." Wilson performed the sign of the cross on her chest.

"Your husband drove for Straightline Trucking which frequented that stretch of highway."

"He must have killed her then."

"People say he had a bad temper and—"

"He never hit me once."

Paige wondered about the mental state of the woman. Her eyes veiled over periodically as they spoke, and the records showed domestic abuse was a prevalent occurrence in her past. They would have to handle this delicately.

"He broke your nose. Do you remember that?" The words came out, and Paige wondered if she went about it tactfully enough.

Wilson laced her arms. "I…" A few seconds later, she picked up again. "I do now, come to think of it. He did that? Frank?"

Paige nodded, doing so with a skill she had acquired over time. It communicated empathy and established a common ground.

"No, he was a good man."

"He may have been, Mrs. Wilson—"

"Don't be condescending to me." She flipped the lever on the side of the chair and pushed the footrest down with her legs. "Out. I want you out of my house."

"We don't believe your husband killed that girl."

Her movements halted. "Then why, why are you here?"

"We want to know if your husband had any close friends he worked with, anything he might have mentioned about any of them." Paige knew it was unlikely that Wilson would recall even if he had. It had been many years.

"No, not that I can…"

"It was possible he mentioned something to you around the

time he was being accused of the murder," Zach said. "Can you think back to that time? I'm sure things were upside down in your lives."

"You have no idea, young man."

"Did he get along with his employer, his coworkers?"

Wilson chewed on the inside of her bottom lip. "He…"

"Why don't you sit back down again? Relax. It will come to you."

She gave them a look that said, *whatever you think, I'm not buying it.* She reclined back in the chair again.

"Now close your eyes."

Wilson's eyes pinched shut and opened, not even a fraction of a second later. "Oh, no, you don't. Don't you be hypnotizing me."

"This process is not hypnosis. It is a relaxing of the mind so that it can recall certain things with clarity, even what you may not have considered to be important at the time."

She didn't seem to buy his line. "Not hypnosis?"

"No." Zach reassured her with a smile.

"All right." She closed her eyes, and the wrinkles in her forehead relaxed as she did.

"Think back to when the police first came and got your husband. What happened?"

"There were two police at the door, but a bunch of cop cars on the road. One drove up onto my front yard. I was so mad." Wilson opened her eyes. "I had a beautiful garden started that year. He wrecked that."

"Okay, move past that. Did your husband say anything to you?"

She closed her eyes again. "He said to call a lawyer. Oh, and he said, 'I love you, sugar.'" Wilson smiled, but it faded quickly. "He said, 'they have the wrong man.'"

"Okay, did he give you any names?"

Wilson kept her eyes shut but shook her head. "No…wait!" She paused for a second, and then opened her eyes. "He said Ladies' Man."

"Ladies' Man?"

"Yeah, all the guys gave each other nicknames on the road."

"Do you know the real name for—"

Wilson shook her head before Paige asked the full question. "I'm sorry I couldn't have been more help, but it is what it is."

"Did your husband bring home any friends from work?"

"No. He liked to keep work separate. He had a couple friends, but they rarely came over or went out."

"What were their names?" Paige rubbed the flat of her hands on the top of her thighs and leaned forward.

"This is real important to you, isn't it?" The older lady studied both of them. "Is this about those recently missing women and that body they found? You know my Frank's been dead for years. He couldn't have done it."

"Your husband is no longer a person of interest in the murder of Melanie Chase, but we believe he may have had contact with the person who is responsible for recent abductions."

Wilson gripped the top of her shirt, bunching the material in a nervous manner. "Dennis was a good friend of Frank's. So was Ken."

"We're going to need to know their last names if you—"

"Smith and Campbell. Dennis has passed on, though. Ken is in a nursing home in town here. Not sure how helpful he'll be. Alzheimer's has left him stripped of dignity. He was a good man. It's not fair what happens to us when we get older."

Paige offered a sincere smile. She didn't like to think about the future and what it held. She preferred living in the now and experiencing all that life brought her way. "Thank you for your time."

The woman reached for the lever on her chair and seemed to spring from the seat to a standing position. While age may have affected her mind, it didn't limit her mobility.

"Not really sure how much help I was, but it was nice having company." She squeezed Paige's arm.

The contact made Paige think of her own mother, and, in turn, her father. She had a good relationship with them, it just wasn't cultivated often. She was busy on the road a lot with her job. Her parents had their clubs and interests that kept their time occupied. It had been at least six months since she saw them. She had only spoken to them via e-mail once or twice. It was pretty sad as they only lived a half hour away.

Paige pulled on the door handle of the SUV and got inside. "Curious why you used your hocus pocus trick. I thought it only worked on victims who escaped brushes with death or a life-changing situation."

Zach put the key in the ignition, bringing the engine to life. "The process can be used to bring back anything from a traumatic situation. Her life may not have been threatened, but her way of life was. While she was used to police dragging her husband off on assault charges, murder was a new one. She was likely contemplating if she would have been the next victim. Either way—"

"I get it. Traumatic." Paige smiled. "Well, now we know a couple things. We need to find a guy from the seventies nicknamed Ladies' Man and speak to Ken Campbell."

"Yeah, it's going to be a fun day, that's for sure."

"Sure, if that's how you see it." Paige laughed. Her mind was no longer occupied with Brandon and their relationship, or lack thereof. It didn't matter—it was what it was, and she would be fine.

The onboard system notified them of a voice mail message.

They had their cell phones on them, but a third was always connected to the SUV. Paige found it strange the caller used that one and not the phones they carried.

Zach hit play. Jack's voice filled the car.

Chapter 26

THE SHOVEL WAS HEAVY IN his hands. His purpose never clearer. He needed to let the FBI know he was in charge. He would show them he was someone to fear and not take lightly.

He dug around the body and small quakes ran through him. His eyes kept drifting to where Nina had been laid to rest—where she had escaped from.

He had the urge to make the sign of the cross but held off, his mind judging him. How could he believe himself pure when he did the things he did—and where had such a silly notion sprung from?

But the women—the whores—deserved everything that came their way. He had come to accept that. They willingly offered themselves as pieces of flesh to be taken advantage of, to be fed off of, by men whose carnal desires penetrated any supposed boundary of matrimony.

You are worthless. The voice barked at him from the shadows.

The wind blew, bringing a chill that gripped the back of his neck.

What are you doing?

Do you want to get caught?

Stupid idiot!

"Shut up!" He stopped working the shovel and rested his hand on its handle as he swept the surrounding area with a flashlight. He wouldn't see anything, but every time the voice spoke, he wondered if the outcome would change if he searched hard enough. He asked himself many times how he would react if he saw it there—the source of the voice. While he convinced himself he could handle whatever it was, he knew he'd buckle in strength and fortitude. He wouldn't have the willpower to carry on doing what he did. He would fail the voice. The voice must know this, and, therefore, kept in hiding, taunting him from the darkness.

Go back to the girl and show her you're a man.

Why are you doing this?

The voice called out to him, now questioning his actions, wanting an accounting. If he refused to acknowledge it, the inquiry would transform to a demand. It would insist on being told why he was doing this, why he had the need to unbury the dead but he would tell it nothing.

Sweat dripped from his forehead, despite the cool bite in the evening air. He stood there, looking down at the head he had revealed.

He lifted the shovel a few feet from the ground. Ironically, despite having been digging with it, the very tip of the steel shone. He came down on her neck with the force of his full strength.

Resistance traveled back through the handle—metal on bone.

His stomach heaved when expected to see her head, separated from her body, but it was still attached, albeit barely. He would have to come down on it at least one more time with equal power.

He raised the shovel, the tip no longer shining in the cast of his flashlight. It was stained red.

Bile rose in his throat, but he suppressed it.

What are you doing?

The voice proceeded to laugh at him.

You are a loser. You are not—

He cut the voice off with a scream as he wielded the shovel into the sweet spot that had once been her neck. With the pressure applied, her cords severed, and her head rolled free and to the side.

He vomited on the ground beside it.

He ran the back of his left hand across his mouth. Chunks of stomach contents were now lodged in his nostrils, and the smell of it nearly drove him to a repeat performance. But he got it under control and bent down beside the freed head.

He stared at it, partially in denial that this had been his work. This would be his first for this, but would it be his last? Even he didn't know the answer to that question.

He lifted the head from the long strands of hair and dangled it there. Blood dripped at the source of the trauma, along with cords and veins.

His stomach tossed, but he stifled the overwhelming need to vomit again with a gut-wrenching scream.

Chapter 27

The news Jack had given them repeated in Paige's mind. They could have their guy.

Nadia had found out that Wesley Keyes, Brad's father, owned a trucking company that had been in business from 1965 until late 2005 and held contracts with local meat vendors. According to the information on the business, they offered refrigerated trailers and targeted their marketing to butchers. They even went so far as to mention meat hooks. Wesley had passed away years ago, but, a background on Brad Keyes showed a cabin north of Dumfries registered in his name. It was conveniently close to Phillips's property where the remains of Nina Harris were discovered.

Jack and Brandon were posted outside of Fitness Guru waiting on the warrants to come through for the gym, Keyes's house, and the secondary property.

Agents outside of the cabin described it as appearing vacant. They said the curtains were drawn, and there were no vehicles in the driveway.

When Paige and Zach filled Jack in about how they made out at Wilson's, they were told to continue on to see Ken Campbell at the retirement home. They had a photograph of Wesley Keyes to show to him.

The woman behind the front counter at the home smiled at them until the realization must have hit that they were cops. Her expression then contorted into a scowl, and her arms crossed over her bosom, tugging on the fabric of her pink nursing uniform which was already a tight fit. Her skin was black, and her eyes darker than midnight.

"What do y'all want here?"

Paige glanced at Zach and enlarged her eyes.

"I'm right here. I did see what you just did. No cops in here. It upsets some of our patients."

They both held up their credentials in unison.

"*Ef-bi-ai.*" The nurse drew out the acronym, assigning it a lower ranking than local law enforcement.

"We're here to visit Ken Campbell." Paige slipped her creds back into her pants pocket. Her hand barely brushed her holster. The woman didn't miss it. She let out a puff of air and tightened her arms.

"What business do y'all have with Ken?"

"That is a private matter, and it is rather urgent that we talk with him."

"My name's Ester, and I run this home. I can't have cops coming in here and disturbing the peace. I hardly believe a seventy-year-old man can help with any investigation you have going. The man's all but mostly lost his mind."

"I can appreciate you're trying to protect those under your care, but freedom of rights is in effect here, is it not?" Paige paused, but Ester said nothing. "We have the right to speak with Ken Campbell, and he has the right to talk with us."

Ester jutted her hip to the right. "He also has the right not to talk with you."

"Let him make up his mind. We'll be right here waiting for him."

"Oh, no. He's not coming to you." She looked past Paige to Zach. "Follow me."

JACK AND I SAT OUTSIDE of Fitness Guru. Brad's Kia was parked out front, and, when we called the gym, we were told he was in. The girl put us on hold to get him, and we hung up. I didn't understand why we weren't making a move. This was our guy, or at least it seemed like it on paper.

Here we were sweating in the SUV, the AC doing little to offset the beating sun—something that shouldn't be a problem for mid-

September. To make it worse, Jack lit up his second cigarette. The smoke hovered in the air and formed an ominous fog around his face.

"You ever think of quitting?"

Jack took another pull on the cigarette and let the smoke draw out on a steady exhale.

"You are going to give me lung cancer."

He tapped the ash into the tray. "Worried about me or you?" He drew on the death stick again.

"Both of us, actually, truth be told. Every day I go home saturated in nicotine. It leaves a slimy coating on my skin that, sometimes, I fear a shower won't even remove."

Jack laughed. "You're whining."

"Come on. Look at the pack."

"Hmm."

"Amuse me."

Jack pulled the pack from his shirt pocket and tossed it in my direction. I caught it before it landed in my lap. I started reading without giving it much thought. "'May complicate pregnancy.'"

Why did I start with the last item?

I didn't glance over at Jack but heard another pull and exhale of air. The waft of smoke burnt my sinuses.

"'Smoking causes lung cancer, heart disease, emphysema.'" I could tell I was losing the man. His attention was on the front doors of the gym. I continued. "You don't want to be like Jed Chase. These things will kill you given time."

"A lot of things will kill you Kid." Jack got out of the SUV.

I should have known better than to show I had emotions or even a hint of affection for him. He was likely starting to view me as weak.

I got out and rounded the back of the SUV to take up position beside him.

"Thought you'd prefer I smoke outside. Then you follow me."

"Since when do you listen to me?"

"You know, you speak your mind an awful lot."

"I thought I was paid to do so, to express an opinion, to—"

"Keep your thoughts focused on the case and off me." Jack

stayed leaning up against the SUV and took another pull on the cigarette.

"I don't understand why you get like this. Every time I try to talk to you about your personal—"

"That's the problem right there." Jack extinguished the glowing butt with a twist of his shoe. "It's not your concern."

I let out a deep breath. It was the same every time. I didn't even know why I kept trying. Paige tried to tell me Jack's problem was he cared too much. At times like this, I wondered if he cared at all. His focus was aligned on a track, closed cases being his target. He didn't allow himself to get detoured or delayed along the way. No, that would add complications to an otherwise set lifestyle he had going—keep everything business.

Jack got back into the SUV. No sooner had he closed the door than he opened it.

We had our warrant.

Chapter 28

Ester knocked on the door frame of room number eighteen. "Mr. Campbell? It's Ester." She waited a few seconds, and, when there was no response, she said, "Mr. Campbell, I'm coming in." She turned to Paige and Zach. "You two stay here."

She tucked her hands into the pockets of her shirt and headed into the room. "You have visitors."

Paige heard a deep moan and a man's voice that had a low register, making it hard to understand and hear from a distance.

"Yes, they are with the *ef-bi-ai*."

Paige rolled her eyes at Zach who went cross-eyed and smiled at her. It was one of the things she liked about him. He had the mind of a genius but held the maturity level of a college student.

"All right, he'll see you, but if you upset him, know I'll be in the hall and back in jiffy if need be." Ester brushed past them.

The room only had enough space for a dresser, a single bed, and two chairs. An older television sat on top of the dresser at the end of the bed. Paige couldn't help but think how the reward for living to old age was coming to a place like this and waiting to die.

Ken Campbell sat in a wheelchair, positioned in the corner of the room. His head was full of wiry silver strands of hair, complete with wild sideburns. A blue blanket lay draped over his lap, and a pair of prescription glasses dangled from a chain and rested against his chest. He held a paperback in his hands and looked up at them. He smiled at Paige. She gathered from the glaze in his eyes he was lost in a memory. It was possible he confused her with someone else. Barbara Wilson had mentioned Alzheimer's robbed his mind.

"Hi, Mr. Campbell. I'm Paige Dawson, and this is Zachery Miles. We're agents of the FBI."

He dropped his book and stared at her.

"We have some questions and think you may be able to help us." Paige moved closer to him and took a seat on the edge of the bed. Zach came in behind her and sat on a chair near Campbell.

Campbell's nearly non-existent eyebrows pinched down over his eyes. "Who are you?"

"Mr. Campbell, that is Zachery Miles. He is with me."

His head turned in her direction. "Who are you?"

The only thing Paige believed may be their saving factor was that Alzheimer's patients could typically remember things further in the past easier than more recent events. She reached into her pocket, pulled out her smartphone, brought up the picture of Wesley Keyes, and extended it to the man.

Campbell reached for the technology that he predated by a few decades and held it in his hands as if it were a foreign object. He let go of his grip on it, and Paige was thankful she had kept hers in place. He pulled up the glasses he wore around his neck. Paige noted he wasn't wearing them before—he had been pretending to read.

"We were speaking with Barbara Wilson." Paige held back the urge to ask if he remembered her. From her limited dealing with Alzheimer's patients, she recognized the question as offensive and, depending on his memory, could initiate a defensive response which wouldn't get them anywhere.

He tipped his head back and gazed through the smudged glasses that sat down on his nose like Geppetto in the fictional tale of *Pinocchio*. "I remember Barb."

Paige smiled at him, hoping it would encourage him to continue talking.

"Nice woman. Pretty little thing too." He leaned in toward Paige. "Don't tell Frank I said that. I'll never hear the end of it."

She winked at him. "Your secret is safe with me."

He reached for the phone Paige held. "Now who is this?"

"We were hoping you could tell us."

"Ain't never seen him." He handed the phone back to her.

Again, it was another delicate position. To press him could make him shut down completely, to leave it could mean useful information went unheard. She opted for silence, and, after a few seconds, Campbell broke it.

"I can tell the way you're looking at me." He pointed a finger at her, his hand waving unsteadily from age and loss of motor functions. "You think I've plum lost my mind. Well, there are days I believe it." He took his glasses off and let them dangle from the chain. "I'd lose them if they weren't attached, and there are some moments I do anyway. That man," he pointed to the phone, "is not someone I know." His eyes rose to Paige. The old man believed what he told her.

Paige nodded. So, he didn't know Wesley Keyes. "What about Ladies' Man? Does that—"

"Oh my, I haven't heard that one in a long time." Ken's eyes reflected deep thought.

"I take it you know him, and this is not his photo?"

"No." The older man's tone took on a deeper register. "I'd never forget ol' Steve. Not ever. He could have any woman he wanted in his day." Ken let out a whistle. "He'd have you begging for an evening out with him." He gestured to Zach. "He'd give you a runnin' for your money."

Paige smiled at Zach who returned it. Ken Campbell had truly lost his mind and had likely already forgotten they were the FBI and not a couple. There was no need to correct him as long as he kept talking. "Steve?"

His tone turned aggressive and suspicious. "What do you want with Steve?"

"We are looking for an old friend. Do you know a last name?"

His eyes glazed over and pinched narrow. "No."

Paige slipped the phone back into a pocket and got up. "Thank you for your help."

"If he were an old friend of yours, wouldn't you know his last name?" Campbell adjusted his blanket. His eyes clouded over and went distant, but he appeared at peace.

Chapter 29

Jack held up all required documentation, his badge, and the warrant. "We're here to see Brad Keyes."

I stood a few steps behind Jack, ready to pull my gun if the need arose. Jack told me to have his back but not to anticipate too soon. He'd call it a rookie mistake. Coming in with all guns blazing, people screaming and running for cover—he'd prefer that scenes like that stay in the movies. In real life, the FBI had standards to uphold, a professional reputation which wouldn't be sullied by an inexperienced pending agent—especially one from Jack's team.

I scanned the gym after studying the girl behind the counter. Both her hands were in the air as if she were being arrested. Panic and fear mingled on her facial expression, her mouth gaped open and her eyes enlarged.

Three people were on cardio equipment located at the front of the gym where we were. One man was in an outright run on a treadmill, another lady, carrying easily an extra fifty pounds, was in a fast walk on another one, an electronic reader in her hand. The third member was a woman on a bike who was sweating profusely. None of them paid us any attention. They were intent on their workout.

"I'll get—" The girl lowered one hand and went beneath the counter.

"Let me see your hand," Jack barked.

"It's just the release…for the…" Where her words failed, the wild gestures of her hand toward the bar blocking our entrance filled in the missing syllables.

"You've got to go. Now."

She stared at Jack as if in a daze. She moved slowly, and then there was a soft click. The bar gave way and as we walked in, she left.

I looked past Jack, taking in the room. The gym was laid out in a simple fashion. Circuit machines were grouped behind the cardio equipment and beyond that there was a free weights area. Two men worked out there but didn't pay any attention to each other. All of this was off to the left of the main ceramic tile walkway where we were standing. I assumed the route would lead to the back of the gym and the change rooms.

Off to the right, were bar-height tables and chairs. This would be where they signed up new members and gave them the details on what they would get for their bi-weekly payment.

The room next to that had a schedule for cycle class. The glass wall that faced the rest of the workout area revealed a darkened room. No class right now. That was a relief.

I sensed someone watching us and turned to see the heavier woman from the treadmill facing us.

We needed these people out of here. That was my responsibility. While we didn't expect any trouble at the gym, we needed to be prepared. If Keyes were the man who kidnapped, raped, and murdered all those women, he would fight for his freedom and wouldn't be opposed to taking others down in order to retain it—unless Zachery's theory about him wanting to be stopped was correct.

"Got this?" I asked the question close to the back of Jack's head. He nodded, and I went off to gather the people working out while he set out in search of Keyes.

I went to the heavier woman on the treadmill first. She had since slowed down her stride and watched me approach. The machine let out a beep and the tread halted its cycle.

"I'm going to have to ask you to come with me," I said.

Her eyes went over me for only a few seconds before she hopped off the machine and hurried in the direction of the change room.

"Miss?"

She stopped and turned around.

"You stick with me." I didn't need her going on ahead and falling right into Keyes's hands. I wasn't losing my place on the team today.

"Okay."

She was shaking, and I wasn't sure if it were her nerves from our presence or from an amped-up heart rate. Her cheeks were a flaming red and sweat beaded on her forehead. Her ponytail was dangling loosely with the elastic somewhere near the base of her neck.

"Come with me." I headed to the man who was in a run on another treadmill. Buds were in his ears, the cord leading to a bright blue MP3 player, clipped to the waist of his running shorts. He didn't notice me until I was right beside him. He pushed some buttons on the machine and the speed slowed down. He walked at a fast pace.

"We need you to leave," I said.

"I pay to work out here."

I pulled out my identification.

Another beep and the machine came to a halt. He grabbed the towel he had hung over the machine and ran it down the length of his neck, behind his hairline and across his forehead.

"What's this about?" He stood with his legs on the starter plates on both sides of the tread.

"Official FBI business. We need you to leave."

"Okay." He drew out the word and got off the machine. While doing so, he passed a judgmental glance to the woman who had peacefully been reading and getting a workout before we became involved in her life.

As I gathered up the other gym members, I couldn't help but think how much easier this looked in the movies, but it had taken less than two minutes to get the five members out of the building.

They just cleared out when Keyes burst around the corner with a girl who appeared ten years younger.

Jack followed, his hand gripped on Keyes's shirt, leading him with the bunched fabric—a makeshift rein on a horse.

The girl ran toward me, tears streaked down her face, but I

sensed more from fear than anything else. She hit the door, and, when it wouldn't give, she banged on the glass.

"Let me out of here."

"It's locked," I said and went to help her out. By the time I reached the door, she had already slipped out to the freedom of the street. I re-locked the door.

Jack pushed Keyes forward.

"What the fuck are you doing here?" Keyes's cheeks were red from anger. His eyes were no longer those belonging to a man hurt over his lost wife, instead they contained a darkness that was hard to penetrate.

"We have a warrant to search this place." Jack slammed the paperwork on the counter and signaled me to open the door again.

I noticed the investigation team was here, with their collection cases and gear, ready to get to work. Six of them came in and spread out over the place, like dispersed metal shards being drawn to magnets in four corners. It was moments like this I was proud to be with the FBI.

"What do you expect to find?" Keyes leaned against the counter. His body registered defeat, not fight.

I continued to watch him closely.

Jack ignored his question. "As we speak, investigation teams are going through your house and your cabin—"

"Tristan? He's going—"

"He's in good hands. The babysitter's going to be fine too," I said.

"Where are they, Keyes?"

He shook his head. "Where are who?"

Jack got within inches of the man's face. "The missing women—Rogers, Poole, and the others. Where are they? Are they still alive?"

"How the hell would I know?"

"I'm not going to ask again."

"I don't know."

Jack gestured to me. "Cuff this shit."

"I'm telling you, you have the wrong guy."

"They all say that." I snapped the cuffs without care about cutting into his wrists. He tortured all those women—he deserved payback.

Keyes spoke over his shoulder. "In my case, it's the truth. You guys are going to pay for this. You can't just come into my business and—"

"We just did, and now it's time to go for a ride."

Chapter 30

"She must have been sixteen. We'll add statutory rape to your list of charges."

Jack sat in the chair opposite Keyes in an interrogation room inside the PWPD.

Keyes patted the flat of his hand on the table in an uneven rhythm. "She's twenty-one."

"Did she turn that last week?"

"You're the FBI. Don't you know anything?" He stopped tapping and leaned forward. "Like the fact I'm innocent?"

"Tell us about your father." Jack tossed a photograph from the file across to Keyes.

Keyes sat back in his chair and didn't reach for the photograph.

"I take it you weren't close."

"What does that matter?" Keyes's eyes traced to the ceiling and then back to Jack. "What does any of this have to do with anything? Why do you even think I'm involved?"

"We don't think you're involved, we think you're the one taking these women. Where is Amy Rogers?" Jack slid her photo across the table. "Where is Sydney Poole?" Her picture was placed beside the one of Rogers.

Keyes touched his brow with an index finger and pressed. "Besides hearing the news, I wouldn't even know their names, let alone what they look like." He dropped his hand. "I'm telling you, I'm innocent."

Jack leaned back, patted his shirt pocket, passed me cursory glance, and went back to focusing on Keyes. "Your father owned

Hartland Packers. They hauled meat for local farmers and butchers starting in the mid-sixties."

"So what?" Keyes lifted the glass of water in front of him with both hands. He set it back down heavily.

Jack went back into the folder and pulled out crime scene photos of Nina Harris. He laid out a spread of seven shots. With each one he took out, he placed them down with a distinctive thump from the side of his hand against the wood, stacking them with emphasis.

Keyes closed his eyes. "Please take those away."

Jack made no motion to gather the photos back into the concealment of the manila jacket. "How was your childhood?"

Keyes twisted his lips with his fingers for a second. "It sucked."

"Tell us about it." Jack clasped his hands on the table.

"He never touched me if that's what you're thinking, but I never got along with the man. At least, most of the time I didn't."

I noticed he had no apparent emotional connection with his father. His articulation never carried anxiety, and his words were stated stoically.

"You got along just fine when you were abducting women together." Jack didn't phrase it as a question.

"You want me to talk or not? I can lawyer up. Isn't that how you phrase it?"

Jack let Keyes's threat lay out there in silence.

Keyes spoke again. "My mother was a good woman. She'd do anything for anyone."

"Then she wouldn't be too happy to find out that you and your father killed together?"

I was wondering why Jack was pushing him so hard. I feared Keyes would shut up, demand representation, and everything would get delayed. The more time that passed without the missing women in our hands, the higher the likelihood they wouldn't be coming back to us alive.

Keyes didn't bite Jack's bait. He remained silent.

"Tell us more about them. Did your mother cheat on your father?"

Keyes's eyes glazed over. "I don't think she did. Like I said, she was a really sweet woman, still is a very sweet woman."

"Still is? She died in a car accident years ago."

"She's here with me." He balled a fist and held it over his heart. "She always will be."

"Okay."

"Don't say *okay* like that. I know what you mean by that. You think I'm crazy because I carry a dead woman around with me."

Jack paused for a few beats. "With him being on the road all those hours, she never got lonely?"

"How did she have time to be lonely? I was around. Do you have any idea how much work it is to have a kid? Let me guess, no."

"I know."

I pushed off the wall I had been leaning against. Jack didn't look in my direction.

"You know how much is involved? She wouldn't have had time to *get* lonely."

"Your father—"

"What about him? I hardly knew the man."

"Spend any summer vacations with him, on the road, learning the business?"

"I don't like what you're implying."

"I wasn't implying anything. Should I have been?"

"You are driving me mad. Listen, my father was one of those never-in-the-picture kind of deals, all right? I believed he loved me in his own way until I was about fifteen. Then I stopped living the fantasy and let him go from my life. It was either that or go crazy trying to seek approval from someone who was never going to give it to me."

"What happened at fifteen?"

I knew where Jack was headed with this—that age group was right on target.

Keyes didn't answer.

"Fifteen? What was it?" Jack pulled a photo from the file, rose, and paced the perimeter of the table, walking so close that he nearly brushed against Keyes's arm. He came to a standstill beside Keyes and bent over to the level of his ear. "Did he make you rape this woman?" He slapped the photo of the female victim from two thousand in front of him.

Keyes turned to face Jack. "I want that lawyer now."

"You'll be needing one." Jack didn't gather up the pictures he had laid out on the table. It resembled a montage of faces and places, the colors blending. The only thing he picked up was the file folder before we left the room.

We watched Keyes from the observation room. He fanned his fingers through his hair, and then rested his elbows on the table. His head was facing down and seconds later he had scooped up the photos into a pile and flipped them over. He pushed them to the far end of the table.

"You think he did this? That he has Rogers and Poole?" I asked and shoved my hands into my pockets.

Jack reached into his shirt pocket, pulled out a cigarette, and let it perch in his lips. "It doesn't really matter what I think. It matters what the facts show. The facts show our unsub had a traumatic childhood. His mother died when a transport truck skidded through an intersection. The ruling was careless driving. The driver never even faced jail time."

I nodded. "But there's nothing traumatic that exists, on record anyway, of his relationship with his father. We felt that was our trigger, right? An older man took a younger one along in his abduction and murder of women."

"I'd say you don't sound too convinced about his guilt."

"I'm not sure how I feel and we thought maybe it was a father's or uncle's voice that directed him in the abduction and murders, but maybe it was his mother's. It could explain why originally there was no rape?"

"Then all of a sudden, in two thousand, mommy turns the other way while her son rapes a victim?"

I heard it in Jack's voice. Thinking that Keyes's mother was a trigger at all was a far-fetched notion. I pulled it back to the basics we knew. "It seems everything was really triggered with Leslie, Keyes's wife. That girl Keyes was with at the club. Was she married?"

Jack shook his head.

"That means he abducts and kills one type of woman while he dates another kind? I'm not sure I'm buying it."

"Well, it is possible he holds more respect—"

"More respect for the one who will make out in the change room of a public business?" I let out a laugh. "Hardly respectable."

"Hmm."

"Well, you have me here for my opinions, right?"

Jack faced in the direction of the one-way mirror but gave me a sideways glance.

I continued knowing what I had to say applied to my adultery but dismissed its implication. "How could anyone have respect for women who cheat on their husbands? They've made vows, whereas the single, promiscuous woman is only accountable to herself."

"He did bury Nina Harris with her ring."

"Maybe that factors into the equation?" My attention went to Keyes. He sat there staring in our direction as if he was able to see us. "Why did you push him so hard? We could still be in there."

Jack pulled the cigarette from his mouth. "Keyes is a narcissist. I sized him up as one the first time we met. He takes pride in running the gym, in being a father, in being in good shape."

"Nothing wrong with those things."

"But he also needs to be heard and to be in control. I pushed him because I didn't see him pushing that control on to anyone else, even a lawyer."

I didn't say the words, *seems you were wrong in this case*, but it took all my self-control. I didn't have any left to hold back the question about Jack's personal life. I cleared my throat. "You have a kid?"

He bobbed his head toward the glass. "Turns out I was right."

Keyes was motioning for us to go back.

"You have a kid?" My repeated question fell to Jack's back as he already cleared the doorway, headed to the interrogation room.

I'll be damned.

"You're waiving a lawyer then?"

Jack slipped into the chair across from Keyes.

I took up my position in the corner of the room again.

"Just don't go accusing me of things."

"I can't promise that." Jack took the pile of photos Keyes had stacked, flipped them over, and laid them back out again.

"No. God, please don't do that." Keyes put a hand on the photo closest to him.

"Why did you kill your wife?"

"See? You're accusing me again. Stop doing that. Fuck!" Keyes swiped a hand through his hair. "I would never have touched a hair on her fuckin' head! Ever! I loved her. We had a child together. We were happy."

"Until she had an affair."

Keyes shook his head. "She didn't...well, if she did, I didn't know about it. She was a great actress."

"You weren't around all the—"

Jack's cell rang.

"I don't know, all right? Maybe she was, maybe she wasn't, but I didn't kill her."

Jack read his caller's identity and held up a finger to Keyes. "Harper."

Less than a second later, he was on his feet, his phone pressed to his ear, and I was following him out the door.

"Where do you think you're going? Are you just going to leave me here?" Keyes called out.

I ignored Keyes and kept up with Jack. The odd word from his phone conversation was making it through.

The case just took another turn.

CHAPTER 31

THE CALL CAME FROM RICK Lane, a supervisor with the FBI Evidence Response Unit, and he told us we needed to get to Keyes's cabin immediately.

The smell reached out of the cabin like an invisible hand, grabbing hold. Maybe it was because I knew what was inside.

It overshadowed the scent of Jack's cigarette, reducing its strength to a talc powder. Glancing over at the rest of the team, I saw they were experiencing the same reaction, except for Jack of course. The man seemed untouchable.

The stout forensic supervisor waited inside the front door. If I didn't know better, I would have sworn he wanted to run out of the place, but his legs had him grounded to the floor. Lane shook hands with the four of us, ending with Jack.

"What I told you over the phone? Yeah, it doesn't even begin to describe the real thing. This way." He turned and we followed him through the living area to the bathroom. "Found it in the toilet. The smell's enough to really make the eyes water in here."

Jack went in ahead of us and stood over the toilet. We were in the hallway watching him. His eyes pinched shut for an instant, and I wondered if the smell, combined with what he saw, got to him.

I had rushed to a conclusion too quickly. His energy spoke of angry determination.

"Nothing's been touched?"

"Coburn took photos. That's all. I wanted you and your team to see her just as she was found."

Jack stepped out, and the rest of us took our turns inside the little room of horror.

I worked to prepare my mind to handle what I was going to see. I factored in the smell, the obvious level of decomp, the size of a toilet bowl. My fortitude slipped some when Paige came out and placed a hand on my shoulder.

It was my turn.

I took a deep breath, coughing on the acrid scent, instantly sorry for having done it. The team's eyes were on me, but, more importantly, Jack's were. I had to prove to him I could handle this type of thing—prove, in fact, that I could manage anything thrown my way.

I had seen a lot in my few months as part of this team. I looked down. How bad could this—

The gagging sensation gurgled in my throat and rushed up my esophagus like a speeding train.

"Looks like Pending's gonna blow, boss."

"Shi—" My hand snapped to my mouth. Bile coated my tongue in its acidic, slimy texture. I tried to swallow. My stomach heaved. I needed to get out of there. Now. If not, I was going to—

Time was up.

I turned to the sink beside the toilet and emptied the contents of my stomach.

"Whoa Pending." Zachery was clapping. "Nice job. At least you missed the remains."

Another round struck—the bile shooting up like a geyser, splatting the sink again.

Paige came behind me and placed a hand on my shoulder. "Come on, let's get you out of—"

"Can't handle it." Zachery was laughing.

"Shut up, Zach. You're not helping," Paige said.

I glanced over at the doorway and saw Jack. I shrugged Paige off me. "Leave. I can." The only way I could talk was in short bursts.

"Yeah, it sure sounds like it." She left the room, possibly angered and embarrassed by my rejection.

I had just vomited twice. Her pride was really the last thing that worried me. What if Jack thought I was incompetent for the job? What if he kicked me off the team?

I rinsed out the sink, swished the water around, and watched chunks of my stomach contents do a dance around the drain opening before they disappeared. I splashed cold water on my face and slapped my cheeks. I would take a glimpse at the remains again. This time with focus. This time without vomiting.

I braced myself on the sink for a few seconds and willed myself to go through with this. I closed my eyes and centered my vision. I coached myself—I had been there, done that.

Okay. I sprung up and positioned myself in front of the toilet.

The head of Amy Rogers sat in a bowlful of light pink water. Her brown hair swirled around her head, floating there like a twisted halo. Maggots the size of quarters fed off her flesh, crawling on her, coming out of her nostrils, mouth, and ears. Her eyes, clouded in milky decay, were wide open, as if screaming from death at the atrocity that had come to her remains.

My stomach compressed, but there was nothing left to expel. Instinctively, I laid a hand over my abdomen.

"He's gonna blow again," Zachery said.

When I straightened out, I was happy to see that only he was standing there. I walked past him to the front steps and took up a standing position beside Jack who was talking with Rick Lane.

"She was dead when she was decapitated," Lane said.

Both men acknowledged me with a quick glance and then carried on with their conversation. Lane continued his point. "For one, there would have been a lot more blood. Question is how, or even why, would Keyes put the head of a victim in his toilet? That doesn't make any sense."

"Hmm."

Zachery and Paige joined us outside.

"Agree, boss," Zachery said.

Paige put her hands on her hips. "Like we said before, he could have wanted to get caught."

Jack's eyes took in his team. I wondered what was going through his mind.

He addressed Lane. "We need to figure out when she was put

in there. If it was during the last six hours, we know it wasn't Keyes. Any time before that and Keyes could still be our killer. We need to find out where Sydney Poole is and if she's still alive."

"Absolutely. I've called in for more backup here too. We'll be tripping over each other, but it will mean everything is covered. We won't miss anything."

"I have faith in that."

Was Jack smiling?

"Of course, it's not forensics that solve crime, it's the investigators."

"You've been drinking martinis on shift Harper? We've been through this. Without forensic evidence to back you guys up, nothing would be open and shut."

After seconds of staring at each other, both men laughed.

"Come on guys. We've got work to do." Lane snapped his fingers, and his expression turned serious. "We have evidence of sexual activity in the bed, and, looking at things under the ultraviolet light, there are possibly several contributors. Of course, the bedding's been collected and will be fully analyzed. If there's DNA to be found anywhere, we'll find it."

"Expect no less." Jack pulled out a cigarette and lit up. The smoke ascended heavenward with his exhale. His eyes were on me until it dissipated and then narrowed a trace. "Want one, Kid?" He smiled the way he did when mocking me, crooked, with the right side of his mouth rising higher than the left.

"One thing that really stands out, next to the dirty bedding, is the cleanliness of the place. Anyway, I better be going." Lane excused himself and went back into the cabin.

Jack turned to Paige. "Fill me in on your visit to the nursing home."

"Ken Campbell was just as Barbara Wilson told us he'd be. He's in advanced stages of Alzheimer's. He went in and out on us a few times."

She filled us in on a person nicknamed Ladies' Man. "Campbell gave us the name Steve but no last name. I had Nadia do a quick check on the employees at the trucking company where Campbell and Wilson worked, but there weren't any Steves."

"Hmm." Jack extinguished the cigarette on the ground.

I wondered if I were the only one thinking along these lines. "I have a question." A second's pause to make sure I had their attention. "Why would Keyes put the head in the toilet?"

"Pending's got a good question. If Keyes wanted a trophy, why keep it there? He wanted to get caught? Why cut it off in the first place? None of the other victim's heads have been found. It's the only bathroom in the cabin too. If he needed to go, did he pee on her head?"

"Forensics will confirm or deny that," Jack said.

"Listen, guys, it doesn't make sense. If Keyes is the killer, where is Poole and the remains of the other missing women? Dogs have been combing the back lot, and I haven't heard anything from their handlers. They are down as far as the riverbank. Surely something would have come to light by now."

"You think the head was planted in Keyes's toilet?" Paige asked.

"I do. Yeah. I mean it would make sense, really, wouldn't it?"

"Hmm."

"What?" I turned to Jack. "Why *hmm* me right now? It makes sense."

Jack's intense gaze went through me.

"It does make sense. I agree."

Paige stood ground beside me. Her agreement caught me off guard.

"All right, then, if that's the case, where are we with other suspects?" Jack asked with his eyes glued on me. I sensed, due to my brief disrespect, not that I needed to answer.

"We still need the employment records from the gyms in the area," Zachery offered.

"We also need the financials from Lindsay Parks," I said.

"Okay, first thing we're going to do is press Brad Keyes. We need to know what women were in that bed. We need to confirm that the male DNA belongs to Keyes. If our unsub was brash enough to hide a head in the man's toilet, maybe he's been coming here to have sex with the women."

I nodded. "We also need to really dig deep into Keyes's life. It started with his wife."

"Agreed." Zachery smiled at me.

"What are we doing standing around here then? We'll head back and let Keyes know we found his treasure."

"Boss—"

The team stopped moving and turned to face me. "We just said we didn't think that it was Keyes who put the head there."

The three of them shook their heads and kept walking.

HE WATCHED THEM FROM A HILLTOP, about a mile down the road. It had a clear line of sight to the cabin. The crime scene technicians and police cruisers were parked in the driveway and at the road, and there was a black SUV. The FBI had arrived, and they were there because of him.

He watched through the scope of his father's hunting rifle, having adjusted it until he felt he could reach out and touch them. He had waited patiently for them to arrive. Now the world would take notice of him. He would make sure of it. He would prove he was something. Someone to fear. Someone to respect.

"See," he yelled at the voice.

You are a loser.

The voice carried through the long grass that rustled in the breeze.

He focused his scope on the female. Petite with red locks of hair that reached her shoulders. The gun holster she wore was large on her frame. She looked out over the field in his direction. She was older than his regular targets, but she was beautiful.

He put a hand on his cock and rubbed until it fed him to full erection. No one was around. He unzipped his pants, freeing himself, and finished it to conclusion.

Kill her!

Do it. Prove you're a real man!

The tremors that took his body to climax relaxed, leaving him blanketed in warmth.

The voice was loud and demanded his attention. He would satisfy it too, but this time he wouldn't do exactly as he was told—at least not yet.

Chapter 32

An officer led a handcuffed Keyes into the integration room. He took the cuffs off and pushed Keyes toward a chair. The officer's thought was clear in his eyes, *crucify the son of a bitch.*

Like before, Jack sat at the table, and I took up position in the corner of the room. The observer. Again.

"As you know, we searched the gym, your home, and your cabin," Jack began.

"And you found nothing."

"Actually, we didn't find anything at the gym or your home initially, but we're combing through them even closer. Your cabin gave us quite the find however."

"What are you talking about?"

Jack slammed the flats of his hands onto the table. The action made Keyes jump and sit farther back. "Where is Sydney Poole?"

The plan was to push Keyes to a breaking point. While we questioned his guilt, he still needed to prove his innocence.

"What? I don't know. What are you talking about?"

"Is she still alive?" Jack asked.

Keyes's eyes blanked over.

Jack repeated his question, leaning across the table—his butt off the chair and his face inches from Keyes. "Poole. Is. She. Still. Alive?"

Keyes shook his head. "I...I don't..."

"Simple question, simple answer. Last time I'm asking."

Keyes's eyes shot to me, but his gaze settled on Jack. "I wouldn't know."

"You wouldn't know?"

"Why would I? I didn't take those women!" Keyes's face flushed a bright red.

The two men locked in eye contact, a battle of the wills as to who would back down first. I knew it wouldn't be Jack.

"What did you find?" Keyes asked and turned away.

Jack kept his eyes on him a few seconds longer before retreating back to his side of the table. He opened up the file folder.

My stomach tossed, thinking about the photograph. If we leaned toward Keyes being innocent, I wondered why we'd put him through that. Jack must have agreed. He shut the file without taking anything out.

"What did you find?" Keyes repeated his question.

"We found remains of Amy Rogers in your cabin."

"What? No. That's...that's not even possible."

"Well, it was, and it is."

"Where did you? This is crazy. I knew I should go up there more than I do."

I pushed off the wall.

Evidence indicated that Keyes, or someone at least, held up regular attendance at the place. The cabin was kempt—no dust was on any of the furniture or floors. There were sexual fluids found on the sheets which, if not from recent activity, could have degraded beyond usefulness to a lab.

Jack told me a long time ago not to interrupt his interrogations unless it was for a damn good reason. In this case, I had to take a shot. "When was the last time you were there?"

I had expected Jack's eyes to be full of reprimand, but, instead, I saw that he was impressed.

Keyes looked between the two of us and settled on me. "I don't know. Years ago anyway. I tell you that."

"Well, someone must take care of the property."

"Yeah, it's covered. I hire someone to empty the mailbox, cut the grass, etcetera."

"Do they have a key for the cabin?"

"No."

I found his response interesting, and it didn't explain the tidy inside. "You said you were there years ago, but I think you know exactly when." There was something in his eyes. I moved closer.

Keyes blinked rapidly. His eyes misted. "It was…" He swallowed hard. "It was not long after Leslie went missing, but I was starting to accept that she wasn't coming back, that she wasn't going to be found, that maybe she was even dead." Any anger from earlier had abated and the man sat in front of us broken, with nothing more to lose. "I was lonely. I was depressed. Tristan was only a baby. He'd scream for his mother. I…I couldn't give her to him." He choked back tears, evidenced in the gruffness of his voice, the faraway gaze to his eyes, and the odd misalignment of his jaw as it slid right and left.

"You took women there?" I asked the question without judgment. Keyes was only a man, after all, and a man who had been undergoing a life-changing situation.

Keyes nodded.

"Did you take Amy Rogers recently?"

Keyes remained silent.

"We have to ask these questions."

"No." His face fell, his eyes focused down on the table. "I told you…"

"You said you were there not long after Leslie went missing. Did you go there often?"

"What? No?" Keyes swiped the flat of his hands down his cheeks, and wiped away tears. "You think I became a male whore when she died? That I escaped my child and had sex with a bunch of women at the cabin?"

"We never mentioned a bunch of women."

Keyes slammed his hands on the table. "It was a figure of speech."

"And you said she died. Do you know this for a fact?"

"Impossible. I'm trying to talk to you. I've been cooperative, and I'm not sure the hell why. Actually, I'll tell you why. For Leslie. She's the only reason I'm any semblance of a good person at all."

"There was evidence of sexual activity found on the sheets in the bedroom."

"Well, if it's recent, it wouldn't be from me. You said you found Amy Rogers there?"

"Part of her," Jack corrected.

"Part of her? What the hell is that supposed to mean?"

Jack gestured toward me but addressed Keyes. "Answer the agent's question."

"Which one?"

"How did you know Leslie was dead?"

Keyes took a choppy, deep breath. "It was something I felt in the deepest parts of me. I'd have nightmares of her, screaming and calling out to me. I wanted to help. I tried to help, but my reach was just shy of contact." A single tear slid down his cheek, and he didn't move to wipe it. "I tried to go about my day-to-day life. Then one day I felt very dark and empty. I felt cold."

Keyes studied our reactions to what he was saying. "I just knew I was alone. Well, alone with Tristan. I had to be strong for him, when I felt anything but. What's the phrase, life goes on? It's an easy mantra to preach, a little harder to accept."

Keyes's words hung in the room for a few seconds, and then he continued. "Whatever you need from me, I will give it to you. I want to find Leslie—even if it's to give her a proper burial." His last words had his voice constricting and sounding rough. "And if we can stop this from happening to other women."

"We'll require your DNA," Jack said.

"Consider it done." He paused, seemingly unsure whether to continue. "I loved my wife, I still love her. I know what these other men are going through—an absolute nightmare. I wouldn't wish this on my worst enemy."

Jack closed the file and rose. "We'll get someone in here to swab your mouth. I'm sure you've already been contacted, but we'll need the employment records at the gym."

"Sure. No worries."

"The warrant is in place—"

"That wasn't necessary. There's nothing to hide, and if this creep you're looking for turns out to work there, I'll kill him myself."

"Hmm."

Keyes passed a nervous glance to me as we left the room.

Chapter 33

I stood with Jack in the hallway outside of a conference room at headquarters, waiting for Kirk Rogers. We had debated providing notification at his place of work but thought it more beneficial to bring the man in. We also wanted more neutral territory, as opposed to Washington where his friend sat in the chief of police chair.

Kirk Rogers came toward us with another man in a pressed suit. The man was about the same age as Rogers—no older than his early thirties. His eyes were a dark brown and matched the color of his hair. He crossed his arms, shortening the sleeves of his suit to expose his shirt cuffs and designer watch.

"Did you find my wife?" Rogers asked.

I picked up on his efficient nature, which had been apparent from our first meeting. Besides skimming along in the wakes of his father's empire, he had made his own waves in the industry. I thought of extending a hand, but Rogers wasn't in a civil mood so I gestured him toward the room.

This was one aspect of the job I hated the most, and, with this case, I didn't even have a full body to provide the widower for identification. We had a head—a body part no one would want to see severed from their loved one. A vision like that would change a person forever.

We sat around the table, and Rogers introduced the man with him. "This is Bruce. He's my brother."

Bruce poured a glass of water for Rogers and himself, then sat down.

Rogers nodded a thank you to him. "He's also a lawyer."

I didn't really find it surprising that a man like Rogers had lawyers in the family or that he traveled with them.

The image of Amy's head sitting in that toilet bowl knotted my stomach. Identification wasn't necessary. We knew it was her. There was no way to go about this other than to come out with it, and Jack made it clear that he wanted me to handle this. Something about getting used to it.

"We found your wife," I said.

"Where is she? Please tell me she's alive." His gaze faltered as he received the message from my eyes.

"I'm sorry for your loss."

Silence enveloped the room for a few seconds before Bruce broke it. "How? Where did you find her?" He reached an arm out to his brother.

Rogers pulled back and lifted a hand to stave off the act of affection.

Bruce, unaffected by Rogers's reaction, set his focus on me for elaboration.

"She was found at a cabin outside of the city."

"A cabin?" Rogers's lashes were soaked with tears. He pinched the tip of his nose and squeezed his eyes shut.

"We know who the cabin belonged to, and we will find the one respons—"

"Save the speech. I've heard it on TV before. Is he under arrest? I want this son of a bitch to pay with his fuckin' life. You hear me? I will testify in court. I will pay for the trial. Fuck, I'll pay for the lethal injection."

Jack's facial features cut at sharp angles.

"We need you to trust us," I said.

"Trust you?" Rogers let out a mock laugh, and it had Bruce placing a hand on his forearm again. Rogers didn't dismiss the gesture.

"We'll be in touch with you as the case progresses." I hoped that would serve to pacify him for the moment.

"How did she die?"

"There will be an autopsy conducted to determine this." I didn't have the fortitude to dwell on the fact that a *full* autopsy would be impossible. "There is something you can help us with though. Do you have any close friends in your life that may have noticed, or should I say, thought, that you had problems in your marriage?"

"Why would anyone—"

"You're a busy man Mr. Rogers. You have a large company to run. Someone could take that as you leaving your wife to live her own life separately. They may think she was lonely and neglected."

"My Amy was the most spoiled bitch on the planet, and I mean that affectionately. She suited it just fine too. You know that. She had no problem spending my money, getting us involved with charity events and save the world type things. I went along. It's good PR. She said I look great in a tux. You know women. When they want something, they sweet-talk you and either make you think it was your idea or make an irresistible offer."

Part of Rogers's statement sounded familiar, and I knew why. I hadn't thought anything about it at the time. I scribbled it in my notepad to make sure I let Jack know after this meeting.

JACK CAME OUT OF THE meeting room at a fast pace, but I kept up. I touched his shoulder, and he stopped walking and turned around.

"When Poole came in to report his wife missing, I remembered something in the report that said she was involved with charity events. He said that he knew Rogers but only through these types of events. I didn't think anything at the time, but now that we're analyzing things from another angle, from the unsub being close to the husbands and getting to the wives that way, I think it matters now."

"They knew each other and moved in the same circles." Jack summarized what I brought to light.

"Yeah. Like I said before, we didn't think it meant anything."

"Rogers has a payroll for private investigators. We know this because he utilized them when his wife went missing. If he finds out that Keyes owns the cabin where she was found, he could be as good as dead. Do we still have him in holding?"

I dialed the PWPD and a few seconds later had my answer. "He was released about an hour ago."

"We need to get to him. Now."

CHAPTER 34

THE LINES ALWAYS REACHED THE front door, and he loved it that way. In fact, he preferred it because it allowed him to be faceless and become a number—the next to serve in a montage of age, nationality, and gender. He would order what he always did—a regular coffee, black. Typically, he never diverted, giving preference to being predictable, and he hated making decisions. There was safety within the walls of his self-imposed box.

He was satisfied with what he had done. He had let go of the proverbial reins and let himself be reborn. There was liberation that came with that.

Maybe he would have them add a splash of milk.

There was a couple in front of him, holding hands and laughing. He wondered if the blond female would roll her head back in laughter for any number of men or if the guy were special. He sided on the belief the latter held true. Women knew the power they possessed and wielded it to their advantage.

The blonde was trim, and her blue eyes were accented with soft hues of brown shadow. When her hand came up to touch her lover's cheek, her nails were painted red. She leaned in and kissed him—open-mouthed.

His first reaction was to turn away, disgusted by the whorish ways of this woman.

Then again, she was perfect for the statement he wanted to make. He made himself watch.

Seconds later they parted from their kiss, her eyes were partial slits. She would fuck her lover on the floor of Starbucks if given the chance.

She is perfect.

The voice that had fought against him and his next step now urged him forward.

The whore glanced back at him, picking up on his attention. She smiled.

They always smiled when they caught his eye or when they noticed they had his interest. His attractiveness was one thing that had always worked to his advantage. He had died his hair gray to give him the appeal of an older, more sophisticated man, when in fact he had just passed his twenty-sixth birthday. His steel eyes carried his raw sexuality and had a way of reaching into a woman's innate animal hunger. He kept himself trim, a prerequisite for his line of work. Without being in shape, the challenge would be much harder, if not impossible.

He studied her, wondering if her lover were even aware of the whore on his arm. How long had they been in a relationship—did it even qualify as such?

There was no ring on her finger, but he was willing to make an exception. After all, a statement needed to be made.

Take her.

Do it now.

Swells of adrenaline pulsated beneath his skin. He swore his flesh jumped from his bones in anticipation. He tapped the flat of his hand against his thigh—anything to quell the excitement and impulse to act immediately.

Tappity, tap. Tappity, tap.

He scanned the glorified coffee shop. Patrons sat at tables, absorbed in conversations, oblivious to the goings-on around them. They held no interest in human beings outside of their circle—an observation he had made years ago that continued to be advantageous.

The blonde laughed again at something Lover Boy said while rubbing a hand on her abdomen.

She passed him another glance over her shoulder, holding her expression, wanting to make sure he noticed. Her eyes sparkled and hinted at seduction. She was just the kind he searched for.

"Can I help the next person?" A server called out and the line moved up.

The blonde and Lover Boy ordered and moved down the counter to wait on the barista for their beverages.

He placed his order—adding the splash of milk—and he didn't have to wait at the end.

Each time it was the same. Ask for a standard coffee here, and there was always a hesitant pause as if to say, *are you sure that's all you want?*

He turned to the blonde. Her one arm was now latched in Lover Boy's. Her one leg was bent back and the tip of her boot tapped the floor.

She was perfect.

Don't lose her. She is perfect.

You'll probably fuck this up.

He sipped slowly from his cup. His full attention was on her. There was only one way out of here, and she wouldn't be alone. In fact, for at least a little while, she'd have the company of two men.

CHAPTER 35

"I CAN'T SEE ANY LIGHTS on inside the house, but his car is in the driveway," Detective Hanes came over the onboard phone system in the SUV. He had made it to Keyes's house well ahead of us.

"Just hang back and let us handle it." Jack directed.

"Understood."

Jack's response was a disconnection of the call. He addressed the team. "Let's talk."

"Boss?" Zachery said.

He was in the front passenger seat. Paige and I were in the back.

"The unsub's game has changed. What changed it?"

"He knows that we're in town and involved with his case. He's either trying to get involved in the investigation, or he's working hard to pin Keyes. Possibly a bit of both." Zachery answered Jack's question and angled his body to see us in the back as he spoke.

"He knew Keyes was in custody? He could be keeping a close eye on him," Paige offered.

Zachery pulled out on his seat belt and shifted toward the center console to see us in the back seat.

"I think our unsub put the head in the toilet to make a statement."

Paige turned to me. "He made a statement all right. He's even sicker than we originally thought."

"I'm wondering if he did know Keyes were in custody, and, in effect, was waving a flag saying it's not him, it's me. We had discussed the possibility of him wanting to be found."

"Either way, this guy is escalating. Now he has not only invaded Keyes's life once, but twice. First, by taking his wife and now by mocking him." Jack exhaled white smoke out the window into the night air.

I only wished all of it had left the car. I cleared my throat and realized how cigarettes made me cough less than before and how my chest didn't feel any heaviness or tingling from the pollution.

"What is so important about Keyes?" I asked the question out loud.

"You know, that's a damn good question," Paige said.

"That is a great question boss," Zachery said, with his gaze on Jack, as he took another drag on the cigarette and then flicked it out the window.

"Of course, an ID on our unsub might make a world of difference." Jack's eyes went to the rearview mirror. "First, let's secure Keyes."

Jack parked the SUV on a side street near Keyes's residence. "We're going in on foot."

The air carried the warning Jack didn't put into words—be alert and be careful. We put communications gear on which would allow us to update each other.

The evening air was cool, and the breeze brought an ominous feeling which had my nerves tapping beneath the skin—more with excitement than fear.

Paige and Zachery slipped into the backyard with their guns ready. A fence outlined the perimeter of the property, but it was open at the sides. Jack and I would approach from the front. This was all too familiar. The past came back in successive slides. A similar situation had transpired in Kentucky, but I preferred to forget the outcome. I had confidence this scenario would go better.

Jack spoke into his headpiece. "Rogers is here. His Mercedes— to the right."

I confirmed his verbal observation with a peripheral glance, doing my best to follow my training, which dictated keeping my eyes on the target while being aware of my surroundings.

Being a good agent—one that would return home alive—sometimes made me feel like an eagle who took in everything from a distance with acute accuracy.

Acknowledgements came through from Paige and Zachery. We would approach this situation with intensified caution.

"Lights on in the back of the house," Paige said.

"Just like other times. I'll take the door. You stand off to the left of me," Jack directed me.

"Got it."

We walked up the paved driveway, hands over our holsters, ready to pull our weapons if needed. I took in Jack's profile—the hardened edge of his facial features and his eyes intent on the door.

The bay window in front of the house disclosed a faint glow of light inside. I understood why Hanes may not have seen this from the road, but at this distance it was unmistakable. I pointed, and Jack nodded in such a way that my observation was dismissed as fast as it was relayed.

"There are definitely two or more people in there, boss," Zachery's voice sliced into the evening.

"There's stress in the voices. Do we go in?" Paige asked.

"Do you have a visual?" Jack asked.

"Not yet." The change in Paige's breathing told me she was trying to secure a line of a sight.

"What do you see?" Jack asked.

"Just moving around to get a better—" Paige's voice cut off for a second. "They're in the kitchen. He has a gun to Keyes's head."

"That's our cue." Jack turned the handle on the front door, and it was locked. He gestured to me, and, within seconds, I had the deadbolt picked, and we were in.

THE BACK DOOR ENTERED INTO THE KITCHEN. Paige went in first, and Zach followed behind her.

Rogers was there with another man she hadn't seen before, and Keyes was bound to a chair—his arms pulled behind him, his wrists tied with butcher twine. Blood stained his face, and the red had seeped to his clothing. The fabric, acting as a wick, had turned a dark crimson at the collar.

Rogers's eyes shot to Paige and Zach, control of his gun faltering slightly. "He killed my wife." Tears poured down his cheeks, and spittle flew from his mouth. He jabbed the gun barrel toward Keyes's head.

Keyes angled his head away. "I didn't kill her. I tol--"

Paige took a few slow steps toward Rogers, a gun held in one hand, and the other held up to Rogers. The other man eased back, lifting his hands up in surrender. He wasn't armed. Her eyes fixed back on Rogers. "You need to put down the weapon."

"But he killed my wife!"

Paige stopped all movement, training her gun on Rogers's forehead.

"Put the gun down," she repeated. If she needed to, she would shoot to kill.

Zach maneuvered around to the other man and cuffed him, keeping his eyes on Rogers as he did so.

Rogers lowered the gun slightly. "He killed my wife."

"This isn't the way to get justice."

"It's the only way." His voice cracked.

"You need to put your gun down, and we can talk about it."

"Let me avenge her!"

"You have the wrong man. The man who did this to your wife is still out there. Put your gun down!"

She studied his eyes—the crucial moment to decide the next course of action was now. Rogers's eyes went between her and Zach, and then dipped to take in Keyes. He turned when he heard Brandon's and Jack's footsteps behind him.

Both of them had their guns leveled on Rogers, and Jack solidified eye contact with Rogers. "I'd do as she says."

"Put it on the floor in front of you," Paige directed.

Rogers lowered to the floor, his free hand raised in surrender as he did. The metal of the barrel just touched the ceramic when Brandon snapped cuffs on his wrists.

"Are you okay Mr. Keyes?" Paige asked as she untied him.

Rogers bucked against Brandon, struggling to gain ground, but he held him steady. The fight in him gone, he lowered his eyes. "How can you do this?"

Chapter 36

A FEW HOURS HAD PASSED since Rogers had been brought in. Keyes opted out of pressing assault charges, stating he understood Rogers's angst. Rogers overheard the statement and yelled out that Keyes could have no idea until it was his wife's severed head. It became a brief circus performance, with the employees of the PWPD, Dumfries PD, and the FBI as the audience.

Hanes and Stenson were now down at The Earth and Evergreen Restaurant where they often shared conversation, drank a few beers, and fed on chicken wings.

"Ever get the feeling we're like ticks on their backs?" Stenson tilted the beer bottle to the side and then lifted it to his lips. "I mean, they ask for our help but then dismiss us. They run the case like it's theirs—and don't interrupt me to say it technically is."

Hanes rolled his eyes.

"I hate saying it's their case. We had it first. This guy fell into our laps. I was even ahead of you with this." Stenson smiled.

"I hate it when you get that look on your face."

"What? This charming smile? All they want to do is talk about it or jump here and there with the investigation. If I were in charge, I'd have the guy already."

Hanes's brow curved upward.

"Okay, maybe not, but I'd be closer."

"So how close are you, Sherlock? You have a suspect list?"

"I have some ideas, but I'm not sharing them with you."

"Because you don't have any." Hanes extinguished his mockery with a bottle pressed to his lips. "You have to watch your attitude, or you'll never advance rank. I'm telling you."

"You have a damn bad attitude, and you wear a detective's badge. If you can, I certainly qualify."

Both men smiled at each other and clinked bottles.

"Yeah, if you say so." Hanes checked his watch. "I better get going or the little lady is going to pitch a fit."

"She's probably already wound up for a tirade. Come on, one more beer."

Hanes let out a deep breath and settled back into the booth. "One more, but no more daydreaming talk about you advancing rank."

"Oh, you'll be sorry man. One day when I'm your boss," Stenson drained back the rest of his beer and summoned the waitress for two more, "you'll have to kiss my ass to make up for all the times you put me down."

"Trent, you know I have faith in you, but you do have improvements to make."

"What if I told you I had knowledge about this case that no one else does?"

Hanes's face took on dark shadows. "Then I'd tell you to get it out in the open before you're considered an accessory."

THERE WAS HARDLY ANY LIGHT in the room as he watched her sleep. Her apartment was a one bedroom on the main street and two stories up. He had followed her and Lover Boy from the coffee shop and planned his return visit.

The building wasn't secured and it gave him direct access to her front door. He had picked the lock easily, and, as the blonde's chest rose and fell beneath the sheets, he zeroed in on his target.

Kill her now.

The voice reached him no matter where he was. He might as well embrace it and let it become one with him.

Lover Boy had left an hour ago. He saw him walk down the sidewalk—a literal bounce to his step. He had fucked the whore, but it would be his last mistake.

You are going to fuck this up.

He spoke back to the voice within the confines of his mind. *I have everything under control.*

Even with his determination, uncertainty had a way of creeping in on him. He had never gone about things this way. He got to know the women and lured them to him. He would take this one with him, and if she didn't cooperate...

His thought derailed there.

Her breathing exhaled as soft purrs, bordering on snores, into the darkness of night. She kicked the sheets off, and his heart raced as he readied to move. But she hadn't woken up, only moved in her sleep.

He stepped closer to her bed and caught the waft of her smell—woman muskiness mixed with perfume. As he inhaled, he also picked up on something else. She was unclean. The man who had defiled her had left his stench behind, and the air was riddled with cheap cologne. He guessed it was a pharmacy knock-off.

Bile rose in his throat. Rage filled him.

Kill her now!

Do it!

While she sleeps, cut off her head!

You had fun with Amy. Remember Amy.

He tried to forget Amy. She had been beautiful, but he had taken her beauty. He usually struggled with remorse, but, with her, it went deeper. She had been a passionate lover. She looked him in the eye when he was inside her. She was uninhibited. He had loved that about her.

She was poison.

"Shut up!"

The blonde bolted upright and screamed. He slid up the bed and muffled her yells with a well-placed hand over her mouth. Her eyes went wide, the whites obvious in the dim light, as if she were facing a ghost.

"You do as I say, and I remove my hand. Got it?"

She nodded.

"We'll try this...slowly." He peeled back his hand in fragments of inches.

She howled.

He tightened his grip again. "Nope, nope, nope!"

"I'm—"

The rest of her words were mumbled, but he sensed it was an apology. At least that's what he chose to believe.

"We will try this one more time. Do you understand?"

She nodded again.

"All right." He removed his hand.

Her mouth remained closed for less than a second, but she didn't let out a scream.

"It's you. You from the coffee shop." Her eyes blinked tears.

"You remember me? Thought I was cute, didn't you?"

Her eyes never left his as she went to lift the sheets up to cover herself.

"Don't try to be modest now. We're just getting to know each other." He reached out to the strap of her camisole and pinched the fabric.

She clawed his face.

His hand cradled the stinging flesh, and he struggled for control.

Kill her! Kill her!

He pulled the camisole up and exposed her swelled breasts. She was aroused. He ripped off her lacy thong and got to work.

CHAPTER 37

JACK HAD WANTED TO TALK to Rogers about Poole, and, in a roundabout way, he had saved us the trouble of hunting him down.

Jack and I sat in the conference room of PWPD with Rogers and his cohort Neil.

The background on Neil didn't show any charges, but I had my suspicions that, in his case, it was only because he hadn't been caught.

Paige and Zachery were in the room with the crime boards. They figured while Jack and I talked to Rogers, they would study them in the hopes of seeing something that was missed.

"He killed my wife, and you're just willing to look the other way and let him go?"

Rogers's body language communicated the man wasn't open to discussion. He leaned back in the chair and crossed his legs at the ankles. He was convinced that Keyes was involved with his wife's disappearance, murder, and decapitation.

"How do you know Keyes?" Jack asked his question calmly, giving no impression that Rogers's impatient attitude affected him at all. My personal opinion was that it didn't. I didn't think there was much that fazed Jack.

"You need proof? How about my wife's head in his toilet? Isn't that enough—"

Neil put his hand on Rogers's forearm, bringing his stream of words to a halt. It earned him a sideways glare, but Rogers calmed down before speaking.

"I know Keyes from charity events—that's all."

"Nothing on a personal level?"

This was the third mention of charity events. Poole had said he knew Rogers from these types of events, and now Keyes was being pulled into that world as well.

"No. Absolutely not. We walked in different circles. He does what? Manages a gym? I run a communications empire."

"What about Ian Poole?"

"The lawyer? Same thing. Charity events. You don't think this factors in do you?"

"Did you ever approach Poole to work for you?"

Seconds ticked by.

"I did approach him once, but it was a long time ago. Nothing came of it. He said he didn't want to get involved with someone who has such a high profile. Didn't make much sense to me. You're a lawyer? Make a killing off it. I would have paid handsomely."

"Did he say why he turned you down?"

"Shouldn't you be out there finding the rest of my wife?"

Jack remained quiet.

Rogers continued. "Just that—he didn't want such a high-profile company to represent. Are you even looking for the rest of her? I can't have a funeral and only bury her head."

"There was no history before that between the two of you?" Jack opened a manila folder in front of him and consulted some reports. I figured it was more to create drama since Jack remembered mostly everything. "Ian Poole owns one of the most successful law firms in the area. He took on companies as large as yours. Why not yours?"

"Like I said, I can't answer that."

"What about your wives?" I interjected the question. "Women can be petty sometimes. They can hate another woman on sight. I know my wife used to be like that."

"Used to be?"

I had hoped that Rogers wouldn't pick up on the past tense and with having such a self-centered attitude, I was surprised he had. "I'm divorced. At least, it's in the process."

Rogers's face contorted, giving the impression he didn't really care.

"Did your wives not see eye to eye? Both of them were involved with charity events, the organizing of them? Did they compete with each other? I'm sure there's only so many who can afford to attend these functions. Were they fighting for attention?"

"I think I need a lawyer."

"Surprised he's not already here." Jack closed the folder.

"I did nothing wrong. Do you hear me?"

Jack walked to the door. "You went to a man's house, bound him, assaulted him, and held a gun to his head, but you did nothing wrong?"

Rogers sighed and rolled his eyes. "Whatever, man. You just don't like me because I have money."

The energy in the room changed as if a hurricane were coming.

Jack turned to face Rogers.

I prepared for a verbal lash out, but Jack said five words. "Get out of my face."

Chapter 38

"I LIKE YOUR ANGLE WITH the women."

Did I just hear Jack correctly? I trailed behind him, down the hallway toward the room with the crime boards.

"Well, it's another viewpoint on this. Maybe the women had an association, and that might be how our unsub got to both of them," I said.

Jack picked up his cell. "Nadia, one more thing for you. Check into charity events where both Amy Rogers and Sydney Poole were involved. While you're at it, see if any of the other women got involved with this type of thing." He clicked off—he must have had to leave a message for her.

I'm certain I was wearing the smug smile that came with validation. Jack had Nadia acting on my suspicions. I had to bask in these moments. They didn't come along as often as I would have liked. Even when I made a hefty contribution, most of them were dismissed with *hmm*.

We entered the room with the crime boards. Jack just cleared the doorway and was already asking questions. "All right, what do you guys have?"

Paige and Zachery were standing in front of the spread on Lindsay Parks.

"The financials came back on Parks." Zachery turned to face us. "There is nothing that stands out as elaborate spending. She went to Reborn Spa every Wednesday, and it doesn't seem that she belonged to any gym."

"That agrees with what her husband told us," I said.

"No connection that way. What about any cash withdrawals?" Jack pulled out a cigarette.

"There was a regular withdrawal of five hundred a week," Zachery said. "That's not a lot, considering the money the Parks have. To us, maybe a weekly cash spending budget of five hundred would be a lot."

"Tell me more."

"The other thing that stands out is most things that Parks spent money on was via her banking card or Visa. So why this need for cash?"

"Possibly for tipping?" I offered with a shrug. "You said she went to the spa weekly. What about regular salon appointments for her hair? I know if I pay cash to the lady who cuts—"

My words stopped there due to the correction meted out in Jack's eyes. I knew what they were saying, *so you can avoid the tax.* I averted eye contact.

Paige consulted the folder she held. I assumed it must have contained the financials of Lindsay Parks. She bobbed her head side to side. "It could be. I don't think any of the names that showed up on the banking report belonged to any hair salons. Reborn Spa doesn't do hair, just massage, etcetera."

"There aren't any names there that do. You know I remember everything I read." Zachery flashed a cocky smile.

"What else would she need cash for?" I asked the question out loud, not necessarily expecting an immediate answer.

"She pays for a gigolo." Paige laughed after she said it.

"A gigolo?" I smiled at her. The word instantly brought to mind the movie from the late nineties—*Deuce Bigalow: Male Gigolo.*

"Being a male gigolo, professionally known as a male escort, is a thriving business," Zachery began.

"Think about it," Paige said. "It would fit perfectly with our victimology as well. You have lonely wives who need attention. They know the comforts of a secure relationship—"

"At least, when it came to their financial status, Paige. Come on, these women were on their own—married yet single," I said.

Paige closed the folder and tossed it on a nearby desk. "Secure in the sense that they probably didn't want to risk their marriages, their comfortable financial status, on a tryst. There were probably prenups in place for all of them."

Jacked pulled out a cigarette. "Then you believe these women paid our unsub for sex?"

"Not necessarily, Jack. It's quite possible that these wives weren't cheating on their husbands, at least not in the typical sense. If their relationship with the unsub was free of physical interaction, in the least, they would have bonded emotionally. That is cheating to me anyway." Paige's eyes slid to me.

Zachery paced the perimeter of the room. "Let's say these women meet up with him for company. They want to feel needed, wanted, and important. How does our unsub go from being a confidant to a killer?"

"The money withdrawals. You said five hundred a week?" Jack asked.

"Yes," Paige answered.

"We need to find out where the money was taken out. On the statement, there's just code. Was it always the same place or different? It might get us closer. It is possible Parks stopped for money en route to the unsub."

Paige took out her phone and dialed. "That's probably something Nadia can handle quickly. Hello, Nadia, need you to check on something for us…yes, I know. This is an easy one for you…yes, I promise." Paige smiled at us, and, when her expression fell to me, it erased, and she turned away.

The situation between us had become complicated, and, at times I wondered if I were deceiving myself to think everything would be all right. Rarely, when mixing a prior sexual relationship— what I liked to classify as encounters—with business, did everything work out.

Zachery watched me as if he knew what I was thinking. I was giving too much consideration to the situation anyway. Go with the flow. That was typically my motto, and it was one I needed to readopt. Everything would be fine.

Paige slipped her phone into its clip and faced us again. "The money was always taken out at the Capital One ATM machine located on Fortuna Center Plaza."

Zachery's finger bolted up and then he pulled out his phone and started tapping keys. He extended it to us as if we could all get a clear picture on a four-inch screen from this distance. "This is the location of the ATM." He spread his fingers on the screen, expanding the grid of the map. "Right near Route 234. She'd just have to follow the highway straight north."

"Toward Keyes's cabin and the property where Nina Harris was found," I said.

Zachery smirked. He must have found my contribution rhetorical. "She could have hit the machine before heading out of town to meet with the unsub."

Jack addressed Zachery. "Did the withdrawals from Parks's account always come out on a certain day?"

Zachery thought for less than five seconds. "Every seven days, on Wednesdays, and that's the day of the week she was last seen."

"She definitely had a regular appointment corresponding with the withdrawal and easy access from the ATM to the highway." Jack paused, letting the summation sit in the air.

"He made the women come to him," Zachery said.

"Or they didn't want him in their homes?" Paige's eyebrows hitched upward.

"Why go to the trouble?" I interjected.

"Their husbands were never around. They would have had time to clean up any evidence of their infidelity."

She crossed her arms. At the same time, a knock came at the door.

"Hope I'm not interrupting anything." Detective Hanes entered the room. "Forensic results have come back on Nina Harris."

POSITIONED OVER HER, he swept back a strand of her hair with his hand. Her eyes brimmed with tears, and she refused to meet his.

"Shh. There is no reason to worry. You will be fine. You were perfect."

The sobs started again, racking her body.

"Now, now."

When he moved, she would do one of two things—scream and run or continue to lie there without the strength to get up. He put his wager on the latter. Not only was she beautiful, she was submissive as well. She was willing to let him have anything if it meant her life in exchange. Those were the ones he could best control.

"You are going to come with me."

She shook her head. "Please, don't…please, leave me."

"No, I can't now, you see. I'm a wanted man."

"I won't tell the…police…please…just go." Crying fragmented her words.

"Nice offer but unacceptable."

Kill her.

He ignored the voice. He had something in mind for this one— just her high cheekbones, her round facial structure, and the color of her eyes. The FBI was after him, and, if they were going to take him down, he wasn't going without His Angel.

Chapter 39

"RIDEOUT HAS CONCLUDED THE CAUSE of death as a brain hemorrhage due to being hung upside down for an extended period of time." Hanes's eyes surfed over ours, and, when none of us said anything, he continued. "There was evidence of food working its way through the small intestines, but we weren't able to confirm what it was exactly. This does tell us she ate approximately two to six hours before death."

The group of us shared glances.

"That sounds like a last meal. Our unsub feels guilty about what he's going to do so he gives them a last supper?" Paige tightened her arms across her torso, heaving her chest in the process.

"That's exactly what I thought when I read it." Hanes's voice sliced through the room. "But why would he feel guilt before killing them? If he felt this way, why not stop before he followed through?"

Zachery answered. "He had come too far by that point. We also believe that he is being controlled, at least in part, by the need to appease or please someone. It may also be a voice conjured by his mind. He's likely not a natural killer but has evolved into one over time and due to circumstance."

"He follows through on the acts of abduction and rape, but murder is one thing he would rather avoid. If he had his way, he would pamper these women, at least as the term applies in his mind. He might not even have gone back to abduction and torture had it not been for Leslie Keyes," Jack added.

"Back to?" Hanes asked.

Jack took a deep breath. "We feel quite strongly, as we have stated before, he was involved with at least the rape of the victim from two thousand. He would have been a young teenager."

Hanes nodded.

"Were there any drugs found in her system?" Paige asked.

"Not that the tox results show, but—"

"I know. It doesn't mean he didn't drug her." Paige smiled at him. "What about any trace from the sexual assault?"

Hanes's focus drifted as he stoically rhymed off some statistics. "You know the evidence points to forced sex. Rideout feels this didn't just happen on one occasion but that the victim was repeatedly assaulted. No recoverable DNA from semen."

"She probably welcomed death in some ways," Paige said.

"That would never be the case."

Becky Tulson came into the room and stood beside me. "You could never say something like that if you were a victim. I'm surprised the FBI wants you thinking like that."

Paige clenched her teeth, and her arms tightened and lifted again. The two women were going to have a fight, and, even though I wasn't the base of their conversation, it felt like I had added an underlying conflict to the fire.

"I just can't imagine being those women," Paige said.

"No, you can't. I can't either really."

Paige's head angled to the side. I read the expression in her eyes, *why get in my face then?*

The tension between the two fed through the room. None of us men wanted to say anything.

Becky broke the silence. "I was raped. I recovered. These women would too, given the opportunity. The human spirit is strong. I believe they would need extensive therapy, but they would—well, they could if they chose to—get through this."

"When I said what I did, I didn't mean that she would be better off dead. I just can't imagine the horror of what they lived through. I've been fortunate not to have the experience of being raped."

"You would never forget it, but you can choose to let it occupy you or learn to let it go. I chose, a long time ago, that it wouldn't have control over me. I accepted that it wasn't my fault, that he was the one who had the issues."

Paige nodded. Even though she agreed to Becky's point, I never saw the two women getting along beyond this room.

Hanes continued with the forensic results. "The bug recovered from her remains was part of an exoskeleton belonging to an emerald ash borer."

"And I assume there are a lot of those in the area?" I asked.

"The emerald ash borer has infected a lot of ash trees. It might not lead us to our killer, but it might help to put us in the right vicinity."

"That doesn't help us a lot because we already know where we found Nina Harris. I don't remember any ash trees right around her."

"There wasn't," Hanes said. "She must have picked it up at the burial location."

"Well, that gets us somewhere."

"We need to locate areas where it is known to have ash borer infected trees. We'll canvas out from there. Hopefully, the stretch isn't too big, and it can narrow the search to a limited number of residences and properties," Jack said.

Hanes nodded and left the room with the words, "I'll contact the city."

"You know, that might help you, but I'm not so certain. The ash borer was local news," Becky added. She shifted her weight, her hip jutting more toward me, and she passed me a glance. "It was in different parts of the countryside if I remember right. And, if I caught the news, it was big. I rarely listen to the news." She smiled at me, and I returned it.

Paige extinguished my expression with a bitter edge reflecting in her eyes. She addressed Becky. "You're a cop. Shouldn't you be aware of what's going on around your community?"

"Too busy doing the real work as opposed to watching it on television."

Zachery's cheeks rose and balled. He fought back laughter.

"You are an officer, but not with PWPD. I'm not even sure

what you're doing in this room."

I winced. Paige wasn't being her typical self. Was I to blame for the animosity between the two women, or had I glorified the situation in my mind? Maybe I had nothing to do with it.

"Brandon," Becky turned to me, and I shrank back. "Maybe we can repeat the other night tonight."

The room was silent enough that I heard my breathing and my heartbeat as it pulsed in my ears. Everyone's eyes were on me. Despite the glare on Paige, I feared Jack's expression more.

"We'll see."

"I guess that's all a girl can ask. Later everyone." Becky reached the doorway and turned around. "I better get back to my little station and do some paperwork. If I get really good at it, they might even let me out sometime."

Jack's cheek held a pulse. He gave one look at Paige, and she followed him out of the room. They reached the doorway and nearly knocked Stenson over.

He doubled in half, winded, and then straightened out. "There's been a murder, and there's another missing woman."

CHAPTER 40

THE APARTMENT WAS A ONE bedroom in the east end of town. It was modest, and bulky furniture filled the space. The only artwork on the wall was a black-framed photograph of the victim and a smiling blond woman. A wilted plant sat on a side table—its dirt, dry dust.

Rideout hadn't arrived, but a couple investigators collected what evidence they could and took photographs. Detective Hanes was getting updated by another detective while we were left to stare at the dead body.

The victim was male and had already been identified as Andy Gray. He was single, in his early twenties, and had been in good physical shape. Blood from two bullet holes to his chest soaked his white t-shirt. He lay on his back on the living room floor, his head settled to the right. His eyes were open, yet the spark of life—extinguished.

A Chinese man introduced himself as Jimmy Chow, and filled us in on the details. "Two slugs, looks like .22 caliber. Gun type that fired the bullets will be determined by ballistics. Based on the damage, the shooter was only a few feet away from our victim, as indicated by the stippling around the entry wounds. Bullet number one would have done the job. Number two seems to have been insurance."

"There was mention of another missing woman? Our unsub hasn't killed a man before or at least that we know. How does this involve us?" Paige stood over the victim, her arms crossed rigidly, like they were back at the station. The buttons on her blouse strained with the stance, pulled at the neckline, and exposed the top curve of her breasts. She must have sensed I noticed as she straightened her arms and placed them on her hips.

Hanes walked into the room, obviously overhearing Paige. "Her name is Monica Rice. Neighboring tenants say she and the vic," he pointed the tip of a pencil toward the dead body, "were close. She was here at least a few times a week. Patrol was sent to her apartment. No one was there, and, when they went inside, they found evidence of a struggle in the bedroom, along with some blood. So far, neighbors are saying they didn't see or hear anything out of the ordinary."

A smile touched Jack's eyes, but the expression didn't form. The detective had impressed him. He turned his attention to the vic. I followed his lead and studied the body with an eye for something the unsub may have left behind. There was usually something, whether intended or not.

Statistically, it's said that most violent criminals subconsciously want to get caught, and, as was the case with our unsub, he killed to be freed of the impulse that compelled him. He may have taken this action to taunt us, to show that he was superior, but, in actuality, he may really be framing himself. I shared these thoughts with the team.

"The unsub is coming apart. If Monica is missing, this is three women he took in the span of a week and a half. He usually takes one every two months. He is bound to slip up and soon."

"An act of arrogance," Jack added.

"We believe his day-to-day life, which may have been relatively normal up until recently, is likely falling apart or has," Paige said. "We need to follow up on where the employment records stand. Even if we got the ones from Fitness Guru and started there."

Jack picked up on her thought. "We need to see if Keyes has let anyone go recently or if someone is close to being let go."

"And what about him?" I asked. "What does he tell us?"

Officer Stenson came toward us, bypassing the investigator in charge of the scene.

He noticed and rushed over. He placed a flat palm on Stenson's chest. "You have to get out of this room."

"I have information on—"

"Great. Tell us from outside of the crime scene." The investigator in charge was in his late twenties and under six feet tall. His stature was trim but soft. He was naturally a lightweight and didn't work at it with diligent exercise.

Stenson looked past the man to Jack, but didn't say anything.

"Can I talk to you for a moment?" Hanes asked Stenson, but it was more of a directive.

"What do you think you're doing?"

"Trying to find this guy. You're too busy sucking up to the FBI agents. They're too busy talking it to death." Stenson ran his fingers through his hair. "Listen, we have to stop this guy. He has taken three women in recent days—that's three families without a loved one. If we don't do something, he's going to get off." He gestured into the apartment. "Now he's killing men. What next?"

"What do you know that you're not sharing with us? I need to know the answer to that. Now."

"You're kidding me."

"No, I'm not."

Stenson drew in a deep breath. "It's only a hunch I have. I'm not ready to share it."

"You were just going to tell us."

"Yes, I was."

"You are being ridiculous. We share everything. That's how it works as a detective. You speak everything, no matter how small, and hope something sticks."

"It's just something that I noticed with the pattern of the women he's choosing."

Hanes raised his brows.

"We're thinking he was triggered by Leslie, right? I've been staring at these women for years now. I've been obsessed with their cases. I saw something there when no one else did."

"All right, enough of the patting yourself on the back. Point."

"They all have something similar to that initial victim. Sometimes it's so small it would be easily overlooked in a pile of faces and names."

"You're sure the FBI doesn't already know this? Whatever *this* is."

Stenson nodded. "I'm not talking about facial or physical similarities."

"What are you talking about then?"

"Nope. I refuse to say right now."

"You're out of here then. You show up at another one of my crime scenes, I'll have you arrested for interfering with an investigation."

"You kidding me? We're friends. We can outsmart the FBI."

"Your mind's messed up, Stenson."

"Trent. You always call me by the first name."

"Because we're friends, I'm giving you this warning."

Silence occupied the space between the two men until Stenson walked away.

"You are going to regret this," he said over a shoulder.

I just regret not doing this sooner, Hanes thought.

THE CAUSE OF DEATH WAS textbook—two bullets to the chest but the circumstances were far from normal. The unsub was communicating with us, raising his stake of involvement and elevating his risk of being caught. It was apparent he didn't see us as a viable threat. He saw himself as being above the FBI. No longer was he interested in pleasing the voices or the figure from which he sought approval. He was interested in making a statement.

"There wasn't a struggle, the lock wasn't picked, and the vic was caught off guard," Paige said.

"It's possible the unsub followed him here, held a gun to his back, and, once inside, the vic turned around and got shot," Zachery offered.

"Or maybe he simply knocked on the apartment door and got the vic to open up for him?"

Paige studied the victim. I could tell she assessed the distance from the door to where he lay on the floor.

The apartment entered into the living area, and the kitchen was off to the right.

Zachery held the framed photo in his hand, and I reached for it. I wasn't expecting the obvious to hit me.

"Look at the arch of her brows, the way her eyes are inset. This could be a blond Leslie Keyes. Our unsub wanted the boyfriend out of the way so he could get to Monica. This kill wasn't personal to him."

"She does resemble Leslie Keyes, just blond hair instead. He was operating as a means to an end," Paige picked up on my line of thought.

"He saw what he wanted, in this case, who, and wouldn't let anything get in his way," Zachery elaborated. "He targeted Monica Rice. Hair can be changed. He is after a surrogate. I think originally Leslie did something to deeply hurt him. She rejected him. Maybe she was going to leave him and stay with her husband. They had just started a family together."

"He saw it as the ultimate betrayal. If he couldn't have her, neither could Keyes."

Zachery, wearing gloves, picked up the framed photograph. "Exactly, and, because of his background, being exposed to violence, rape, and murder at an impressionable age, this course of action resurfaced. Directed either by himself or by a voice he heard, he started up with meaningless abductions and killings. Leslie projected his past to the forefront. He hasn't been looking specifically for Leslie in other women all these years, but he's escalated. He never abducted at such a fast rate before either. Two in a week, now three, one already dead."

"We don't know how long he had the other women before he killed them," I added.

"True, but I tend to believe he held them longer than a few days. He cared for them in his own way. He left their rings on when he buried them. He fed them. As stupid as it sounds, he respected them while stripping them of human dignitary."

"So now he's going after women who specifically remind him of Leslie. I didn't think any of the other women were similar, except that they were all slender and petite," Paige said.

Zachery looked at Jack. "This is his end game. He knows we're going to stop him, and he wants one last chance to rebuild what he had with her."

"Does that mean that Sydney Poole is already dead?" I asked.

"Very good chance. She was a woman who fell into his victimology. She had a husband who paid her little attention, had money, and she took care of herself. Monica is a surrogate for what he couldn't hold onto."

"You think that up until now he's been acting on pure instinct?"

Jack pulled out a cigarette. "Not instinct, Kid, obligation. We've known for a bit now that Keyes was, or at least became, personal."

"He felt like he was carrying on in life the way he was intended. After things ended with Keyes, he gave up and fell back on what he had been taught at a young age. I believe he may have really loved her," Zachery offered.

"Are such monsters capable of love?" Paige asked.

It was rhetorical, but Zachery answered anyhow. "Technically, not everyone is, but I believe our unsub is. What we may not consider to be a demonstration of love, in the mind of a mentally ill person, can be the epitome of love in action."

"I know, they think it's love." She shook her head. "It's scary the type of people who are out there."

"Well, it's just like the abusive mate. They hurt those they love the most."

"You're comparing that to this?"

"It's the same principle."

"Hmm."

We all turned to Jack.

"What if our unsub isn't punishing the women—in his mind? What if it's a demonstration of his love for them?"

"It would explain the fact he buries them with their rings. We've concluded that's a sign of remorse. He gives them a last meal," Zachery said.

"You're forgetting the decapitated head in the toilet," I added.

Zachery glanced at me. "The decapitation came after death. Even after—wait a minute. We know he buried Rogers because of the maggots. He dug her up to decapitate her. He is calling us out."

Jack's eyes gave plain evidence he was deep in thought.

Zachery continued. "While part of him thinks he can win, in other words, continue on as he has been, the other part of him knows we will eventually stop him. That's why he went after Monica. She reminds him of Keyes, and she is his grand finale."

"We have to carry on as if Poole and Monica are both alive. Until we know otherwise, that's how we proceed," Jack said, the cigarette bobbing in his lips.

"And with Monica, the unsub never left anyone behind to report her missing," I said.

Zachery responded with a finger pointed to the dead body. "He was the calling card."

"SHH. YOU'LL BE JUST FINE NOW. You're home." He set her body on the couch, her blond hair cascaded over her shoulders. She resembled an angel. She truly was special.

He grabbed a throw blanket from a nearby sofa chair and draped it over her. The windows in the home were pinched shut, although he had no fear anyone would see him. Most people didn't pay him much attention. Except for the women.

Kill her!

You don't have the guts.

For all she did to you. You still love her? You are weak.

Despicable.

"Shut up!" He gripped at his hair, pulling on it hard enough that pain screamed through his scalp. He welcomed it. He loved to feel.

"Mmm." The soft moan came from His Angel. He rushed to her side and knelt down.

He had put tape across her mouth and fastened her hands together at the wrists in the same manner. He also strapped her legs together at the ankles. He couldn't have her getting away.

He swept a strand of hair from her face. "You are safe now. We can finally be together."

Her eyes fluttered behind her eyelids. The serum he had given her had put her into a deep sleep, but she could hear him. He laid a hand on her chest and looked around the room.

Everything here had its place. The furniture was modern, but purchased from a big-box store and was probably in many houses across America. He had a large flat screen TV—didn't everyone? Framed photographs of his mother hung on the wall. She had seen his talent if she only had time to catch a glimpse. She had brought him into the world, and it was for a purpose.

The house was a one-story bungalow in the west end, an older neighborhood sought after by families. He had a few offers to purchase come to the door. Most homes in this area were only turned over when someone died, and he had no intention of doing that anytime soon. He only got in here because he had paid attention to an older lady named Mable Smith. She dropped dead of a heart attack two years back and had left the house to him. She had declared in her Will that her children hadn't wanted anything to do with her while she was alive so they would get nothing when she died.

Besides the house, she had left him about twenty thousand in stocks and bonds. Most of them were locked up, and he was unable to access them without a huge hit to the bottom line. With odd jobs he did, he had enough to live on—for now anyhow.

He gazed down on His Angel.

Things always changed, but sometimes they came back full circle.

CHAPTER 41

BECKY TULSON SAT ACROSS FROM me at our table at The Earth and Evergreen Restaurant. "Are you sure you have time for a drink?"

"If you keep asking that I'll wonder if you'd rather be somewhere else." I smiled at her, and she returned it.

"It's just, with the latest homicide—"

"Well, the case technically belongs to the PWPD. I know it seems odd, but we're to be notified of any forensic findings that might lead us to the missing woman."

"You FBI always have to do everything by the book."

"Doesn't the PD?" I hitched an eyebrow which garnered a laugh.

"It's funny you're not the type I would picture as an FBI agent."

"And what would that type be?"

"Well, it's a rumor anyhow, a bad one."

"I'm listening."

"While cops do the real work, the feds sit around thinking and analyzing. By the time they come up with the solution, the cops have wrapped it up."

"Youch." I winced, pretending to be insulted, but I was wondering if she were going to come back with something like that.

"Like I said, you don't strike me as the type." She lifted her glass of scotch and took a sip.

"Well, you wouldn't strike me as the type to like scotch."

"Really?" She moved in her chair, hoisted a leg up, and bent it beneath her. "Why is that?"

"You're a woman."

"Oh. I'll try not to be insulted now."

"I haven't met any who like it. It's nice to finally have that checked off the list."

"You have a list to check off when it comes to women and their drinks. Interesting."

I smiled at her. The easiness that settled into her expression, softened by the alcohol, gave her much appeal. She was pretty, bordering on beautiful at this moment. She must have sensed my thoughts as her eyes lowered, and then briefly turned away.

"Listen, you're not married are you?" she asked.

"Thought we covered that on our last date."

"Date?" She laughed. "Is that what this is to you?"

"A man and a woman sharing a couple drinks."

Her smile faded. "What is the deal between you and the female agent?"

The mouthful of scotch partially went down the wrong pipe. I started coughing.

"Ah, just as I thought."

I held up a hand as I continued trying to clear the burning sensation from my lungs. "It's not what you think. We're close friends."

"Friends don't get so confrontational over another friend."

Her eyes leveled with mine. There would be no avoidance of her observation, no rebuttal that would be accepted.

"We had a bit of a relationship. Once."

"A bit?"

"It's getting late." I drained back the rest of my drink, took out a twenty, and put it on the table.

I REACHED MY HOUSE AND wondered if Deb would ever end up coming after it.

I had always believed in love, but these days I wasn't too sure. Everyone, just like the killers we hunted, had an agenda. It might not include the abduction and murder of several people, it might not even include physical assault, but there was a pattern in each person's life. Behavior wasn't taught, it was learned.

With my wife, we fell into the relationship quickly, everything was perfect—maybe that should have been my clue that at some point it wouldn't be.

Her parents were happily married until her mother decided she had to go find herself. Deb had held a grudge against the woman for years, but, as she got older, the indiscretion became tolerable, even excusable. She began seeing her mother's side in the situation.

"Dad is old school. He doesn't even want her taking classes at the local college. We're talking about courses on gardening Brandon. Just crazy." Deb had accentuated her statements with a shake of her head to drive home the insanity of her father's rein on her mother. "You better never try to control me like that."

I think back on that now, and maybe that's why she needed to get out. As much as she preached about not wanting to be controlled, she didn't like my independence. She was fine when my becoming an FBI agent was talk, not that she encouraged me, but she didn't shut the conversation down when I wanted to discuss it either.

I went up the stairs to the bedroom without turning on the lights. I knew the path by now, and the moonlight creeping through a side window helped detail the edges of each step.

It brought back another memory of Deb. She had insisted on getting a nightlight for the landing. I reached the top and its green glow cast over the hallway carpet. I pulled it from the wall and held it in my balled fist, the prongs sitting between two fingers.

She didn't control my life any longer. She was a part of my past. I had to let her go or become crazy over something that was beyond my reach. No one could make other individuals love them. It was a volunteer job one stepped forward for, from the heart. Deb's heart had simply resigned.

The thought cinched my chest. The pain would go away. I was certain of it. In fact, there were times I felt like my old self, as if nothing life-changing had even transpired. There were good days and bad, and, eventually, the former would outweigh the latter—of that I had no doubt. It was just reaching that point.

I tossed the nightlight in the garbage can in the corner of the bedroom. As I passed my punching bag, it called out to me.

I flicked on the light in the room, wrapped up, and did my best to expel thoughts of Deb and Paige from my mind through jabs into the leather.

CHAPTER 42

"RISE AND SHINE!" JACK'S VOICE was coming over the answering machine on the main level, and I could hear him upstairs.

I rolled over, and the sheets were wrapped around me as a cocoon. I struggled to break free.

"Son of a bitch." I let the expletive go and finally pulled the covers off. My eyes felt like they held grits of sandpaper. I could barely open them to see the clock.

"Seven a.m." I let my head drop back onto the pillow.

I should have thought the FBI thing through more—it wasn't a standard eight to five job.

These days it usually wasn't a problem to wake up, but I didn't crawl into bed until after two a.m. That fault was entirely mine, although, I would like to blame the women in my life for keeping me up and for torturing my good sense into oblivion.

Who the hell needs this thing called love anyhow? I for one was done with it.

I pulled my cell from the nightstand. Three missed calls. It explained why he had moved on to my home phone.

I heard it, and it took a while to make sense of it. The doorbell. Shit!

I gathered my pants from the floor and slipped on a t-shirt that was also there but stopped when I noticed my reflection in the mirror. I couldn't answer the door like this. I had to be ready to go.

"Come on. Answer. I know you're in there." Jack's voice came over the answering machine.

I balled my fists and found my center—something I was desperately trying to do since Deb left. Most times I wondered if I had a central point from which to derive strength.

"Hurry up Kid. We don't have all day." I heard a distinct click. Jack had hung up, but he would expect me at the door in seconds.

I slipped on a pair of dress pants and a white collared shirt. I ran the comb through my red hair, momentarily cursing it for my temper, before racing down the stairs.

"Well, it's about time you answered the door." Jack stood on my steps with a cigarette perched in his lips. Beyond him, at the curb, Paige and Zachery were in the SUV. They both faced my house.

"Just wanted to look good for you." I smiled.

"Hmm."

"What, I don't look good? And after all the extra effort I put in."

Jack's eyes snapped to mine, and he exhaled a puff of cigarette heavenward. He was the human equivalent of a chimney, and there was always a fire. "We have a lead."

HE COULDN'T KEEP HER HERE FOREVER, but it was great having her in his home. When he was gifted the house he had decided he could rise above his past. Too bad it had come barreling down after him. It ravaged him and conquered him, as a lion does its prey. He had no opportunity to flee, no means of escape. It captured him, and it would take him down. He accepted this fate, but he wouldn't leave without at least a menial effort at proving himself.

Her eyes fluttered open. They widened shortly afterward.

"You are safe." He brushed a hand across her forehead, sweat glistened there. "We are finally together. We will be forever."

"Who—"

"Hush now. It is time we—"

Kill her!

Take off her head!

She destroyed you!

He pulled back from her and shook his head. The voice still came to him, haunting him.

Do it now!

"It's time we made—"

Off with her head!

"Shut up! Just shut up!" He paced around the fold-out bed where she was lying.

Her eyes followed him as he moved, but his attention was on that voice—the one that never shut up.

"We made what?"

Her voice broke through the nightmare that lived in his mind which controlled him like a puppet. He would come out of this. He would return to a normal life. She—His Angel—would help him.

He stopped pacing and bent over. "Time we made love again." The phrase make love always came foreign to him, but he hoped, with repetition, he would come to experience it.

Tears seeped from her eyes. "Please don't do this to me. Please."

"You don't want my love? We are destined to be."

You are a loser!

She cried. It stole her breath and heaves racked her body.

"I would never hurt you." He caressed both her breasts. They were round and firm. She wanted him as much as he craved her. "You remember when we had champagne in the afternoon?"

"What do you want? Do you want money?" She pulled on her wrists. They were secured to the bed frame above her head and didn't give her much leeway.

"Why try to escape when you know our love is meant to be? Why leave?"

Her eyes pinched shut and her body became rigid. She had submitted herself to his will.

He unfastened his belt buckle and let his pants fall to the floor. He stepped out of his boxers and made his way to the bed, coming up the end and affording himself the full view of her soft womanhood, open and in want.

"Please...don't...do this." Her words broke through panting breaths.

It confirmed that she yearned for him too. She craved more than his touch—she hungered for his possession. He moved up the bed and positioned himself over her. Her smell reached his nose, and he inhaled appreciatively. Her desire was confirmed.

"NADIA GOT THE EMPLOYMENT RECORDS from Fitness Guru. She's working on the rest." Paige filled me in once I got into the back of the SUV with her. "There's one man of interest. His name is Chad Holmes."

"And we are interested in him why?" I took the coffee Zachery extended from the passenger seat and nodded with appreciation.

"Because he was let go two weeks ago from Fitness Guru. Keyes confirmed the reason was he had become unpredictable. He would show up for some classes and not others."

"Classes?"

"He taught cycle class there."

"It would align with what we've said about him fitting in and being attractive to the women he abducts," Zachery said.

"Very true. Was he always this way for Keyes, or did it begin recently?" I asked. "How long did he work there?"

"Guess he has had issues off and on. He's worked there for over six years. Keyes is digging up his resume as we speak, but from what he remembers his career references were all for brief stints, nothing substantial there," Paige said.

"That would put him there before Leslie disappeared. Keyes remembers all that about his resume?"

"He said that it was one thing that made him leery of hiring Holmes in the first place."

"Hmm." I uttered the expression, and it had everyone looking at me, including Jack, who peered into the rearview mirror.

I cracked the lid on the to-go cup and drained back some coffee. I had a feeling it was going to be a long day, and this might be the last time I'd get a coffee. "Did Keyes remember conducting any reference checks? Calling these places up?"

Paige shook her head. "Said he didn't have time. They needed someone fast."

"Does the guy have a record?"

"Nope."

"And we're certain this could be our guy?"

"There's only one way to find out Pending," Zachery said.

Jack pulled the SUV into an older, established neighborhood.

"Doesn't look like the house of an unraveling psychopath," I said, taking in the grounds, which were well maintained. The garden beds had flowering perennials, and the walkway to the front door looked swept. Heavy drapes were drawn in the front window. "This place is nowhere near where the remains of Harris or Rogers were found."

"Minor details," Zachery said.

"How are we going to approach this?"

Jack turned off the ignition and spoke over his shoulder. "You and I are going to ring the doorbell."

He really had a thing with ringing doorbells today. I buried my sour expression behind the lip of the cup.

Chapter 43

"You give people five seconds to answer the door. After that, it becomes suspicious."

I glanced at Jack. "Five seconds? You must have been ready to break down my door."

"No, but I was right, wasn't I."

"Right about what?"

"The fact that you stayed up too late and slept through your alarm—again. You have a problem with alarm clocks. I'll get you one for Christmas."

I wasn't sure whether to be honored I made his shopping list or insulted by the item I would be getting.

"Second ring. Never a good—"

The door cracked open to a man in his mid-twenties. His hair was slightly disheveled as if we had pulled him from bed. In contrast, his eyes were alert. His hair was gray, despite his age. He studied both Jack and me in less than a second and looked past us, I assumed to the SUV in his driveway and the two other people who occupied it.

"We're FBI Special Agents Harper and Fisher," Jack said. "You're Chad Holmes."

"Yeah." His eyes wouldn't stay focused on us. "What do you want with me?"

"Do you have a few minutes?" Jack didn't pose the request as a proposition that insinuated a choice. He moved toward the man which caused him to step back into the house.

Chad shut the door when we were all inside. He tightly folded his arms.

"I'm not sure what you…I stick to myself." Chad walked backward into the living room.

We followed.

I did a visual swoop of the area. Everything had its place. There wasn't a sign of dust anywhere. This didn't fit with the profile of our unsub, who was apparently falling apart, but it did match the condition of Keyes's cabin. The furniture was from a big-box store but modest and fairly new looking. There was a large flat screen TV that took up residence at one end of the room.

"We have a few questions for you." Jack didn't wait for the invitation to take a seat but lowered onto a nearby sofa.

I didn't follow his lead but walked around the edge of the room toward a staircase that led to an upper floor.

"I stick to myself." Chad repeated.

I detected strain to his voice. He came at me in a few long strides. Inches from my face, he studied my eyes, scanning left to right, right to left.

"What are you doing? What are you looking for?"

I lifted my shoulders. "Nothing really."

"Good then, 'cause you won't find anything."

The exhale of *hmm* burned to eject from the back of my throat. I fought not giving birth to my mentor's audible expulsion of thought. There was one thing Chad didn't realize—when he studied my eyes, I studied his in return. He was hiding something, but whether it was the abduction and murder of many women, I wasn't sure. Yet.

I resumed walking and went into the kitchen. Like the rest of the house, it was modest and kept clean and tidy. No dishes, clean or dirty, were in the sink or on any counters. Everything, again, had its place. I was turning around to come back into the living room when I noticed the door to the right of kitchen. It could be a pantry, but I didn't think it was. I twisted the knob and cracked the door slightly when Chad put a hand on mine.

"You're not going to snoop…what am I guilty…I don't see a warrant."

We stood there for a few seconds, frozen in place, watching each other closely, trying to anticipate the next move. I let go of the handle.

"No, you're right." I passed him a fake smile and went back to the living room. I remained standing.

Chad stood at the edge of the room. "I think it's time for you guys to leave."

"Just a few questions." Jack gestured across to a chair.

"One minute only. I have things I have to do today." Chad dropped down on the arm of the chair. His hand slapped his thigh in a soft, even rhythm.

Tappity, tap. Tappity, tap.

"You worked for Fitness Guru up until recently," Jack said.

"Yeah, until they—I was the best trainer they had." Chad shook his head. "Stupid, stupid mistake…they lost their best employee. But there will be other jobs."

"It seems you have held a lot of jobs."

Anger flashed over Chad's eyes. "I just haven't found the right place. When I think I have…they don't appreciate me. They don't deserve me. Why are you here? I doubt it's about…I remit my taxes."

"That part's the Internal Revenue Service, nothing to do with us. We're here because these three women went to Fitness Guru." Jack extended photos of Leslie Keyes, Sydney Poole, and Nina Harris. "Did you ever have contact with them?"

Chad remained quiet.

"I'd suggest you answer honestly. He can get pretty nasty if you piss him off," I said.

Jack's resultant condemnation burned as if a laser beam were aimed at the side of my head. I refused to let him know I sensed the chastisement.

"I knew this one." Chad pointed to the picture of Leslie Keyes. "She was the owner's wife."

Neither Jack nor I interjected any comments. We wanted Chad to keep talking. If there were something in regards to her abduction that he was hiding, there was a chance it might slip out.

"She went missing if I remember right, didn't she? Well, it was really hard on all of us."

"You were close to her?" Jack asked.

His question met with a shoulder shrug. "She was just really intelligent."

"Intelligent? Most guys will say a girl's got a great ass or a beautiful face."

"See, she had that too. Leslie was the complete package." He moved from the arm of the chair onto the cushion. "She had a way of making you smile even when you didn't feel like it."

"You had a thing for the boss's wife?" I smiled at him, mischievously playing up on the allure while it was really laid as bait.

Chad nodded. "That's probably the real reason Keyes fired me."

"You worked there a long time after her disappearance," Jack said. "I'm sure he never even knew about your attraction."

"Oh, I think he did. He kept me close by to watch me."

His words made me think back to the file when Leslie was first reported as missing. No one was named as a potential suspect in her disappearance. If Brad Keyes held any suspicion of Chad Holmes, why not mention it before now? It confirmed at least one thing—Holmes held an elevated opinion of himself.

"Do you know of anyone who could have abducted Leslie?" I asked.

Tappity, tap. Tappity, tap.

"She probably ran away to get free of Keyes. He didn't treat her right."

"He hit her? They had a child together."

"Children do not a family make." Chad brushed his one cheek against a shoulder. "Sorry, my love of literary art sometimes seizes me."

Although I worked on writing a novel and considered myself to be somewhat influenced by the greats, his garble was nothing that I recognized. When I did a visual sweep of the house, there were no bookshelves. Even in the electronic age of e-readers, dedicated readers had paperbacks around, maybe a few hardcover books. I tucked this fact away.

"Well, thank you for your time." I rose to my feet, and received a corrective glance from Jack who normally was the one to call an end to interrogations.

"Any time."

"And don't worry about getting up, we'll let ourselves out."

"WHAT THE HELL DO YOU think you just did in there?" Jack slammed the driver's door. The energy emanating from him could have started a forest fire.

"We need to do more digging on that guy. Something is definitely not right with him." I would defend that thought to the point of staking my career on it.

"He liked the woman. We have nothing more right now, and we don't because you got your ego into the equation."

Paige and Zachery turned their heads to follow our conversation.

"Ego? This has nothing to do with it. I'm not trying to prove my—"

"You're always trying to prove yourself. It's what you do."

His words bit. Paige sank farther into the leather seat beside me.

"He had someone there with him."

Jack adjusted the rearview mirror so it was focused on me.

"He spoke of his love of literary art, but there were no books in his house."

"That you could see," Jack said.

"That I could see. I suppose he could have them upstairs in an office or study. Maybe he reads in his bedroom."

"Speculation. That's all you have."

"It's a place to start and more than we've had so far, don't you think?" Anger rose within and I feared I wouldn't be able to tamp it down.

Jack put the car into gear. "You said he had someone there? How would you know that?"

"I heard a shower running on the second floor when I was standing at the base of the stairs."

Jack stuck a lit cigarette in his mouth. "It could have been anyone."

I let out a deep breath. "What do we know about our unsub? He's egotistical—" I paused, half expecting Jack to comment on how I should recognize my trait in others. He didn't. Now I was disciplining myself. "He's attractive to women. He's driven to prove himself. Those are just a few aspects. Chad ticks off each one of them. He has guilt, at least to some degree, over Leslie going missing. He said that Keyes kept him around to keep an eye on him, but that was Chad's viewpoint, not Keyes's. Not once has Keyes mentioned a concern with Chad when it came to his missing wife." The words gave birth in a quick rush and sat in the open without comment for at least twenty seconds. "And did you notice how he talked? His sentences were fragmented."

"That is one side effect of auditory hallucinations," Zachery said.

"He never smiled either, even when talking about how wonderful Leslie was," I added, knowing it was another strong indicator.

Jack inhaled from the cigarette, suctioning around it audibly, and the smoke was let out in a *puff.* "We'll do more digging on this guy and go from there."

CHAD WANTED TO WATCH THE cops pull away and leave. Cops, feds, they were all the same to him. Either could put him away for life and take away his freedom. He resisted the urge to make sure they were gone, to confirm they'd left him in their rearview mirror.

His heart raced, and he was lightheaded. What if they called in for backup?

He ran up the stairs, taking two at a time. Opening the bathroom door, he crossed to the tub where he had secured His Angel. He couldn't risk her freeing herself and exposing them. He had done too much, come too far.

No, they would finally be together, for good this time.

He pulled the shower curtain back. The water poured over her flesh, as a cleansing rain. Beads of moisture kissed her skin. He followed the path of the water as it streamed down her chest, over a breast and off the nipple. She was perfect.

His eyes traced her form. She sat in the tub with her back against the end, opposite the faucet—he was too smart to let her drown. Her arms were secured behind her back with a necktie. He had wrapped another around her head and over her mouth to serve as a gag. He didn't think it was necessary, based on the drug he had also put in her system when he heard the doorbell, but it was a precaution. He didn't need an off-chance ruining this moment.

Her eyes were shut, and she was in a deep sleep, evidenced by the rapid eye movement beneath her lids.

Kill her!

He squeezed his eyes shut.

The voice that would never completely disappear—it would haunt him until the day he closed his eyes for the final time. But he would learn to live with it, to ignore it. Things were finally the way they were meant to be.

He reached for the soap and lathered it over her body. Despite the warm water and the heat of his touch, her body shivered in response.

She would come to realize they were meant to be together, and there was nothing she should fear.

When she was bathed, he shut off the water and left the bathroom. He returned with the perfect outfit for her. As he re-entered, her eyes flickered open, squinting at first, likely in objection to the bright light in the room, but he left it on. He had something for her to see, something for her to wear, before they headed out. This was the reason he had to bring her here, and it would be worth it.

"For you." He extended the white dress, holding a shoulder strap in each hand, as if she could get up to reach for it. He pinched the embroidered daises beneath his fingers. "You will look beautiful in this. This I know."

Chapter 44

Paige and Zachery were going to get what they could together on Monica Rice while Jack and I headed to talk to Brad Keyes again. We were hoping, by this point, he had put his hands on Chad's resume, and we would have more to go on then his job history consisting of brief stints.

On the way, he contacted Nadia at headquarters, gave her a push on the employment and financial records, and asked her to dig up anything she could find on Chad Holmes. We waited on the phone while she gave us the basic scoop on him.

"No criminal record," she said.

"We know that. Give us something we don't have. Does he have a gun registered? Does he have any other properties?" Jack flicked the butt of his cigarette out the window into passing traffic.

"There's nothing showing on record. Again, it could just be that—"

"It's not registered in his name."

"Yeah." Nadia let out a rush of air that came across the onboard phone system.

Jack passed me a glance. "Well, keep digging. There's something there."

I held back the impulse to smile at this small victory. Jack and the team had been onto Chad Holmes before me, but I was the one convinced, after speaking with him, that he was our guy. Jack was showing faith in my hunches by having Nadia investigate him further. I turned to look out the passenger window before allowing the smile to give birth.

There were two sides to pushing Keyes about Chad, but the risk of damaging a potentially innocent man's reputation was trumped by the fact that, as of right now, we considered Sydney Poole and Monica Rice to be alive. We needed to find them before that status changed.

Two girls, both different than the one before, and a guy stood at the front desk of Fitness Guru. One of the girls smiled at us as we approached, and the other two employees turned to talk to each other.

The smiling girl's eyes went to our hands, as if expecting us to pull out a slide key that would give us access to the gym. Jack and I both wore dress pants with collared shirts. We didn't have a bag strapped over a shoulder. We certainly didn't appear as if we were here for a workout.

What was it with people who worked in gyms? I had belonged to a few before I decided it was easier, and more convenient, to set things up in my home, but, in my life, I had belonged to a few fitness centers. The employees were usually beautiful and fit, but their brains could have occupied a thimble.

Jack pulled his creds and flashed them to the girl. Her mouth formed an O.

"We're here to see Brad Keyes."

She nodded and walked away.

Seconds later, Brad was at the front desk. "I found what you were looking for." He extended a file folder to Jack.

"We'd like to talk to you as well," Jack said, passing the folder to me.

Brad glanced at the three employees occupying the front area, but the fact they stood around, mostly socializing, didn't seem to faze him. "Sure."

The girl who had retrieved Keyes smiled at us again and gestured for us to come through the entrance.

Brad led us to an office past the area where they signed up new members. Boxes and trays lined shelving behind his desk. A desk calendar and laptop were on the surface of his workspace. Two chairs sat tucked in opposite corners of the room. Neither

Jack nor I made a move to either one of them. This wouldn't be a long visit.

Brad dropped into the leather swivel chair and rubbed his hands together. "I'm not sure how else I can help. I just don't know how much longer I can afford to be a part of this. I can tell by the way you're looking at me you don't understand, and that's fine. But when something horrible like this happens to you, that rips apart your life, as you know it, at some point you have to move forward or risk being paralyzed by it. I chose, a long time ago, to move on."

He sounded a lot like he had when we first met.

"Did you ever suspect Chad Holmes as being involved with your wife's disappearance?" Jack asked.

Brad blinked a few times, passed a glance at me, and I read his eyes, asking the question, *did he hear anything I said?*

"We're asking because he seems to think you were suspicious of him," I said. I remembered Chad's words at his house clearly. *He kept me close by to watch me.*

Seconds went by in silence. All that could be heard was the soft hum of the fitness equipment. Brad stood up and shut the door.

"I never thought he took her. He didn't seem like a real threat." Brad took a deep breath. "I thought he might have been sleeping with her."

I turned to Jack only to meet with his profile. His attention stayed fixed on Brad.

"Maybe I should have mentioned this, but I didn't think it mattered. Leslie was a pretty woman, not beautiful outwardly, but pretty enough. Her inner beauty more than compensated for any default in her physical appearance."

I noticed the contrasting statements between what he was sharing now and what he had said previously. When we talked at his house, he mentioned he didn't think his wife was cheating on him, that she never would. Now he was voicing his suspicions. We needed to figure out the reasoning for the conflict, to expose the truth. "Before you—"

"I know what I said. I said that she would never do that to me. Well, I've since come to grips with the fact she could have.

You have alluded to it, maybe even said it directly. I don't know anymore." He paused a second, his tongue touching his bottom lip. "Yes, at the time, I wondered about their relationship. I was mostly jealous of Chad though. I never thought she was capable of it, but, with Chad, I wasn't so sure. Women always liked him. Leslie liked him. That much was obvious." His eyes fell to his desk. When we didn't say anything, he continued. "It's embarrassing to think your wife, the mother of your newborn child, could have sex with someone else. Shit, we just had a kid together. Were things that bad? It makes you feel like a failure."

I could relate more than I cared to admit. I swallowed the emotion in a thick wad of salvia. "We can't control other people and their choices."

Brad nodded absentmindedly. My words didn't seem to bring him any comfort.

Chapter 45

Outside Fitness Guru, Jack slid behind the wheel, and I got into the passenger seat.

"That guy doesn't know what the hell he's talking about," Jack said.

"He's going through a lot. His past has resurfaced, and he's forced to face it."

Jack looked over at me. His eyes were harder to read than his energy. He thought I was weak for disclosing some empathy. So, convict me for being human. "He's gone through a lot. He lost the love of his life, he's a single father, he—"

Jack laughed.

"What's so funny?" The man hardly ever expressed amusement, and I hadn't told a joke.

"Love of his life? That's a little drastic, don't you think? People fall in love every day. What's the big deal?"

I studied his eyes, and, while I wanted to hold back my thoughts from becoming audible, I wasn't sure I could. There was something I needed answered. "Are you speaking from experience?"

Jack's facial features went back to stone.

"When we first interrogated Keyes he asked what you would know about raising a kid alone at his age. You said you knew." I let the statement sit there.

He lit a cigarette and put the SUV into gear.

"You think that you can avoid this conversation forever? I'm pretty persistent you know."

"Hmm." A wisp of white expelled from Jack's mouth.

"What's the big deal? You have a kid. Is it a girl? A boy? How old are they? Where do they live?"

Jack slammed the brakes at a red light, and the SUV lurched forward from momentum. He inhaled on the cigarette and let the smoke ride out on a slow exhale. "If it's not a big deal, maybe you should focus more on the case, less on my life."

My fists balled in my lap, and I had the urge to punch something. The way he established eye contact with me I knew this conversation was over. He still didn't "win" though. I would revisit the topic. I was too stubborn to let it go.

Chapter 46

Hours had turned into days. She shivered in the darkness of the pit where she had been banished, surviving, somehow, in her own filth. Her stomach ached from starvation. Her bladder and bowels had excreted their matter repeatedly. The smell of feces had lodged up her nose and disarmed her sinuses. It was no longer detectable or noticeable beyond the feeling of it beneath her, against her.

The thought made her gut heave and spin, but with no contents, the gag reflex came up wanting. She pulled on her restraints. The chains that bit into her wrists were no longer daunting. She would not die in here. She couldn't allow herself to be found this way.

Surely, she would be rescued.

Reality extinguished the spark of hope before it set aflame, and tears fell down her cheeks. She remembered the drive out here, how remote it was. No one would find her.

If only she could break free.

She pulled on her bonds with more force, letting out a scream as the metal tore flesh. Succumbing to the realization she would not be leaving this room without him releasing her, she let her body fall limp and welcomed death.

Her head had fallen to the side when she heard the noise—a distinct moaning in the floorboards above her. He was coming.

She strained to listen closely, trying to discern where he was on his path to her. The top of the stairs. When his boots hit the wood, she heard something else—another set of footsteps. He was not alone.

The light turned on, nearly blinding her. She turned her head to face who was coming. Her heart raced. Her nightmare was that he had brought another man to rape her. He had always talked about a three-way—when they were mutual lovers—and she had shot the idea down.

Tremors ran through her, and she willed herself to die.

"I have someone I want you to meet," he said. There was a woman beside him in a white dress. "You two will get on fine, for now. This is my angel Leslie." He kissed the lady's forehead as if a doting lover. "And this, Leslie, is Sydney. You may recognize her from the news. She is famous now. I made her—"

Leslie lurched forward, bent in half, and vomited on the floor. Her eyes were wide when she resumed full height.

His eyes were on her filth. "What have you done?" He gripped Leslie's wrist and said, "You stay right there, or I will come after you."

He went to the corner of the room and pulled out a hose. "We'll have to get you cleaned up, won't we? Crap everywhere."

Cold water hit Sydney's flesh, each droplet as a plunging needle.

He put down the hose and moved to a ratcheting system above the end of the table.

"No! Please! No!"

He turned the crank until Sydney was suspended upside down, her legs splayed open. He picked it up again and blasted water, first on the table to clear off the rest of the visible excrement, and then back on her.

He ran the hose water down her torso. She bucked against the chains, but they didn't give much. He moved closer to her and sprayed her inner thighs.

What he did next had her wishing for death.

CHAPTER 47

JACK AND I WERE GOING to meet up with Paige and Zachery at the PWPD. The onboard system rang, and Agent Lane came over the speakers.

"The cabin sheets gave us vaginal secretion and DNA. Two of the missing women can be tied to that bed—Amy Rogers and Nina Harris. There was also DNA gathered from male ejaculate. It didn't match Keyes or anyone else in the database, but it matched the rape case from the victim in two thousand."

"That means our unsub takes them up there, has sex with them, and then kills them. The burial site needs to be near the cabin," I summarized, "but there was a full search—dogs, the entire gamut. Nothing was found. Evidence shows two victims were taken there, assuming he didn't change the sheets. Why them?"

"Good question, and we may not get it answered."

"There are not many houses near the cabin, and we already focused on the ones closest to the river. What's to say he didn't come from a little farther away? Also, what about the places where no one was home?" Jack asked.

"There were a couple of those, and the backgrounds were pulled on the homeowners and came up empty. No rap sheet, no priors. Unfortunately, there's no way to pull that information for all the houses in the area. In the nearest vicinity alone, investigators visited twenty homes. Full background checks, usually two per household," Lane said.

"And now I'm suggesting we move farther out."

"Certainly won't hurt."

We had just disconnected when Paige called with the results of the autopsy. Everything that Rideout had provided her was pretty much what we knew at the crime scene. She also told us that Monica Rice wasn't an active member of any gym that they had found.

"Brandon is going to get started on contacting Holmes's former employers based on the resume given to Keyes." Jack announced this without a sideways glance to me in the passenger seat. "We'll be back at the station soon. We can revisit all we know about Holmes and discuss the next step."

Holmes's resume was on my lap, and my cell was in hand.

Jack disconnected the call without a good-bye and lit up another cigarette. The air went stale between us, an uncomfortable silence—at least to me. He never felt the need to fill the void.

There was one way to break the monotony. I dialed the first reference listed and followed through the list of four, talking to the manager of each one. It only took seconds to determine they all had the same thing to say, Chad was chronically late or a no-show.

The last gym on the list was answered on the third ring, and I was connected with a manager by the name of Wendy Pollard. Her voice revealed hesitation. She wanted to know what the FBI wanted of her.

"I'm calling to inquire about a past employee—Chad Holmes." By this point, the introductory statement rolled off my tongue.

The line went so quiet that I wondered if we were still connected. I waited it out.

"What about him?"

"What resulted in him leaving his job there?"

"Are you really asking if it was a mutual decision? No. He was constantly late. Sometimes he never even showed up for his class. I'm not sure why he put me down as a reference. I don't have a lot of good to say about him, but I guess I'm not supposed to say that either."

Any misgivings Wendy experienced about talking to the FBI had obviously vanished. I also picked up her words 'I'm not sure why he put me down as a reference.' She must have been called about his employment on many occasions because I didn't mention I had gotten her number from Chad's resume.

"You said he had a class?" My last word raised in volume more than a question required. Jack had come up rather fast on the back of a MINI Cooper sitting at a red light and applied the brakes at the last minute.

He kept his focus straight ahead.

Another drag on the cigarette. Another exhale of smoke.

Wendy answered. "Yes, he taught a spin-cycle class. He had the studio packed. You can imagine how unimpressed I was when he didn't show. All those angry members."

"Did he ever give a reason for being late or missing classes?"

"Never. He'd look at me like it was none of my business, even though he never came out and said it. If he had, I would have fired him on the spot."

"You were all right with that?"

"I fired him, remember?"

I deserved the tone of voice that fired back at me. There was just something more about this, maybe it was a feeling more than anything. "I know if I was late on a regular basis, and missed my shift," I turned to Jack's profile until he faced me, "I would be fired."

Jack nodded, and I believe a smile started to form before the cigarette went back into his mouth.

The line went quiet again. "Miss Pollard?"

"Please don't call me that. It sounds so formal."

"Were you in a relationship with Chad Holmes?"

"A relationship would involve feelings."

I got Jack's attention and pointed a finger at my cell. "So, you slept with him? That's why you gave him some slack."

"It couldn't go on forever the way it was. If he missed one more class, or was late one more time, and one more member complained to head office, I'd be out of a job. It was his or mine."

"How did the relationship—the arrangement—between you two work out after you let him go?"

"How do you think? By firing him, I was also telling him I wasn't going to fuck him again."

I could tell by the emphasis she put on the word, she attempted to shock me by her brashness. It would take more than that. "How was it anyway?"

"Excuse me."

"The sex. How was it?" My question had Jack swerving the SUV to a stop at the curb.

Seconds went by.

"This could be very important to the case we're working on."

"What do you want with Chad anyway? You haven't told me."

"I'm sorry. I can't. It's part of an open investigation."

Another few seconds went by before she answered my question.

"The sex was great. Some of the best I've had, but he was a little kinky."

"Was he aggressive?"

"He could be forceful at times, almost like he was angry. Like he wasn't even there with me but somewhere else. Then other times he could be so delicate with his touch, you know? Like he loved me even." She paused. I never spoke in case she had more to add. "Does that help you?" The snide tone was obvious.

"It does, actually. Thank you for your—"

The line went dead.

"The manager had a sexual relationship with Holmes." Jack didn't phrase it as a question, but an assessment. "And how was it?" His eyes contained a spark of amusement.

"He's got control issues, like we pegged for our unsub."

Chapter 48

"Any word from Nadia yet?" Paige asked as Jack and I walked into the room with the crime scene boards.

"Nothing yet." I answered.

Paige's eyes skimmed over me and settled on Jack.

"The ballistics results came back on the bullets imbedded in Gray. A .22 caliber, shot by a Ruger Single-Nine revolver. I already had Nadia check to see if one is registered to Holmes. He doesn't show any guns, period."

"Hmm." Jack placed two hands on his hips, and his gaze took in the room without focusing on one particular area. He had a way of doing that—taking in everything and making a summation in seconds.

"That revolver is a rather common gun." Paige drove the statement home with a sharp tone and a glare. If looks could silence me, that one would have worked.

Jack addressed Zachery. "We need to find a way to connect the other victims to Chad Holmes. Have you come up with anything?"

"I would have told you if I had. Nothing that I remember from the case files connects them directly. As it shows on paper anyhow."

"We know that Lindsay Parks took out cash every week at an ATM." I started brainstorming out loud.

"Okay Pending, point?"

"It is a convenient location to stop before heading up Route 234 to the cabin."

"We know that already." Paige crossed her arms.

"What if Chad Holmes also had a side business? Maybe he offered his training services outside of the standard gym scene? He could pocket more money, make his own hours. Maybe that's why he's chronically late for his places of employment."

"Or he's too busy abducting, raping, and murdering women," Paige said.

"Boss, he's on a good line of thought with this. Let me see the guy's resume." Zachery extended a hand for the file I held. "I assume that's what's in there."

I nodded and handed it to him.

"All right. Okay." His eyes went down the resume.

"Zach?" Paige asked.

"Now we're onto something. I recognize the name of these establishments." Zachery let us hang there as he went across the room and pointed to the pictures of two women. "Both of these victims were members at two locations noted on his resume. We should call all the gyms that the missing women went to and confirm if Holmes ever worked for them."

Jack scowled. I hadn't caught the fact the names were familiar, and, when I saw the pictures Zachery pointed to, these victims dated back a few years. We had been so focused on the more recent cases that their details had slipped my memory.

My stomach tightened. I hated missing things. I hated incompetence as much as Jack couldn't stand tardiness, but, to admit such an oversight, would mean admission of guilt. However, with Jack's eyes on me, I had to say something.

"We've been so focused on Poole and Rogers, and now Monica."

Paige, who used to come to my defense, smiled and tucked the expression into her shoulder.

"Fine, I messed—"

Jack's cell rang, and I experienced the truth in the saying "saved by the bell."

Seconds later, he got off, and the fire in his eyes was electric. "Nadia's working on Holmes's financials, but a quick look didn't show any businesses registered to him."

There was something Chad had said when we spoke to him at the house. I coaxed myself to remember. Chad had talked about how Keyes was suspicious of him after the disappearance. He said that he was really upset when Leslie went missing. "Let me see the file again."

Zachery handed it to me.

Inside, Keyes had noted the start date for Holmes. It was only a few months before Leslie went missing. If he was our man, he must have become fixated quickly with her.

"Holmes was a relatively new employee and part-time at that," I said. "Why was he so upset when Leslie went missing? Why did he think that he was suspected by Keyes?"

"Kid, what are you thinking?" Jack took a cigarette from the pack in his shirt pocket.

"There's something he said—at the house when we were talking to him—something that's right there, on the tip of my—"

My eyes enlarged and my heart pounded. I remembered. "He said that he was the best trainer. Why not just say the best instructor? That's what he was at Fitness Guru and these other gyms. Nothing more. He could run a business off the books."

Jack and the rest of the team were already on the move. I hurried to catch up.

CHAPTER 49

"WE'RE GOING IN HOT AND fast. We don't need this guy using Poole or Rice in a hostage negotiation." Jack laid out the directions as to how we were to go about it once we arrived at Holmes's residence. As normal, Jack and I would take the front, Paige and Zachery the rear.

Jack continued. "The warrant should be signed, even if the ink is wet, by the time we bust down his front door."

Jack had referred to the women being used as hostages, but I'm sure we were all thinking the same thing—if they were still alive.

Jack pulled the SUV to a stop on a side street, and we all slipped out. Holmes's bungalow was dark, and all the curtains were drawn. There wasn't a vehicle in the driveway.

There was no response to our knocks or to the announcement that it was the FBI.

Jack and I entered. We swept the front rooms of the house, the living room and offshoot bathroom. We reached the base of the stairs at the same time as Paige and Zachery did coming from the back door. Jack gestured that they go up. We headed to the kitchen. My mind was on the door that led to the basement.

The thought of going underground brought back the one case I was certain would haunt me for my lifetime. I suppose this was all part of the job. We put our lives on the line to bring about justice and an end to the madness. An idealistic thought, but one I wanted to believe.

The basement door closed, but turning the handle revealed it wasn't locked. I nodded to Jack, and he acknowledged. I opened it, gun ready, and was met with darkness.

Light from the kitchen seeped down the stairs and revealed a light switch on the right. I turned it on, my gun aimed to the base of the stairs and started going down.

I was relieved to see the clearance on the stairwell was well over my six-foot height, and the width was comfortable. The walls didn't feel like they were closing in on me. I took a deep breath, my mind transferring back to Kentucky, the underground burial chambers, the tight space, and the compression on my chest as it heaved to derive a full breath.

I took the steps slowly, preparing my mind to handle what we might find when we reached the base. The women's dead bodies could be down here, or they could be found constrained and stripped of their dignity. With each step, I went over what we already knew.

Chad Holmes had connections to the victims, easy access.

He was an attractive man and would have no problem gaining interest from women.

He had a trustworthy face.

I thought about how his lust, or, in his view, love for Leslie Keyes had propelled him into a spiral of events that could have pulled him to his past.

My thoughts halted there.

My feet hit the unfinished floor of the basement.

Nothing stood out. Everything was as one would expect to find in any house. Storage shelves lined the walls. They were mostly empty, except for a few cardboard boxes.

Jack and I made our way around the perimeter of the room.

"Clear." Zachery's voice came over the headpiece.

Not long after, Paige and Zachery made their way down the stairs.

"We'll have a team pull every inch of the place apart. If the women were ever here, they'll find it." Jack pulled out his cell, dialed, spoke a few minutes, and then hung up. "Forensics will be here in about an hour." He never got his cell put away before it rang again. "Supervisory Agent Harper."

I waited for Jack's expression to change, to give some sort of a telltale sign as to the news he was receiving. Nothing registered there—good or bad.

He hung up a few seconds later.

"They have a match to the blood found in Monica's apartment. It's the same as the unidentified male from the cabin sheets," Jack said, "and the murder victim from two thousand."

"There has to be proof that the women were here."

"We've been through this entire house, and there's no sign of what would have been used to kill the women," Paige gestured, "no pulley system."

"He has a secondary location where he does the killing. The fact that a woman was even here—if she was," Zachery faced me, "assuming the shower that you heard running was regarding one of the missing women, tells us that he really admires Monica. She's his ideal, or why bring her to his home?"

"She looked the most like Leslie of all the women," I said.

"But it makes you wonder, why did he bring her here at all?" Paige asked. "Did he need to pick something up? Did he have to take care of something before heading north?"

"Nadia hasn't gotten back to us on the property owners yet, has she?" Jack dialed on his cell. "It's Jack…all right." He hung up. "She's in the process of sending the list over. Said there's no Chad Holmes noted as a property owner in the surrounding area where Harris was found."

All our phones chimed at once.

Chapter 50

Zachery didn't even take a full ten seconds to recognize a name on the property owner list. "Ken Campbell."

Paige glanced up from her cell. "The reason we couldn't find a Steve working at Straightline, who was nicknamed Ladies' Man, was because there wasn't one. It was Campbell all along."

Jack was already on his cell phone with Nadia, demanding the man's full background. He put her on speaker.

"Ken Campbell is the adopted son of Steve Manning, but there was never a name change done. Based on records, Campbell never had any children."

"Is there any connection between Chad Holmes and Ken Campbell?" Jack asked.

"Just a minute." There was a bunch of keyboard clicking coming from the other end. "I'm pulling up the record on Holmes—"

"Nadia?"

"Whoa, you're not going to believe this. All right, Campbell did share an address with Chad's mother."

"Her name and address?"

"Jenny Holmes, but she's dead. Died in ninety-eight."

"Chad would have been eleven. Potentially, two years later, Campbell has him go along with him to rape and murder a woman," I said.

Paige rubbed her stomach. "I'm going to be sick."

"Was his mother sharing the address with Campbell at the time of her death?" Jack asked Nadia.

"It looks like it, yes."

"Who was given legal guardianship of Chad?"

"You'll have to give me some time to work on that one."

"Who was Chad Holmes's real father?" I asked.

"On the birth record, it was put down as unknown. Manning is long dead, but the good news is Ken Campbell is still alive."

"We know. We visited him." Paige shook her head. "He was right in front of us, but there's no way that man could be doing the abducting and killing now. It has to be Chad."

"Like we figured. Who's paying for Campbell's care?" Zachery asked.

"I'd need some time to figure that out too, but Holmes's health records just opened. Seems he does experience auditory hallucinations. He received a prescription meant to help quiet the voices." Nadia provided the exact name of the drug.

"That one has been known to quiet the good voices and increase the intensity of the destructive ones," Zachery said. "Those pills, combined with Leslie rejecting him six years ago, would explain a lot."

"The records show he started on them—oh God."

"Nadia?"

"He started on them in the fall of two thousand. Didn't we figure the unsub raped the victim in the summer of that year? Also, Campbell shows a Ruger Single-Nine revolver and a hunting rifle had been registered to him, but it expired years ago."

Jack disconnected the call. The determination in his eyes told me he felt the same way I did. We were close to catching a killer.

TRENT STENSON WAS READY TO make full disclosure, but only to Hanes. He wouldn't be going to the FBI and letting them take the credit for all the hard work he put into solving this case. Sure, they went around and did all the questioning, but it was only because of him that their jobs were easier. He had pieced together that there was something more serious going on before anyone—despite their rank or position. He rang Hanes's doorbell and stood back, waiting for an answer.

The door opened wide. Hanes stood there. "What are you doing here?"

The way judgment and concern married in his eyes had Trent questioning their friendship.

"Can I come in?" Trent asked.

"The wife is finishing up, and, if I ruin Sunday dinner, I'm a dead man." Hanes drew a finger across his throat but stepped out onto the front steps. "I have two—"

"Lenny, who's there?" The question came from his wife inside the house.

Hanes mouthed the word, *see*. "It's Trent. I'll only be a few minutes."

"Okay. Dinner's almost—"

Hanes closed the door and remained outside. "What is it?"

"I'm going to tell you what I've pieced together. It probably doesn't mean anything, but it might. I'm sure the FBI is close to putting it together for themselves."

"You should be talking to them."

"They're probably going to find out the unsub had a stepfather."

"Now you're talking like them? Unsub? Come on, Trent. We both know they're onto Chad Holmes."

Trent took a deep breath. "Chad had a stepfather, but the man never adopted him."

"Okay. What does it matter?"

"All the victims," Trent paused for emphasis, "had more in common than good looks and slender bodies. They—"

Hanes's cell rang. "They what—" He lifted his cell and looked at the caller ID. "It's them."

He answered. "Detective Hanes...yes...okay...I'll be right there." He clipped the phone back in the holder on his hip. "They've tracked Holmes down to a rural property north on Route 234. So much for not ruining Sunday dinner. I've gotta go."

"Not without me you're not."

Sydney heard his footsteps long before his shadow cast across the room. There was something different about his pace and the way his boots hit with each step. He was here to kill her.

"It's time, Syd."

His voice was flat, carrying no emotion.

Her thoughts were clear and the one that keep repeating was she didn't want to die. There was a part, deep in her soul, wanting to cling to life, to continue fighting, but another side, a darker side, begging her to succumb.

"Why are you doing this?" Her own voice was foreign. It had been so long since she had spoken a word, let alone formed a sentence.

"We had fun, didn't we? But all good fun must come to an end. I have Leslie now." His eyes were on her, but with the distant gaze of a stranger, a cold spirit inside him. It was the same each time he had taken her since she had shown up at his Wooded Retreat for a 'time she'd never forget.'

"We used to be happy." Her words roiled her stomach.

He paused a few feet away from the end of the table.

She had his attention. She had to try to change his mind about killing her. "I really cared for—"

Emotion welled in her throat. All she had been through and had suffered over the last while.

He leaned over her and studied her eyes. "Do you love me?"

She was terrified to say no. What would he do to her? Would he make her death even more unpleasant?

"I do." She swallowed bile.

He moved closer to her. There was a light that appeared in his eyes. He swept back her hair with his hands and cupped her face. There was softness there, dare she even compare it to tenderness. She recognized his touch from when they were truly lovers, an innocent tryst between two consenting adults. From a time when he satisfied her and made her crave his fingertips. Now the thought of him made her instinct recoil. She had to fortify herself when he bent farther down and took her mouth.

"IN THIS TRAFFIC IT'S GOING to take us an hour to reach the place." Jack flicked the butt out the driver's side window. "I don't want anyone going in before us. They follow our lead, our strategy. This could turn into an ugly hostage situation, and that's the last thing we want."

Here I thought the last thing was Holmes killing someone. I

kept that to myself.

"How do you want to play this out, boss?" Zachery asked.

Jack laid out his plan to us.

Chapter 51

Chad entered Leslie's room and went toward her. "We're going to have company for dinner tonight. I hope you don't mind." He undid her restraints and told her quietly, "Don't try to escape."

She looked at him blankly. Her eyes were slits. She must have still been feeling the effects of the drug he gave her.

He led her to the dining room where he had set out food. A large steak was on a platter, and there was a bowl of baked potatoes. There were three plates and one complete place setting.

Sydney was sitting at the end of the table. He had dressed her in the cream colored suit she wore when she had arrived. He had tied her legs to those of the chair and secured a rope around her torso.

He helped Leslie take a seat at the other end and did the same with her.

He walked behind Sydney. "We're going to have a last meal together. Sydney's going to be leaving us soon."

He ran a hand down the length of Sydney's hair.

She shivered under his touch, possibly even withdrew. He chose to ignore it so that dinner wouldn't be ruined.

Sydney had watched him bring Leslie into the dining room. She swayed on her feet and leaned heavily into him.

Sydney knew the woman was trying to get her attention, but she feared getting caught. When she could, she'd get in quick glimpses and sensed Leslie wasn't feeling as drugged as she was acting. Her eyes were clear, except for when he'd start to turn in her direction. Then she'd lower her eyelids, as if she were dozy.

He worked at cutting the steak into pieces—one for each of them. He placed the portion on their plates and followed the meat with a baked potato.

"You can make it up the way you want. The butter…I love steak." He cut off some beef and slid it into his mouth.

"Please, eat up." He spoke between chews. "You have to eat with your hands. I can't have you…God, this is good."

Sydney glanced over at Leslie at the wrong time, and their eyes connected. Leslie was up to something. It was in her eyes. Sydney blinked and held her eyes shut for a few seconds to show her that the message was received.

CHAPTER 52

"THANKS FOR LETTING ME COME ALONG." Trent Stenson sat in the passenger seat. Hanes drove.

"You should have talked to the FBI as soon as you knew about the connection between the victims."

"Then what? Let them have all the glory? I've wanted to make detective for years now."

"You know the expression that goes around the department?" Hanes shifted his focus from the road to Trent. "Shit floats."

"So you're calling yourself a shit? From this perspective, I'm starting to see it."

"Don't be like that. Shit." Hanes pounded the wheel with his palm.

"Shit. That seems to be your word at the moment. I'll tell them as soon as we get there."

Hanes let out a deep exhale and shook his head.

"What?"

"It's just you've been obsessed with these women's cases for how long now?"

"Not long after I became a cop."

"And you want the glory for piecing them together? But when you can make an actual difference, you keep quiet? What is it anyway? What all have you figured out? You never finished saying." Hanes turned onto VA 234 and headed north.

SYDNEY KEPT WATCHING LESLIE AS she scooped out some of the potato from its peel and put it into her mouth.

"Careful, it's hot," he said.

A second later violent, racking coughs seized her and had Leslie pulling on the rope that held her to the chair. Her hand went to her throat. Some potato must have gone down the wrong way.

He was quick to his feet. "Leslie?" Concern filtered into his voice.

He went beside her and rubbed her back.

Coughs continued to grip Leslie, fragmenting her words as she tried to speak. "I...I can't....bre—" She pulled out on the restraint against her torso again. "Pl...please."

"Leslie." He hurried to undo her. "Can you? Are you...you will be fine."

She continued coughing. "Wa...ter...pl...ease."

He passed a glimpse at Sydney before he rushed out of the room to the kitchen.

Leslie's coughs became quieter, less aggressive, with some louder ones. She hoisted on the balls of her feet, lifting the back legs of the chair off the floor and reached over to the man's place setting.

Sydney realized what the woman was going to do.

She was only one inch away from what she needed. One inch. She could do it. Sydney coaxed her on mentally.

Leslie's movements stopped. Her eyes enlarged from fear— nearly large enough to serve as a mirror.

The man was on his way back.

Sydney heard his footsteps tapping on the old wooden floorboards of the house. They had mere seconds. Leslie made one final effort to reach what she needed.

"What the fuck are you—"

He dropped the glass to the floor and shards scattered across the surface.

He lunged at Leslie and pulled back on her hair.

From Leslie's expression and outcry, Sydney wondered if he tore scalp from bone, but she continued to pull against him. She must have been infused with adrenaline. She had plans not only escape but to kill him.

Leslie's fingertips brushed the wooden handle of the steak knife and it seemed enough to propel her forward. She wrapped her fingers around the knife and got a firm grip on it.

When she stopped fighting and let herself go in the direction of his pull, the chair toppled the opposite way, petering on a precarious angle backward. He wasn't prepared for her to give into him, and, with the momentum, couldn't hold her upright. She fell backward, and, thank God, Sydney thought, let go of Leslie's hair.

"Why?" he yelled.

Leslie was lying on her back, flesh against the spindled back of the chair. He came at her quickly, straddling over her in an effort to pin her down. He worked at securing her arms above her head with the excess rope that was tied around her torso.

She struggled against him and let out a scream. He grabbed her wrist and squeezed it tightly. Her grasp on the knife handle weakening, and the outcries getting louder.

With the way he had her pinned, Leslie's hand only bent at the wrist. He continued to squeeze, and then he twisted it to the right.

Sydney heard the crack. And the knife fell to the floor.

Chapter 53

Backup was coming in from all possible directions, and the meeting point Jack had set up was about a mile down the road from Campbell's property. We wouldn't be knocking on the front door. We would be coming from all angles, and cruisers would create blockades in each direction.

Paramedics and ambulances were there on stand-by.

Satellite imagery showed an old drive shed a couple hundred yards from the house.

A car came toward us and had Jack moving to the middle of the road. When he noticed it was Hanes and Stenson, he stepped to the side.

Hanes killed the engine, and both men got out.

I was curious why Stenson had come along, but this was one of those cases where we needed all hands on deck.

"There's something Stenson has to tell you." Hanes gestured toward Stenson, who shifted his focus over the landscape—anywhere but in direct eye contact with Jack.

Three seconds passed.

"What is it?" Jack's anger and impatience were unmistakable.

"I know of a connection among the victims. I've known for a while." Stenson paused and swallowed roughly. "They were all from broken families. For example, Leslie Keyes had a mother who left her father, Amy Rogers had a father who was a drunk, and Sydney Poole's mother abandoned her, but that's not all. I've heard you mention that most of the victims didn't have kids."

"To the point."

"Well, we know that Leslie Keyes was special to him and that she had a kid."

"Tell us something we don't know."

Stenson's chest extended and he remained quiet for a few seconds. "I spoke with Monica's mother."

"You what? You spoke to—"

"You saw the similarities between Leslie and Monica. He picked Monica for a reason. She's pregnant. He wants to make a family with her."

"How long have you known this?"

A pulse tapped in Stenson's cheek.

"How long?" Jack's voice boomed with the question.

"I found this out after her disappearance."

"Get out of here. I want you out of my sight." Jack pointed a finger down the road in the direction they came from.

"But, I just told you." Stenson fought off Hanes's efforts to pull him away.

"Here are my keys. Go. Do yourself a favor. Do as he says." Hanes's eyes locked with Stenson's.

Paige and Zachery weren't returning my eye contact.

"Fine." Stenson scooped the keys dangling from Hanes's hand and took off in the direction of the vehicle. The engine roared, and, seconds later, the wheels kicked up dust as Stenson gunned it in reverse and pulled a quick U-turn.

Hanes rubbed his forehead and Jack directed him to the back of the SUV where we had set up a computer with graphic imaging of the surroundings.

Chapter 54

Sydney couldn't take her eyes off the knife. It had come to rest by her feet. If she could stand on the balls of her feet, she might be able to reach it.

She looked over at them. He had Leslie's hands tied above her head.

Sydney took a deep breath. She could do this. She had to do this.

A cry escaped from Leslie. "Please don't…"

He stopped moving and stared down at her. "You tried to kill me!"

"I didn't…no, I wasn't…"

"We were going to be a family." He ripped her dress, starting at the bottom and working his way up.

"How did you—"

"You are rubbing your stomach all the time."

"Would the drug you gave me hurt the baby? Please."

"You only care about you!"

Leslie was pregnant? She had to act now to save all three of them. There was no room for debate—it was live or die, and the time to decide was now.

He was transforming into a rabid dog, his movements abrupt. He undid Leslie's legs and moved her off the chair to the floor beside it. He was getting ready to violate her.

Sydney moved, the legs of the chair dangling in the air beneath her. She could almost reach the knife. Just a little farther.

She took one quick glance over at them. He wasn't paying her any attention, his intent and focus was on Leslie.

Sydney buckled down the amount she needed. She got a good grip on the knife and quickly sliced through her ropes.

She came up behind him and burrowed the blade into his back.

He arched backward and let out a wail.

The adrenaline pulsing through her had slowed everything down. She pulled the knife out. Her hands were wet with blood and shaking badly.

He shot up from the floor.

She plunged the knife into his chest. He faltered back a few steps, his eyes fixated on the knife embedded in his flesh. Blood poured from the wound.

She didn't think she possessed the strength to pull it out and stab him again.

Behind him, Leslie got to her feet. She grabbed a plate, ready to hit him on the head when he pulled something out from the back of his pants.

He stepped to the right, placing himself to the side of the two women and held a gun on them. He flailed it between them.

"I will kill both of you!" He jabbed the barrel forward, gesturing for them to move in the direction he wanted. "Back to the shed now! Do as I say!"

Sydney and Leslie locked eyes for a few seconds as he led them back to the depths of hell, a gun at their backs.

STENSON BEAT THE HEEL OF his palm into the steering wheel. "How dare he fucking do this? He can't take me off the case when I'm the one that found it."

He swerved hard to the right and pulled to a stop. He had followed directions his entire life. He played within the lines. He was a momma's boy. He didn't even remember crossing the woman. Possibly his greatest offense being the length of his hair.

Now there was too much at stake. He needed to solve this. He needed to bring Holmes in, before the FBI did. Then he would have his pick of any high-ranking position within law enforcement, local or federal.

He pulled out his smartphone and brought up Google Earth

and smiled when he noticed his entry point. The FBI would likely hit the house first. He'd go about it his own way and beat them all to the find.

CHAPTER 55

JACK ASSIGNED PAIGE AND ME to go about things from the right side of the property. For that, we would go through the field in front of us, scan the back of the property, and make our way west to the shed. It would take effort to reach it, but I was ready. A group of five more, consisting of local officers and detectives, would be going with us.

"You sure it's necessary to have all this backup in each location?" Paige asked.

"Since when do you question my directions?" Jack made eye contact with her, and her shoulders lowered slightly.

I knew what her question really alluded to. It wasn't about the number of people. It was the fact she was matched up with me. We needed to talk when all of this was over.

Jack gave out the rest of the directions. He separated himself from Zachery, assigning them each two seasoned detectives and two officers. Jack's team included Hanes.

"All right, let's stop this bastard and get those women out safely. Stay alert. Stay safe." Jack dismissed us with a clap, and we all headed out.

The ditch at the side of the road went down at a steep angle, at least seven feet. Paige and I led the way, local law enforcement followed behind us.

"You don't like being assigned with me, do you?" I asked. A few seconds after saying it, I dared to look over at her.

"I don't care." She continued facing forward and kept an even pace.

"We should really talk about what's going on between us."

She stopped walking. The local officers followed her lead.

"Do you see something already?" The officer who asked appeared to be mid-thirties and was likely carrying twenty extra pounds, but distribution on his frame made it appear as more, tipping the scales toward obesity.

"No." She let the single word out, on a puff of breath. "Why would I have a problem?" She continued to avoid eye contact.

The others walked around us.

"If we're going to die today, I want you to know something."

"You're off to a bad start."

"A bad start?"

"Yeah, if you think negatively like that you'll make it happen."

"You mean a self-fulfilling prophecy?"

"Yeah." She smiled at me weakly. Instinct told me that she might not want to hear what I had to say, and, since part of me wasn't sure I wanted to say it, I let it go.

"We'll all walk out of this alive," I said.

"Now that's a better attitude."

STENSON RACED AROUND THE PERIMETER. He would go straight to the shed.

It took him fifteen long minutes, but he was comfortable with the timing. The FBI was starting off on foot, a mile down the road from the opposite direction. He was only about a quarter mile away from the property coming at it from this end.

He slowed his approach when he noticed the roadblock ahead. A cruiser was parked at an angle, its lights flashing. An officer stood in front with both hands on his hips.

"Sorry, but I'm going to have to ask you to turn around."

Stenson smiled when he recognized the officer. They had gone through the academy together.

"Walsh, long time no talk. I was told to come at it from this end. Special Agent Harper told me—"

"I'll have to call it in. I wasn't told to expect you." He went for his radio.

"Come on, man, you don't trust me? If I wasn't told to come

here, don't you think I would be home having a barbeque and kicking back with a few beers?"

"Yeah, well, I suppose."

"Speaking of beers we should get together soon." As Stenson carried on the meaningless conversation, seconds ticked off in his head.

"Yeah, we should." He smiled and pulled up on his pants.

Stenson pointed to the field on his right. "You going to stop me?"

"Nah, go ahead."

Stenson was already into a run before all of Walsh's words got out.

I COULD MAKE OUT THE house from where we were. If Holmes looked out a back window, he would have no problem seeing us. We had to keep going until we reached the other end.

"Keep low," Paige said as she crouched down and kept in a forward movement.

The rest of us followed her lead and duck waddled behind her, dividing our focus between the house and the path in front of us.

"At the back side of the property," Paige said to let Jack and the other teams know where we were. "No sign of Holmes. We're still clear."

"Us too. Approaching the front of the house now," Jack responded.

Chapter 56

Stenson reached the shed in less than two minutes. He was happy that he kept up at the gym and favored running as a workout. He leaned his back against the building and steadied his breath. He didn't need heavy breathing to disclose his position. He paused when he heard footsteps and what sounded like the dragging of metal pass through the shed.

He strained to listen—the sound traveled through to the back, and then a door opened. He didn't hear it close.

Stenson went down the exterior of the shed and peeked around the back. He saw Holmes walking away, a shovel in his hand. Holmes followed a worn dirt path toward a wooded area.

There was a blood-stained hole in the back of Holmes's shirt—one of his victims had fought back.

Had he just killed her? Was he getting ready to bury her?

Now was Stenson's opportunity. The women must be nearby. He had to move. He didn't know how far away Holmes was going or how fast he would return so Stenson moved around to the front of the shed. The main door was open and so was a regular doorway at the back. A soft breeze blew through, bringing with it the smell of freshly cut grass mingled with floral overtures.

He found irony in the contrast between beauty and horror. No doubt hell awaited him. The women could be beheaded or hanging upside down on their way to death. He had to hurry.

His eyes swept over the walls, searching for any hidden rooms or doorways. There was nothing that stood out. Manual harvesters hung from long nails on the wall. A large riding lawn mower was tucked into a back corner. His hand snapped to his nose in time to stifle a sneeze. It was then he noticed the door in the floor.

He pulled on the door and found it unlocked. Holmes must have been confident no one would come along and free the women.

Or were there women to free?

The thought pulsed through Stenson's veins.

The door opened to a narrow stairwell and went underground. There was a light on down there. He put his hands on the walls as he descended. The air was stale, but that wasn't what had his attention.

Two women stood, one at each end of a large table. Their wrists were bound to chains that led to a suspension system above them and fed into a ratcheting mechanism.

This was Holmes's torture and murder room.

Sydney Poole stood closest to him and Monica Rice was at the far end.

"Please help us!" Sydney's eyes were full of tears. "He's coming back. He's going to kill us."

Stenson checked their restraints. Each woman had a small padlock securing the chains. He needed the keys. His eyes darted around the room. If he could find metal cutters or something…

He moved to the other side of the room where a counter lined the wall. It had storage cabinets above, drawers below. In the third one he got lucky and found an awl.

"I'm a cop with Dumfries PD." He worked at freeing Monica.

"He'll be back soon. You have to hurry." Monica wiggled her wrists.

"Just keep still. One more…" He snapped the lock open.

"Please! He'll be back." Sydney cried.

It pulled at Stenson's heart, thinking about all she had been through. "Just one more wrist, and I'll be right there." Stenson rubbed the back of an arm across his brow to clear the sweat. He had to hurry.

Monica's nervous energy radiated through her hands as he worked on the other lock. Seconds later, the chains gave way, and he tore them from her wrists.

"Thank you!" She ran to the other end of the table and wrapped her arms around Sydney. "Now her. Hurry."

Stenson heard the steps overhead. Holmes was coming back. "Back to the other end of the table. Wrap the chain around your wrists."

"No. No, please don't make me." She shook her head wildly before consenting.

"I'll take care of you. Just do it."

Monica squeezed Sydney before returning to the other side of the table.

"Well, what do we have here?" Holmes stood at the base of the stairs. He had a knife embedded in his chest and a revolver in his hands.

Stenson tucked the awl in a back pocket, and then raised his hands in surrender.

CHAPTER 57

JACK CONFIRMED OVER THE RADIO that Holmes's car was in the driveway along with a BMW registered to Poole. We listened as he verbalized their approach to the house.

"It's closed up, but we're headed in." A few seconds passed and he continued. "We've got blood and what looks like a last meal. Good news is it looks like the two women are still alive."

"What about the blood?" Paige asked.

"My guess is it belongs to Holmes. He was the only one with a fork, and I'd assume a knife which I don't see."

There was a pause.

I spoke into the earpiece. "Jack?"

"They're in the shed."

Jack's observations caused my heart to speed up, along with my team's pace.

"We're closing to within fifty yards of the shed," Paige said over the radio. She turned around and started to lay out how we were going to approach. It mimicked Jack's advance to the property—cover all corners.

CHAD COULD BARELY STAND. The blood loss was making him dizzy. After taking the shovel out to the burial site, he wasn't sure if he had it in him to dig a hole. He might just throw them into the river, but now he had a bigger obstacle to attend to—a man.

"Are you FBI?"

"I'm an officer with Dumfries PD."

You're not even worthy of the FBI!

Loser!

The voice taunted him, mocking him with laughter. He tapped a hand against his thigh.

Tappity, tap. Tappity, tap.

Chad caught the reflection in the man's eyes. He was scheming. He thought he had a way out of here with the women. He lifted the revolver and pointed its barrel at the officer.

Another wave of nausea passed over him. His legs buckled, and his eyes went to the knife in his chest. He'd die if he pulled it out.

Before he could steady his balance, the man lunged toward him, a flash of metal flailing in the air as if he were a madman.

Chad pulled the trigger.

"A SHOT WAS JUST FIRED. It came from the shed!" I gave the update and the other two teams echoed back—they had heard it as well. In seconds, we would all reach the shed.

"The report was subdued. They must be deep inside, an underground room maybe."

Paige and I entered the front of the shed, guns drawn. Inside, relics of another era were mounted on the walls. My eyes followed it through to the back side where a door was open. A couple officers came through, and we stood there for a few seconds before we spread out.

"Over here." One of the officers called out the find. Off to our left was a door in the flooring. It was open.

I pointed to the floor. "Blood. We have him."

STENSON BARELY DODGED THE BULLET. Sydney dropped to the floor, as far as the chains would allow. Monica dropped too. The fact she was no longer restrained was now obvious. She crouched and made her way around the exterior of the table.

Holmes fired another round. This time the bullet chewed into the flesh of Stenson's shoulder.

"You are all going to die!" Holmes wobbled on his feet as a drunken man.

"Not if you die first!" Stenson's move would blend bravery

with stupidity, but he didn't know how much time he had before the others would reach the shed. They must have heard the gunfire, but he couldn't be sure. He had to go at it as if he were the women's only savior.

He roared as he launched at Holmes intent on only one thing—killing the man.

Another round fired.

Blood burst from Stenson's chest and bloomed red around the wound. It was surreal, as if he were in a first-person-shooter video game. It hurt like hell, but he couldn't fail these women. He charged at Holmes again, staggering, each breath a challenge as pain cinched his chest, and each heartbeat reverberated in his skull. He needed to reach Holmes before he lost all strength.

He heard the click of the revolver and prepared for impact, but no bullet came. The chamber must be empty. Now was the time.

Stenson pulled the knife from Holmes's chest before his vision darkened, and he hit the floor, a burning in his chest. He closed his eyes and wondered how long it would take for death to claim him.

"THAT'S TWO MORE. Move. Move." Paige hurried down the stairs. "FBI!"

Holmes sat hunched forward on the floor, blood draining from his chest. Staring into space, his breathing was erratic, and his words came out in a low tone. "The graves lay silent. The graves lay untouched."

I picked up the revolver at his side, clearing it from his reach.

Only a few feet away, Officer Stenson lay on the floor, a gunshot to the chest and a bloody knife in his hand.

Paige hurried over to him and called in for medical assistance. "Officer down."

Monica rose from behind the table, her arms in the air.

"We're FBI. We're here to save you." I extended a hand to her and helped her come out from around the table.

I then noticed an awl on the floor, and the chain wrapped around Sydney's wrists. It must have been how Stenson freed Monica. He was a hero. Time would tell whether he was a fallen one.

CHAPTER 58

WE FOUND THE GRAVES ON the slant of a hill, in a wooded area near the river. An FBI helicopter hovered above, while on the ground investigators worked to uncover the remains of fifty women. This had been a killing ground long before Holmes. There was speculation that it dated back to Steve Manning, Campbell's stepfather, since he had inherited the property from him.

Nadia's digging had uncovered that Barbara Wilson was the sister of Holmes's mother and the one granted legal guardian status. With her husband working with Ken Campbell, it would have kept Holmes within easy reach. If that weren't enough, up until now, Barbara had been the one paying for Campbell's healthcare.

She had been brought in for questioning, and, of course, she swore she had no idea that Campbell was even capable of such acts. Without evidence to hold her, she was released. She swore that he wouldn't see another red cent from her.

The accessibility to Melanie Chase was also there. We were still working on the connection to the other two victims, the one from nineteen seventy-three and two thousand. It was possible that they were random targets.

Inside the house were a bunch of books—it must have been the literary collection Holmes had alluded to. Campbell was more likely than Holmes to be the reader, accounting for a fictitious quote he tried to pass off on Jack and me. Paige saw the books and said Campbell had been reading when they showed up to visit him at the home.

Holmes had been taken off in an ambulance with a couple FBI agents who were entrusted with making sure he remained in custody and didn't take action to terminate his life. He would pay for his crimes against these women.

It was stated that before they put the oxygen on him, he had repeatedly chanted what he had said when we found him.

"The graves lay silent. The graves lay untouched."

Campbell would face multiple charges, but it was unlikely we would get a sentence passed against a seventy-one-year-old Alzheimer's patient. When questioned about the remains on his property, a sinister smile had lit his face. Those who witnessed it wondered if it were the Devil himself.

I had no doubt the revolver we collected would tie back to the bullets pulled from Andy Gray. I also believed the DNA left behind in two thousand would be a match to Holmes. We also needed to know who belonged to the epithelial Chase took from her attacker.

Stenson was rushed to the hospital. Sydney and Monica were tended to by paramedics—Monica with a broken wrist—and both followed behind him.

The women would either be inseparable, bonded by their experience, or repelled because it would remind them of what they had lived through together. I sensed it would be the former.

Sydney had confessed to an affair with Chad Holmes but said she knew him as Brad. Holmes had wanted to assume the life with Leslie so badly he had adopted her husband's name. He had dyed Monica's hair brown, like I had suspected he would.

It was hard when Monica peered into my eyes and asked about Andy. I had to let her know he had been shot and killed. But the hardest part was when Ian Poole came running toward his wife and held her tightly.

My heart ached from the reunion. I missed Deb, but I had to learn to let her go.

PAIGE HAD NOTICED THE EXPRESSION on Brandon's face when Ian Poole hugged his wife. There was definite heartache there. She'd had the urge to hold and comfort him, but he would be all right.

He was a strong man. She also knew, in that moment, she had to let him go. He needed time to heal.

She had stepped back from the group and headed to the burial sites where she'd watched the remains being recovered. She'd stood there for hours until Jack came and got her.

Despite the early hour, it was now technically Monday, Becky Tulson was at the front door of PWPD to greet them. She hurried toward them but slowed her pace when she got near.

She extended her hand to Paige. "Great job." She smiled at her and Paige returned it, along with a nod as she kept walking.

Paige turned to see the female officer stop in front of Brandon, but, instead of a handshake, she hugged him and kissed his cheek. Paige saw happiness wash over Brandon's expression.

Chapter 59

Paige didn't know if this were a good idea, but she had no choice. She didn't know what she would find once she got there, but she convinced herself she could handle anything.

It was the wee hours of the morning, and she couldn't sleep. While she stood outside Brandon's house, she tried to talk herself out of it but couldn't bring herself to turn around.

She softly rapped her knuckles on the door, subconsciously giving herself a way out. If he heard the knock, he was awake, and they were meant to talk. Ringing the doorbell would leave nothing to chance.

Her hand was braced to knock again when the door opened.

There was no hint of a smile, but his eyes said it all, *what are you doing here?*

"Can we talk?"

"Now's not a good time." He glanced over his shoulder toward the stairs.

Paige's stomach sank. The female officer was with him. He was moving on, and it was without her. She had to say the words she came to say before she was unable to form them. "I'm leaving the team."

His eyes went through her. He gave her no reaction. "You don't have to do that for me."

"I'm not doing it for you."

Brandon nodded.

He was dismissing her. He didn't buy her line and didn't care. She swallowed back the emotion that threatened tears.

SHE WOKE UP IN A SEATED POSITION, her heart beating rapidly. It had been a dream, a horrible nightmare. Surely Brandon would care if she left the team, wouldn't he? She had to believe he would.

She let her head fall to her pillow but couldn't fall back asleep. Her stomach was tight with the tension that cinched it into a compact ball.

Maybe the dream was telling her something. Was it possible her future no longer included the BAU?

"I'm leaving the BAU?"

Epilogue

A couple weeks later...

"You son of a bitch. You had us all scared." Hanes stood to the side of Trent's hospital bed. "What were you thinking anyway?"

The shot to his shoulder had been a through and through. The bullet that had gotten him in the chest entered a mere fraction away from his heart. The doctors said he was extremely lucky.

"Here we go. Another lecture by Lenny." Trent tried to smile, but, with the pain medication, it didn't fully form. "Guess I can make detective now that I risked my life."

"Let's not get carried away. You were reckless." Hanes smiled at his friend. "I will put in a word for you though. I almost forgot, but the lead agent had a few words about you too."

"Oh? What was that?"

"Stupid kid could have gotten himself killed."

"Maybe I don't need PWPD. I could be FBI."

"Now you're really getting carried away. I don't think he liked you all that much."

Both men laughed.

It had been a long day but all the answers had finally come back. The revolver registered to Campbell was a match to the bullets that killed Gray, and the epithelial pulled from Chase also tied back to him. The soil collected from the burial sites, as well as the presence of the emerald ash borer in nearby trees, had confirmed that Nina Harris had been buried on Campbell's property.

Holmes had found his victims, Leslie surrogates, through

teaching spin class and being an in-home trainer. Nadia had dug up that he had also attended a few charity events, a couple of which Sydney and Amy hosted.

The drug Holmes had used on the women was herbal based and wouldn't affect Monica's baby.

Paige knew she should have gone straight home, it was after midnight, but she was drawn to a bar within walking distance of Brandon's house. She had a couple of drinks and did her best to talk herself out of what she was thinking.

An hour later, when she rung his doorbell it felt like a bad case of déjà vu. She was no longer hindered by the dream she had. She didn't care if she woke him up. She didn't care if he was dating that female officer from Dumfries and was lying naked in bed with her. She had to talk to him, and it couldn't wait until the light of a new day. She had already waited long enough.

The porch light came on, followed by the one inside. The door opened, and Brandon stood there, his eyes barely open. "Paige?"

Just like her dream, his eyes said the rest, *what are you doing here?*

"I'm sorry if it's not a good time, but I need to talk to you."

"Don't be crazy. Talk. You already woke me up." He smiled lazily.

She couldn't allow fear to hold her back. Her stomach churned as she thought of the words to say.

"I'm leaving the BAU."

Brandon opened the door wider and gestured for her to come inside.

"It's just that I've been doing a lot of thinking about this lately. It would be best for everyone if I--"

Brandon took her mouth with a hunger she craved to elicit in him.

A few seconds later, he pulled back and peered in her eyes. "It wouldn't be the same without you."

She blinked away the tears that formed and swallowed hard. She studied the eyes of the man she loved but wasn't sure she could ever possess. She nodded, wondering how long it would be before she woke up from this dream. In this moment, in his arms, she wasn't sure she even cared. She pulled herself into him and rested her head on his chest.

But as she breathed him in, uncertainty loomed. How long could she continue to put herself through this? Her thoughts quieted as he led her to his room.

Note to Readers

If you've enjoyed this novel, please tell your friends and family about it. If you have time to write a brief, honest review on the retailer site where you purchased this book that, too, is appreciated.

Carolyn loves to hear from her readers. You can reach her at carolyn@carolynarnold.net.

Upon receipt of your e-mail, you will be added to her newsletter mailing unless you express your desire otherwise.

Keep on reading for a sample of *The Defenseless*, book 3 in the Brandon Fisher FBI series.

Do you, or have you, worked in law enforcement?

If so, Carolyn would love to know how you thought she did when it came to the police procedure in this story. Her goal is to provide the most realistic and entertaining police procedural novels in the marketplace. Your feedback would be much appreciated. Please e-mail her at the address noted above.

Read on for an exciting preview of Carolyn Arnold's next thrilling novel featuring Brandon Fisher

THE DEFENSELESS

PROLOGUE

Twenty-six years ago

He should be celebrating at home with a bottle of Cristal. Instead, he was outside of his neighbor's house, frozen to the bone, his hands like ice.

He hadn't had a moment of peace and quiet all day. His project was getting further behind, the deadline ever looming, but the new resident next door gave no consideration to those around him. First it was his barking dog, but when he came to complain, the sight of it whelmed up pity into his heart and fueled his rage toward its owner.

With the canine now tucked away back at his home, warm and secure, he trudged back out through the snow.

The heavy-metal music that had drowned out the howls of the animal, now vibrated the deck.

All he needed was silence. So he could think. So he could get what he needed to get done, done.

He pounded on the door, and it sent pain flashing through his knuckles—the combination of determination and the bitter temperatures against flesh and bone.

The wind howled between the two houses, gusting up the snow into miniature funnel clouds of ice crystals. They assaulted any bared skin—his neck and face taking the brunt of it. A quiver wracked his body and prompted a deep exhalation, which created a cloud of white in the night air.

"Open the fucking door!" He pushed through the discomfort and knocked again.

Still no evidence the man was even listening.

He surveyed, left and right, glancing over his shoulder, feeling eyes on him. Were the neighbors watching him? Did they call the cops?

The light was on in an upstairs room, but otherwise the nearby house was enshrouded in darkness. The only other illumination were the streetlights that cast dull beacons amidst the blowing snow.

He went to bang again, but his hands refused. They had seized up from the cold. He blew on them to warm them. Surely, the occupant was drunk and would awaken from his stupor to—

The door opened and with it, the music got louder.

"What the fuck do you want?" The man stood there, six feet tall, a few inches shy of his own height, and his face was unshaven. His suspicions were confirmed by the pungent smell of whiskey that flushed out of the house and exuded from the man.

But it wasn't his neighbor's appearance, or even the odor that burned his eyes and had his attention, it was his identity.   He would never forget that face. It had scarred his childhood, and it wasn't until this moment, until this *reunion* that he realized how much. Ken Bailey was the man's name.

A warmth encased his insides and his vision grew clearer.

"Freak, what the fuck is up?" Ken leaned against the doorframe but lost his mark and stumbled to regain his balance.

This arrogant son of a bitch didn't recognize him. It provided him clarity—and strength. A shiver laced down his spine as he stepped inside the house.

"Hey!" Ken slammed a hand against his shoulder.

It shuffled him back a few feet, but he never lost his balance. He was sober as a priest, thanks to Ken interrupting his evening's plans.

He pushed past Ken into the house. He shut the door behind him and stood there, facing his opponent, breathing as if he'd run a marathon. His heart beat so fast, it pained in his chest. Whatever happened next, Ken would deserve it for what he had done to her.

"Get out of my hou—"

He felt cartilage shift under the impact of his fist to Ken's nose.

Ken instinctively cradled his nose and blood poured down his face. A red mist spewed from his mouth as he spoke. "What the—"

"It's your past calling, asshole."

He landed another blow. Ken's nose was broken.

Still, Ken retaliated, coming at him with force, and pinned him to the back of the door. It knocked the wind out of him.

He doubled in half, clenching at his injured abdomen, his eyes only seeing one color—red.

At that moment, adrenaline fused through his system, cording his sinew into tight springs ready to pounce. He would make him pay, make him beg for his next breath. He would no longer be viewed as weak and puny, instead, as powerful and in control.

He thrust his fist toward Ken's jaw but missed when he diverted to the side and dipped low. He took aim again, but a blow to his face stopped all movement.

White, searing pain hindered his vision. A constant rhythm pumped in his head, the music now a deadened cacophony.

Ken stood across from him, winded, each exhale exuding alcohol blended with nicotine.

"You don't even know who I am, do you?"

"I don't need to know you to kill you." The man charged at him, the motive clear.

He had mere seconds, if not merely *a* second, to assess his surroundings and calculate the odds. They were in the kitchen. Dishes were piled on the counters and in the sink. Empty beer bottles covered the table. On the floor next to them were, easily, twenty to thirty alcohol magnums waiting to be returned for a refund.

He ducked just in time.

Ken's fist met with the wood door and had him howling in pain—but not for long. He came at him again, wrapped his hands around his middle and worked to pull him to a straight position. "You think you can come in here and attack me!"

The jab met his cheek, sliding his jaw askew and sinking his teeth into his tongue. He tasted blood.

He glanced back to the bottles again. They were close enough that he could…

Ken yanked on his coat and pulled him upright. His opponent threw a punch and he returned one. They continued to come at each other, both men juking to avoid the other's blows, the odd one making purchase.

It was a misstep that had his foot twisting at a precarious angle, the move to divert, working to his detriment. He fell. Hard. He scrambled to regain equal footing.

It was too late. Ken came down on top of him with powerful force, straddling his mid-section and constricting his airflow.

The music came back into focus. The droning guitar and screaming singer.

The blows landed consecutively, meeting with his face, his shoulders, his gut, and his sides until Ken paused, panting, and looked down at him.

"Now I know who you are." Still mounted over him, his laughter shrilled above the noise disguised as music. "I recognize your shriveling nature." More mocking laughter. Ken was driven to tears with his amusement.

He saw the one color again. Did he have what it took to take a man's life? He used to be peaceful…until he was eight and this man stripped his innocence. Life *wasn't* but a dream, sweetheart.

He bucked, trying to break his arm free, but Ken applied more pressure.

It was time. He had a decision to make. Would he continue to loll back and let the Baileys of the world overpower him forever? Or would he make it clear, once and for all time, that he wasn't a man to be fucked with?

His insides warmed. His extremities cooled.

He assessed the bottles that were beside his head and he figured out what he had to do. But did he have the guts to do it? He had come over here prepared to fight, hadn't he? Well, he found one. He just hadn't expected it to be with Ken Bailey.

But what real difference did it make? It only reinforced the direction and power of Fate. He had been brought to this point in his life for a reason. He was tired of letting everyone down—especially himself.

His fingertips grazed the edge of the closest bottle—a clear rum bottle. His fingers danced across the glass until he had a hold on it.

The hyena laughter stopped. Ken came to, realizing the intention in his eyes.

Ken drew his arm back to make a fatal blow—it was too late.

"For Molly, you asshole!" He let out a roar that challenged the music and ripped the bottle from the floor. He would be the last thing this man would see.

He wailed against him with the bottle until, finally, the glass weakened and shattered, raining over him, to reveal jagged edges.

Minutes later, he hoisted the lifeless body of Ken Bailey, off of him and onto the floor.

His legs were rubbery when he went to stand, but he had proven himself. He had stood up to the bully and had come out the victor.

He gazed down and noticed Bailey's chest still rose softly. Scanning the room, he found the perfect thing to fix that.

When he was finished, he decided he had something to celebrate after all.

CHAPTER 1

THE PLANE TOUCHED DOWN AT Denver International Airport just after six in the morning. I was happy to have the tumultuous flight over with and thought it should have been canceled, but apparently those responsible for that sort of thing had cleared take-off.

Flying typically didn't bother me, but high winds and various temperature pockets had buffeted the plane, rocking it almost like a ship at sea, only we were thirty thousand feet in the air. Land never looked so good.

Zachery slapped me on the back and had me lurching forward from the momentum. "We made it, Pending."

Months into my probationary period but still not clear of it—something I was reminded of all the time by his beloved nickname.

Jack brushed past, leading the three of us through the airport, no doubt driven by the undying urge for a cigarette. Paige hung back, and when I turned, she pushed a rogue strand of hair from her eyes and dipped to the left as she shifted the position of her suitcase strap on her right shoulder.

We were called to Colorado because some old-timer detective by the name of Mack McClellan was confident the area had a serial killer. He believed it strongly enough we were convinced as well.

The label *serial killer* no longer fazed me, and it only took a few horrid cases to rub off its shock value.

Regular people, who didn't have to hunt down murderers, lived life as if they were merely characters fabricated for entertainment purposes. The dark truth was, conservatively, there were an estimated thirty-five to fifty serial killers in the United States at any given time.

The local FBI office was to provide us with transportation, but it was the local detective who insisted on meeting us at the airport and bringing us up to speed.

Stepping out of the warm cocoon of the airport into the brisk winter air of Denver stole my breath. It had me wanting to retreat back inside for the warm, blowing vents.

For recreational purposes, Denver would be an ideal location to spend the Christmas season, with its mountain slopes and deep snow. Even facing the search for a killer, I'd rather be here, miles away from home, than facing the emptiness of the house on Christmas day.

This would be the first year without Deb. The only thing that could make it better was reconciliation, but we were beyond that point. Truth be told, I wasn't even sure if I'd take her back. The divorce was already filed, and knowing my penchant for attracting negative events, it would be official in time for the holiday. It didn't matter though. I had found a way to move forward in my life—at least I told myself that. Maybe I was burying my feelings, but I preferred to think I healed faster than most.

"Hey, there they are."

A man pushed off the hood of a Crown Vic, the cup in his hand steaming in the cold air. At full height, he was all of five eight. His hair was sparse and reminded me of a Chia Pet just starting to grow, but what he did have was a dark blond. He wore a thigh-length wool parka, zipped up shy of his collar by about six inches. It revealed a white collared shirt and a blue tie with white dots. I wondered if he dressed this way all the time or only when the FBI was in town.

He put his cup on the car roof and came toward us with another man who wore a fur-lined leather jacket paired with blue jeans, which appeared stiff due to the mountain air.

It had me wondering which scenario was more uncomfortable, frozen stiff jeans or breezy dress pants. I experienced the latter and questioned the wardrobe I had brought, wondering if I'd be warm enough.

Curse winter and all that's white.

"Gentleman, I'm Mack McClellan." The man in the parka extended his hand, first to Jack. He must have sensed his authority despite the lit cigarette.

Jack took a quick inhale and blew a stream of white pollution out the side of his mouth as he shook the man's hand. "Supervisory Special Agent Jack Harper and this is my team." Jack left us to introduce ourselves.

McClellan's gaze settled on me, and I surmised what he was thinking—I was the young guy on the team, the inexperienced one he'd have to watch.

He gestured to the man with him. "This is Detective Ronnie Hogan. He's also with Denver PD. We're not partners, but he's of the same mind. There's a serial at play here."

Hogan bobbed his head forward as a greeting but made no effort to extend a hand. His eyes were brown and hard to read. Crease lines etched in his brow, but he also had smile lines, so there was some promise there. Not that we witnessed the expression.

McClellan grinned with a warmth that touched his eyes, giving me the impression he was used to Hogan's aloofness. "Glad to see you made it all right. It's quite the weather we're having these days. How was your flight?"

Jack took another drag on his cigarette. "Over now."

His retort killed the expression on the detective's face. "A man who is all business, I see. So, the dead body. You know the name and details."

Another pull on the cigarette and Jack flicked the glowing butt to the ground and extinguished it with the twist of a shoe.

"We know what the file says, but we like to go over everything in person." Paige smiled at the detectives, no doubt trying to compensate for Jack's crass behavior.

"Well, let us fill you in on the way to where the body was found.

My, it's mighty cold out here." He rubbed his hands together and grabbed his cup before going around to the driver's side. "For everyone to be more comfortable, two of you can come with me, and the other two can go with Hogan."

McClellan seemed like an open book—what you saw was what you got. With Hogan, there was something about him, whether it was his skepticism or what, I wasn't sure. A quality that should repel actually made me want to get to know him.

"I'll go with Hogan." Paige and I spoke at the same time.

Our eyes connected. In the past this symmetry in thought would have elicited a smile from both of us. These days our relationship was more complicated.

Paige stepped back and sought Jack's direction. "I'll go with whoever you want me to."

"It's fine. You guys go with Hogan. We'll all catch up at the crime scene."

She went past me and held out her hand to Hogan. "I don't think we've been properly introduced."

Hogan stared at her extended hand and, eventually, conceded to a handshake. The greeting was over quick.

As he was getting into the driver's seat, I whispered in Paige's ear. "He's not really the touchy-feely kind, is he?"

I received a glare in response.

Chapter 2

"Things must be slow for you guys if you're willing to come all the way here for this case." Hogan kept his eyes on the road, his voice level as he spoke. He made a quick pass of a slower-moving vehicle.

My fingers gripped the armrest on the door, indenting the foam beneath it. "You're not buying that it's a serial at work?"

A small snort, which could have been construed as a laugh. "I'm not saying anything. McClellan can be a convincing man. I agree the situations surrounding these men are similar. Whether that means anything more, I haven't fully decided."

He touched the brakes, and the back end of the car lost traction and swayed to the right. No one else seemed to notice or care.

"How long have you been with Denver PD?" Paige asked.

It warranted a quick, sideways glance from Hogan. "Is this where you try to get to know me better?"

Paige's jaw tightened. "If you don't like people, why are you a cop?"

I settled into the seat, happy that I wasn't on the receiving end for a change. Part of me wished to be elsewhere, the other part wondered who would come out the victor.

"Who says I don't like people? I like people. I just don't like feds."

"And what have we done to you?"

Hogan kept his eyes straight ahead. "McClellan feels the latest victim was left there for us to find. Like this guy wants to get caught."

"So that's how you get by in life? You shut people down who try to get close."

"You want to get close to me, sweetheart, we'll do it after hours, but now's the job."

Air rushed from Paige's mouth, skimming over teeth and making a *whooshing* sound on the exhale. She knotted her arms and kicked her back into the seat as she did so.

Hogan didn't give any indication he was affected by her response. He took a street on the right, made a quick left, parked, and cut the engine. "We're here."

"I'm glad you told us," Paige mumbled and got out of the car.

We had beat the other detective and the rest of our team, but as we made our way toward the dumpster, the department-issued sedan pulled in, crunching snow beneath the wheels.

When we were all standing around the dumpster at the back of Lynn's Bakery, McClellan pointed to the right of the bin.

"The body was found right there. He was covered in snow, with only the tip of his boots showing. The waste removal company found him when they came to empty the bin. At first they thought someone was too lazy to pick up the trash and dispose of it properly. They stepped out to lift it and got more than they expected."

"Something that they even got out of the vehicle. Most would carry on and not care. They're hired to empty the container, not clean up the surrounding area," Paige said.

"Exactly what I thought."

"Did you question the garbage man?"

"Yeah. Even pulled a background. Nothing came of it."

"Name's Craig Bowen," Zachery interjected.

McClellan seemed impressed by Zachery. "Read that in the file? Good memory. The cause of death?"

"Rat poison."

The man had no idea with whom he was dealing.

"Impressive. Now this guy didn't go silently, or easily, that's for sure."

"And you think this is connected to animal cruelty cases?" I asked the question to get things moving forward.

"Yes, I do. The vic's name was Darren Simpson. Twenty-six years ago he was charged with feeding his dog rat poison, but the charges didn't stick. The guy walked. It was big news around here."

"Animal cruelty cases are big news?"

"Well, there's a spot for them in the paper. Bigger news years ago than it is these days."

"So this guy was accused of poisoning animals twenty-six years ago and you think someone's coming back for revenge now?" Paige asked.

"Exactly what I'm thinking."

Hogan rolled his eyes.

I gestured to him and addressed McClellan. "Your friend here doesn't seem convinced."

McClellan smirked. "Nothing much fazes Hogan, but he does concede to the line of thought that *something* is going on here."

"The file mentions there are a few missing men, and this is why you're convinced there's a serial killer," Zachery said.

"Yes. Two date back a bit ago. Dean Garner went missing in two thousand nine. Charges against him were microwaving a Chihuahua. They were dropped because there wasn't enough evidence. Karl Ball was charged with pit-bull fighting but got off on a technicality. He went missing in two thousand ten."

"So, our victim poisoned his dog and then dies of poisoning," I made the summation. "It certainly sounds like more than a coincidence."

"Our unsub is targeting animal abusers who beat the charges. He carries out his own sort of vigilante justice, bringing the same punishment upon them as they inflicted," Zachery said.

Paige tossed some hair behind her shoulder. "Is it wrong to side with a killer in this case? What kind of monster abuses animals? They rely on us for protection, for food, for shelter, for love, and how are they repaid? Abuse. The thought makes *me* angry enough to kill."

"He?" McClellan picked up on Zachery's reference to gender. He rested his hands on his hips and drummed his fingers there.

"It's a logical deduction to presume the killer we seek is male.

The targeted victims are men for one," Zachery explained.

"But poison? Isn't that a common method for females?"

"It is, however, no women that fit the profile of being animal abusers are missing, are they?"

"No."

"That lends it toward being a man hunting other men."

Hogan stepped toward Paige. "All I know is this guy needs to be stopped. These are people he's killing, not animals."

Paige's jaw jutted up. "You sure?"

"I agree they were charged with barbaric acts, but they deserve to be heard and have a fair trial."

"Guess you do like people." Paige secured eye contact with Hogan. He turned away first.

Jack slipped a hand into his coat pocket. "While the background is good to have, the real reason we're here is because you feel the threat is still viable, and you convinced us of that. What really got our attention was the recently missing man."

McClellan nodded. "His name is Gene Lyons. His wife reported him five days ago, but after Simpson, we realized the similarities. He was charged with animal neglect, resulting in a beagle barely hanging onto life. They nursed him back at significant expense, only to find out, in the end, the dog's mind had snapped. They had to put him down. The charge against Lyons was made twenty-five years ago."

Anger ripped through me. The man we hunted—was he a monster or a hero? What sane human being wouldn't consider, even with a passing thought, the execution of revenge on those who abused animals? This case would be a tough one.

"The file said that all four men were married," Zachery said. "Four, including Simpson, our murdered victim."

A slow nod from McClellan. "Not all happily, but in somewhat committed relationships."

"Did you speak with them?" Jack asked.

McClellan answered. "Oh yeah. Let's just say the women in these men's lives are interesting. We'll leave it at that. They had alibis if you want to call them that. Of course, you say you're looking for a man…but the strongest defense was Simpson's wife, who was spending the night in jail for a drunk and disorderly. Let's just say some people dance to the beat of a different drummer. These would be them."

"The file said Garner's wife, Jill, was home watching TV when she decided enough time had passed and her husband should be home. Ball's wife, Renee, was out drinking with her girlfriends at the time of his disappearance." Zachery burrowed his hands into his coat pockets. "With Lyons, the wife was trying to hunt him down for some spending money and couldn't find him. She didn't really know exactly when he went missing."

"Correct on all counts. Lyons and his wife were separated but making it work like that. They led separate lives, except when it came to finances. He carried her."

"His line of work?"

"A computer geek."

"You've got to be kidding me. Just when you'd think he'd be harmless, he's at home abusing the dog." Paige bounced, in what appeared to be an effort to fend off the cold.

"Why don't we go inside Lynn's? She's got hot coffee and baked goods you would die for. Besides, there's no sense us standing outside and freezing."

"Sounds good to me." Paige smiled.

Jack nodded and the team followed the local detectives.

LYNN'S BAKERY WAS A FAMILY-RUN business. It hadn't been touched by corporate America with their flashy monikers that signified a franchise. Stepping inside, the warmth made my cheeks tingle and encased me in a metaphorical hug while the smell of cinnamon buns and apple pie baking in the oven tantalized.

In a front display case, there was an assortment of baked goods, which included cookies, muffins, scones, donuts, pastries, and cakes. Everything came in a seemingly endless variety. On the counter were more tiered confections, with slices missing, displayed in glass domes. A wooden easel held a chalkboard sign that read *Please seat yourself.*

We followed its direction and pushed two tables together.

McClellan gestured to a waitress. She was maybe twenty and

had long brown hair that was swept back into a loose ponytail, with the exception of two curly strands that dangled in front of each ear. Her eyes were pale green and she didn't wear any makeup. Stitched onto her uniform was the name, *Annie*. She held a pen in her left hand and a small notepad in her right.

"You guys all here 'cause of—" She gestured with the end of the pen behind her shoulder, denoting the back alley.

"Now, what have I told you, Annie?" Detective McClellan sustained eye contact with her.

"Dad, I'm just curious. It's not a big deal. You guys are all FBI?" She smiled at me.

Paige didn't miss the attention I received and raised her brow.

"We're here to warm up, not to meet and greet," McClellan directed her.

Annie's shoulders sagged and her hips jutted to the right. "Fine."

"All right, so we'll each have a coffee and a Christmas special cookie."

Annie's pen never met paper and she walked away. I was left wondering a couple things, one being, what was a *"Christmas special cookie?"*

I voiced my other observation. "You never told us your daughter worked here."

McClellan waved a dismissive hand. "What does it really matter? She didn't kill that man."

"That you know of."

"You're serious? I thought you said that it was a—"

I smiled at the detective.

He grimaced in return and rested his hand on a napkin. He fanned up its edge and repeated the cycle a few times. "As we were starting to discuss out—"

Annie put a coffee in front of Jack. "You must be the boss. It's easy to tell."

Did I deduct an underlying smile from Jack?

"I am." He reached for a sugar packet from a small glass bowl in the middle of the table.

She set the tray down with the rest of our coffees and extended a hand to Jack. "I'm Annie."

He shook her hand. "Jack Harper."

"Annie, we don't have time for this."

Annie ground one of her shoes into the floor. "My Dad likes to control everything I do. He drives me nuts."

"Well, until you pay your own rent."

"Yadda, yadda." She looked at me. "You ever get the as-long-as-you-live-under-my-roof speech from your parents?"

How young did she think I was? I had at least seven or eight years on her.

"You're kidding? He still gets that." Zachery, who was sitting beside me, patted my back.

Annie laughed. The expression suited her—well. She was probably a heartbreaker. I had a feeling McClellan was well aware of it too. His attention narrowed in on me.

"Annie, please, we have work to do."

She rolled her eyes and distributed the coffees, then held the round tray against her chest when she was finished. "If it's true that murdered man killed a dog, then he deserved what he got." Annie gauged us for a response, but when none of us offered one, she left.

"You discuss open cases with your daughter?" Jack asked.

"I didn't discuss anything with her. The news was all over it."

"The news?"

"You know what they're like. They sniff out murder like ants do a picnic."

"Hmm."

"We were talking about the missing men's significant others," Paige interjected, "before we came inside. Tell us more about them."

McClellan pulled his eyes from Jack. "None of the women have a violent history. Even with Simpson's drunk and disorderly, she wasn't hostile, she was half-naked in a public place. Charges of indecent exposure should have been pursued."

"Why weren't they? You said she spent the night in jail."

Color saturated the detective's face. "That's all she got. The chief thought formal charges were excessive."

"She is a nice-looking piece of ass." Jack pulled out his pack of cigarettes and placed it on the table. His hand covered it, but he didn't light up. There were no smoking signs posted all over.

"Yeah."

"What about here? Anything about this site that seems significant?" I asked.

McClellan shook his head. "None that we're aware of at this point."

"We need to know who wrote the articles on all of these men. We need to speak to the garbage man who found Simpson, his significant other, along with those of the other missing men," Jack addressed his team. "I'd say things possibly started with Karl Ball, who went missing in two thousand and nine, but we've got a fresh body and a new missing persons case. We dig into those first."

"Agree, Boss." Paige blew on her coffee and took a sip.

"I believe we're after a male killer who targets those who specifically abuse dogs." I offered a summation.

Zachery popped a piece of cookie into his mouth and jabbed the uneaten part toward me. "Good point. He probably also experienced something at a younger age that made him predisposed to—"

Hogan coughed and held a hand over his mouth. Its source, clearly, was derision.

We all looked at him.

"You can tell all of this from what we have so far?"

"Hogan, please." McClellan leaned into his chair and flung his arm over the back.

"It just seems like, what's the point of local law enforcement as long as we have the FBI." He tossed a five on the table and stood.

McClellan shot to his feet and leaned in toward Hogan. He spoke low, but it was easy to hear. "Why are you acting like this? You said you'd be of help."

Hogan scanned McClellan's face but addressed us. "I want this killer stopped just as much as all of you, but a serial at work? Unsub? Your fancy terminology for what we would call a perp. You have to do everything different. And, if that's not enough, you have to pry your nose into our cases." Back to McClellan. "I've gotta go do some police work." He left, and his wet boots squeaked across the floor of the bakery.

McClellan's inhale expanded his chest. He took his seat again. "I'm sorry about him."

"From the file, one journalist reported on all these cases," Zachery said.

"Yeah." McClellan's hand went for his coffee. Disappointment radiated from him, but he tried to counter with a smile. It didn't fully form. "The guy's name is Kent Fields, now a giant in the publishing industry. He's got three Pulitzers to his credit and many other awards. I highly doubt it's him behind these murders."

"He might have information, from behind the scenes, that will prove useful to the investigation."

"You sure about that? Remember these cases go back twenty-six years. That's a long time."

"We'll see if it feels that long ago to him."

Enlightenment dawned on the detective's face. "Ah, so you'll set a trap for the rat. If he bites, he could be our man."

Zachery nodded. "Precisely."

"It might not be a bad idea to talk to the main animal activist group in town either. I'll get you their information."

"There's a lot of people we need to speak with and we're not getting it done sitting around here." Jack stood and the rest of us followed his lead.

"You guys take my car. I'll call for a ride." McClellan's gaze went to the window. Outside large snowflakes fell in quick succession.

"Don't worry, Detective, we get snow in Virginia." Jack slipped out a cigarette and tucked the package back into his pocket.

McClellan's eyes went to it. "Of course you do. I didn't—"

"We'll head to the station first, see if our rides are there, and get someone to come back for you."

"I'd appreciate it."

I can't say that I was excited about Jack driving in this weather. Behind the wheel, the man typically scared me on sunny days, but I hurried, hoping to call shotgun first

CHAPTER 3

HIS HANDS SHOOK EVERY TIME, but someone had to clean up the
city. The government certainly wasn't going to do anything
about it. Those who were elected put on a show for glamor and
fame with no real purpose. They slept in their million-dollar
homes and shut out the ugliness of the world around them. For
appearance's sake, they went to their charity benefits while being
too lazy to deal with the issues. The promises made to those
who'd voted them into office in the first place were forgotten. It
was a disgusting irony that defined politics. The very men who
swore to deal with issues, to rectify injustices, sat on the sidelines,
more incompetent than most.

This is why he was left to take the power into his own hands
and make a difference to society. He brought justice for the
Defenseless by condemning their Offender.

It was this reasoning that added justification for his actions.
Everyone had a purpose. His was to speak for the victims who
have no voice. He was their Advocate.

Placing Simpson's body on display was a message to the world
to let them know crimes against the Defenseless would not be
tolerated, and that those who inflicted abuse upon them would be
held accountable.

This Offender, his latest captive, would take patience, but that
was one thing he had developed over the years. A tempering of
knowing when best to strike, and whom.

The Advocate watched his captive through a camera he had
placed in the man's cell. The Offender was extended the same

courtesies he had provided his canine companion—a dank corner with an empty food dish and a shitty water bowl. To complete the retribution, he put a tight choker around his neck and attached it to a short chain.

For hours, the man had protested his captivity, but now his cries for help had lost conviction. What was once a high-pitched fervor had dulled to a mumbled whisper. Despair and hopelessness were taking over.

The thought made the Advocate smile. He was making a difference. He offered no mercy for these men. The Offenders deserved what was coming their way, and if he was the one destined to exact the punishment, he would see it through. Exacting revenge and punishment on these mongrels had become his driving purpose in life. It was what he was meant to do.

The Offender was alternating between balling his fists and pulling out on the choker, but his efforts were futile. The collar was latched tight and secured with a tiny padlock.

"Aw, is it getting a little harder to breathe?" the Advocate said to himself. Laughter had his eyes pinching shut and tears seeping from the corners.

The man kept trying to reach the bench to sit down, but the length of the chain had been adjusted so there was no possibility of that happening. He would stand or hang himself.

Still, the Advocate experienced no remorse. The Offender should have thought through to the consequences of his actions before he outworked his madness on one of the Defenseless.

"Why are you doing this?" the Offender called out.

Rarely did the Advocate respond. They didn't deserve to be heard, to be granted a say. He had tried that in the beginning, but their speeches about their being guileless fell not only on deaf ears, but on a mind forged by retribution.

The Advocate pushed the button that would allow his voice to carry into the room. He wasn't worried about being identified—there would be no escape for an Offender—but he had modified the output anyhow. The speech distortion would toy with their minds even further.

"You brought this on yourself."

"I—" The Offender buried his face in his hands, the muffled sobbing still loud enough to hear.

The crying always reaped the opposite of their desired outcome. Instead of it tugging on the Advocate's humanity, his mind went to the Defenseless, to those who wept internally, in darkness.

"You deserve to die!"

The man slid his hands down his face and sputtered, "I haven't done anything."

"Drink your water, animal." It pained the Advocate to equate this mammal to the four-legged variety. The Defenseless were superior to Offenders in many ways.

The man's legs buckled beneath him, the choker, doing its job, tightened its hold against his larynx. The Offender righted himself and his hands rushed to his throat, where he tugged on the collar without much success.

"Drink!"

"Why are you—" Vomit spewed across the room, splattering some on the camera lens.

The Advocate rubbed his hands, sat back, and swiveled in his chair.

Now things were coming together. The man would break, and when he did, the Advocate would be there to watch him take his final breath.

Also available from
International Best-selling Author
Carolyn Arnold

THE DEFENSELESS
Book 3 in the Brandon Fisher FBI series

The first victim was poisoned. Three others are still missing. One more turns up dead. But there is one connection that ties them all together.

This case has FBI Agent Brandon Fisher and the team in Colorado to stop a serial killer targeting men who beat charges of animal abuse over twenty years ago. With the method of murder changing to match what his victims had allegedly inflicted on the defenseless, the team questions who is on the side of justice— them or the murderer. After all, their unsub is seeking retribution on behalf of the victims who have no voice.

While facing this moral dilemma, Brandon's integrity to the Bureau is also tested. But Brandon is up for the challenge— anything to get his mind off his pending divorce and the upcoming holiday. Being thousands of miles from home, the forbidden relationship between him and Paige becomes more tempting but is he willing to risk all that he's worked for?

**Available from popular book retailers or
at carolynarnold.net**

CAROLYN ARNOLD is the international best-selling and award-winning author of the Madison Knight, Brandon Fisher, and McKinley Mystery series. She is the only author with POLICE PROCEDURALS RESPECTED BY LAW ENFORCEMENT. TM

Carolyn was born in a small town, but that doesn't keep her from dreaming big. And on par with her large dreams is her overactive imagination that conjures up killers and cases to solve. She currently lives in a city near Toronto with her husband and two beagles, Max and Chelsea. She is also a member of Crime Writers of Canada.

CONNECT ONLINE
carolynarnold.net
facebook.com/authorcarolynarnold
twitter.com/carolyn_arnold

And don't forget to sign up for her newsletter for up-to-date information on release and special offers at carolynarnold.net/newsletters.

CPSIA information can be obtained
at www.ICGtesting.com
Printed in the USA
LVHW090200180219
607850LV00001B/104/P